Dave,

Hope you enjoy the read!

Vince

MIDNIGHT ETERNAL
First Edition Trade Paperback, June 2016
All Rights Reserved

Dark Recesses Press
6273 132A Street, Surrey, B.C. V3X 3T2
Canada

Copyright © 2016 by Vince Churchill

All rights reserved. No part of this publication may be reproduced in any form or by any means without the prior written permission of the publisher, except in the case of brief quotations embodied in critical articles or reviews. All characters in this publication are fictitious. Any resemblance to real persons, living or dead, is purely coincidental.

Editor:	Kelly Dunn
Inset Layout and Design:	Bailey Hunter
Cover/Interior Artwork:	Ken Leinaar

This book is dedicated to all my fellow old school comic book geeks, and especially fans of Batman and The Joker.
I'd also like to dedicate this book to a good man who left this world way too early for everyone whose lives he touched in so many wonderful, positive ways. Thank you for being my friend, Varba.

TABLE OF CONTENTS

The Rotting Heart Of San Angeles 7

Old Scratch 18

Getting Some Religion 26

Winner Takes All 30

Awakening From Death's Slumber 39

A City Mourns 44

Bad News Travels Fast 49

Paying Respects 59

A Whole Lotta Good Fighting Evil 69

The Lord Gave 78

The Hellidays 85

Allenby Asylum 91

A Simple Question 103

But Fear Itself 106

Good News And Bad News 120

TABLE OF CONTENTS

Choosing Sides 134

While The City Sleeps 149

The Beginning Of The End 155

And Nothing But The Truth 160

Rome Is Burning 169

Split Screen 172

The Spyder And The Geek 174

Exorcising Evil 180

An Itsy Bitsy Spyder 191

Meeting One's Match 195

Oh What A Tangled Web We Weave 203

The Endgame 207

Goodnight, San Angeles 221

Midnight Eternal 226

Chapter One

THE ROTTING HEART OF SAN ANGELES

Nightfall.

Midnight, the night-fueled crimefighter, squatted on the edge of the downtown skyscraper, staring down through the black curtain shadows into Skid Row. He loved December and the shorter days. Early nightfalls meant basking in the warm pool of his power for an extended time. Those minutes just after sundown and just before sunrise sometimes meant the difference between life and death.

The hero stood, gazing out across the newly formed metropolis. To the south, lights twinkled without end. When he was a boy, Los Angeles and San Diego were separate Southern California cities, but their continued growth eventually swallowed up Orange County, and the two combined to become San Angeles, the largest American city by population and square miles.

There hadn't been a sunset. Severe thunderstorms headed inland, masking the vibrant San Angeles sun. The cloud cover would make the night darker, improving Midnight's visual acuity. He used the shadows like windows to watch over the innocent. The city sheltered so many potential nameless and faceless victims. The Skid Row population was like a herd of foul-fleeced and confused sheep awaiting slaughter. Their sheer numbers drew predictably lazy predators to the area, hungry and eager for easy pickings.

Turning to face west, Midnight could see the high-walled neighborhoods that began in Beverly Hills and continued all the way to the ocean. The press called them "kingdoms." Midnight chuckled under his star-speckled, blue-black stocking mask. Crime had become a malignancy, with no cure in sight. The rich thought they could buy safety, but these entitled types hadn't experienced firsthand the powers of enhanced criminals capable of making their armed protectors piss down their legs. Old Scratch and his minions could spill out of the sewer system like an overflowing toilet and lay waste to their precious communities anytime they wanted. Midnight's jaw flexed under the skintight fabric as he raised his hand and pretended to crush the nearest stone-and-steel wall with his thumb and forefinger.

Idiots.

Crime would always be a part of any society. He'd accepted that, and chosen to apply his special abilities to a more challenging mission. After all, cops could handle the muggers and arsonists and counterfeiters.

He stepped away from the skyscraper roof's edge and turned his back to the daily downtown exodus below, entering the building's freight elevator and stabbing the garage-level button. The elevator started its smooth one-hundred-story descent.

As soon as the doors opened, Midnight burst from the elevator like an Olympic sprinter, moving around and over the backup of cars leaving the skyscraper like a Parkour champion. Commuters yelled and honked as he slid over a pickup's cab roof or hurdled a car's hood. Ducking into an unlit alley, the hero smiled under his mask at the reactions. He loved the people of San Angeles. Thinking about the irate commuters also made it easier to ignore the assault of putrid sweat, feces, and vomit the dark passage offered.

This world had supervillains. There were superheroes to hold that line. And then there was the dark-presence hellspawn Old Scratch represented.

Midnight vaulted over a series of overflowing trash dumpsters, ignoring an Asian family of four battling a swarm of flies for their recycled dinner. He used the last dumpster as a springboard to launch himself close enough to grab the railing of a nearby building's fifth-floor fire escape.

A little farther down the alley, a pair of young men masked with sunglasses and hoodies broke into the rear entrance of a jewelry store. Midnight paused an instant to take a mental snapshot, then scrambled the rest of the way to the building's roof. He covered the next several blocks sprinting and leaping from roof to roof.

Midnight didn't fight crime anymore.

At the top of an apartment building nearing Skid Row, a teenage Hispanic girl stood barefoot on the edge of the roof. She must have heard Midnight's approach, because she turned and stared into the deep shadows where he'd paused. Her long, dark hair hung to her waist, and she wore a sheet of notebook paper pinned to her white t-shirt. The message written on it was short and not so sweet.

DEMONS ARE REAL

The young woman turned her back to him, and then stepped off the roof as casually as she'd step off a curb to get on a bus. Midnight caught just enough of a glimpse to see the numerous cigarette burns on her arms and legs. Most were scabbed over, but a few looked fresh. There was a momentary silence, then the sound of the young woman's body striking a parked car down below. The impact ignited the vehicle's alarm, and its relentless wail, along with bystanders' anguished screams, chased Midnight as he continued his hunt.

He fought evil. Crime and misery were just symptoms of evil, like a runny nose or a cough signaling a cold. Over the years, Midnight's mission for protecting his city had become very specific.

Old Scratch had to be destroyed.

It wouldn't do to merely apprehend and imprison the demon in the new supervillain containment center deep within the earth's core. Nor would any kind of reason work with a being like him. Base mortal desires like greed and envy didn't motivate Old Scratch. He definitely wasn't human. All but immortal, Old Scratch was a monstrous being from another dimension that many, including Midnight, believed must be hell itself.

Midnight hoped tonight would take him another step closer to the demon's demise. So he leapt down to street level and blended into a shadow, refocusing his attention on the beehive activity of the bus terminal. The same scenarios played out there every night. The number of starry-eyed arrivals always exceeded the number of shattered departures. Desperate and naïve young people from all over the country, lured by Hollywood's mesmerizing fame. More than likely, all would succumb to the lure of Old Scratch's dark whisperings. *Exploit your talent. Don't be ignored. Prove the world wrong. Become someone to be reckoned with.*

Passengers spilled out from a bus marked Des Moines, Iowa. It took less than five minutes for a gray-haired, innocent-looking grandmother type to talk a pair of good-looking college kids into her Rolls-Royce. The woman had just opened up a door to a hell beyond their imagination, and the kids just smiled and walked right in.

When Midnight didn't see who he was looking for at the bus terminal, he turned his attention to a quick patrol of the homeless shelters on Los Angeles Street. Then to the overcrowded flop hotels on downtown's eastern border.

Finally, he began to run the maze of back alleys. It was all there, like a Skid Row travel slideshow. Gambling, prostitution, gang initiations, loan sharks, and even an infant being sold by a half-dressed, drug-addled woman whose arms and legs were no bigger than broom handles. Midnight stopped moving long enough to watch a thick roll of money change hands, and then Miss Broom Handle scurried away into the shadows, whooping and cackling like a mental patient. He snorted in frustration. There were moments when his city made it hard to stay on-task. The mist became a drizzle, and Midnight's mood, like the night, continued to darken.

#

"Oooooo baby," the tiny woman cooed. "I'm gonna make you feel so good." The small female showed surprising strength as she tugged the man into the dark alley by the lapels of his second-hand sport coat.

"Wow." It was all the grinning man could say, stunned by his string of good fortune. Earlier in the day he'd landed a job passing out flyers. Since the gig started super early in the morning, he could continue his other money-maker busing tables at Stu's Breakfast Nook. Between the two jobs, he could afford his room at the Hamilton Hotel and avoid moving back into the mission. And now his neighbor Rosie had agreed to give him a blowjob on credit. He'd pay her the fifteen dollars on Friday. Then again, he really needed some new underwear. His three pair were more dingy gray than white, and holes were starting to dominate the thin fabric.

"Just a little farther, sweetie. We don't want to be disturbed, do we?"

Joe Franklin wagged his shaggy head. He needed a haircut, too. Man, fifteen dollars…maybe he ought to renegotiate to just a hand job and save a few bucks. His attention dropped to the shiny red purse Rosie carried. It matched her wig. How many crumpled-up fives and tens did she have stuffed inside? The distraction nearly caused him to tumble over a fly-laden trashcan.

"Easy there honey. Hard to splint a broken dick, and I ain't no nurse."

She shoved him playfully against a brick wall. The passing traffic seemed farther away than it should have. Rosie's plump lips brushed against his, and the jolt in his crotch erased any nagging concerns.

"Now you just relax and enjoy what Rosie does best," she cooed, slowly sliding to her knees, fingernails raking his chest. Despite wanting to watch, Joe's eyes closed, and his large Adam's apple bobbed in anticipation.

He felt her fingers working at his belt and zipper. He was hardening like quick-dry cement. He sucked in a deep breath, anticipating the wonderful sensation.

A deep voice said something, but the words were muffled and hard to make out. Joe licked his lips as he reached for Rosie's shoulders. Confused when his fingers found empty air, he opened his eyes just enough to peek.

His pants flopped open and his thing jutted out. Rosie had disappeared. No, wait…

Rosie stood a few steps down the dark alley, facing away from him. The prostitute seemed to be confronting a large man, her head barely as high as the intruder's chest. Joe could make out the man's broad shoulders and extremely muscular build, but he couldn't see any distinct details. The man's coal-black clothing blended in with the night's shadowy darkness. Shit. Only one man was that massive, and brave enough to be haunting downtown back alleys. "Get out of here. Now!"

Joe understood the words, though they were muffled by the full head-mask the huge man was wearing.

"Joe, you head on back to the hotel, honey. We'll finish our fun in a little while."

Joe Franklin took a couple of steps and could see the masked man had made a fist around Rosie's pale, petite wrist.

"Hey, now..." he protested. No one should be putting his hands on a woman that way.

Something snake-like danced in the air for an instant between Rosie and the man, and a soft, sloppy slurping sound made Joe's blood run cold. He blinked, his mind trying to identify what he'd just seen. What he'd heard.

Fuck this.

He didn't realize he was running until the blaring car horn threw him off-stride as he dashed across Los Angeles Street. Fear robbed him of feeling his feet striking the asphalt. Looking back toward the sound of the horn, the long-time Skid Row resident ran straight into the side of a parked city bus. Joe Franklin lost consciousness before he crumbled to the pavement. The startled bus driver scrambled from behind the wheel to investigate.

From the alley across the way, Midnight stared at what had been masquerading as a prostitute. Rosie's human facial features had dissolved, replaced by multiple rings of jagged teeth like a sea lamprey. A moist pink oval housing a quivering, fleshy tube was set in the middle. A clear fluid dripped to the pavement from its opening. It smelled like rotted skunk.

"What do you want?" Rosie-demon hissed through the tube. Midnight spoke in a menacing growl. Midnight tightened his squeeze on her wrist. His tone was menacing.

"Heard you had some info about Old Scratch."

"Easy, easy..."

Midnight squeezed the creature's wrist tightly enough to crush human bone, but the demon only squirmed in displeasure. "Old Scratch isn't going anywhere. Having a big-shit meeting tonight."

"Where?"

"How the fuck would I know?" the she-demon spat. "Somewhere underground. Shit, it ain't got an address. Everyone knows it's just...down there." Her head tilted toward Midnight's boots and the manhole cover he stood on. When her head lifted, Midnight stared into where Rosie's eyes should have been. The demon shook her head as if annoyed by a question she couldn't answer. "Anyway, that ain't what I have for you. There's a dude on the Westside works for O.S. Supplies him with girls."

"What's the name?"

"Didn't get one. He's supposed to be some preacher in Santa Monica. Little church on one of the higher numbered streets." The thing's wrist all but disappeared in Midnight's grasp. Its tone went up an octave. "Hey, hey…look it up in the fucking Yellow Pages! I ain't a directory!"

Midnight stood perfectly still for several seconds, then let her go. The thing rubbed her wrist. Midnight watched as the demon's face returned to its human disguise as Rosie, Skid Row's good-time gal.

"Okay, well, we done?" she asked. When Midnight didn't respond, Rosie started down the alley. "Hope I can still salvage the date with Joe. A girl's gotta eat, you know?"

He had almost reached the street when a strong hand landed on her shoulder. She sighed and turned. "Now what?"

The Rosie-demon never saw the punch and hardly felt it. She certainly didn't hear the crunch of bone or the squish of soft tissue. The demon/prostitute's body hurtled from the dark alley out into the street. A motorcyclist screeched to a halt, leaving his bike to see about the motionless woman. He started to kneel beside the body, but jumped back when he got a closer look.

Something had punched a gaping, bloody hole through the female's face. It didn't even look human.

From the alley, Midnight shook the gruesome stew from his fist and forearm. His mask hid any emotion as he melted into the darkness.

Midnight didn't fight crime.

He fought evil.

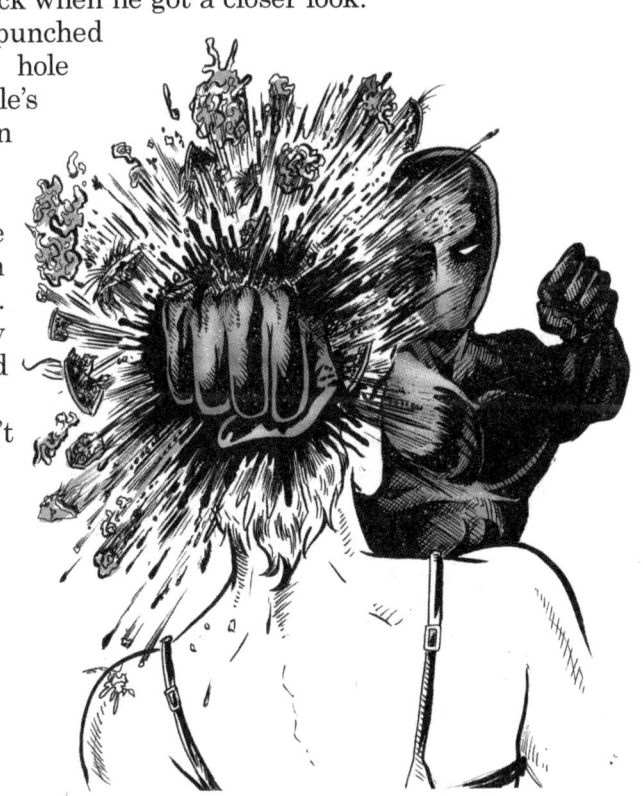

#

From the shadows across the quiet street, Midnight could smell the ocean as he watched the small church. The last greeters left their posts outside the front doors, signaling the start of the sermon.

Other than advertising an unfamiliar, Christian denomination, this church wasn't too different from the one his family had attended regularly just west of downtown Los Angeles. He grimaced at the unexpected wave of emotion that threatened to water his eyes.

His parents, Carson and Katie Waters, had actually been serving lunch to the homeless at their church when Old Scratch had emerged from hell, setting off a string of catastrophes that had taken the lives of hundreds of innocent people. As Old Scratch had burst through the pavement of Sunset Boulevard near Dodger Stadium, a busy underground subway station had been buried under tons of rubble. The panicked driver of a double-decker tour bus had veered off the road and plowed straight into the hero's small family church. More than a dozen people were killed, including both his parents. Instead of meeting his parents for dinner that evening as planned, Dre was rudely introduced to the city's newest archvillain.

Once night had fallen and he'd had discovered the demon had been involved in his parents' deaths, Midnight had put the word out to all the other San Angeles heroes and vigilantes. Old Scratch was his to destroy.

Lightning flashed a jagged streak over the ocean. Rumbling thunder followed. The tiniest raindrop grazed Midnight's cheek, and he focused in on his mission. He started across the street, the evening darkness playing over him like an invigorating shower. The weather reports appeared correct. A rare storm would soon hit Southern California. From the shadows to the church's front doors, Midnight was a blur. His superior physicality included inhuman quickness, a talent that came in handy.

Midnight had no idea what caused his abilities. He wasn't a goodhearted alien trapped on earth. Neither he nor his parents had been exposed to radioactivity. No one close to him dabbled in magic or the dark arts. He'd been born gifted, and over the years he'd had to work hard to understand and harness the measure of his powers.

Comic-book readers called him a mutant. The government had coined an official term, Ultra. Midnight didn't really give a shit what label the world gave him because the general population didn't seem to truly understand his purpose. And why should they? He hadn't for the longest time.

Truth was, Midnight was San Angeles' superhero with the best chance to stop Old Scratch at the stroke of twelve midnight, when he was almost invincible. He might also be the only one willing to give his life to slay the demon.

As he reached the entrance, he used the night's power to shift his appearance. His blue-black, star-speckled bodysuit gave way to a more appropriate white dress shirt and khakis. His shirt's white linen was a stark contrast to his cocoa-colored skin. A pair of black-framed glasses took the edge off his extreme bodybuilder's physique. Now Midnight had morphed into his daytime self, Andre "Dre" Waters, community-college English professor and volunteer football coach.

The church's outdoor message board spelled out the pastor's name in bold black letters. Convenient.

The closed chapel doors squealed in protest as Andre attempted to ease quietly into the sanctuary. Several men in the congregation glanced toward him, but none of the women reacted to the sound. Reciting a Bible verse, the energetic pastor didn't miss a beat as he paced the small stage. For a moment, Dre imagined the clergyman bursting into punitive flame.

Dre sank his muscular frame into a back-row pew. An empty space next to him separated him from an attractive blonde. Her wavy mane of a ponytail spilled to her mid-back. The fabric of her skirt strained against her crossed, tanned thighs. The skirt's high hemline appeared more appropriate for a night out than for a religious service. He offered the blonde a quick smile, but her attention never wavered from the stage. He followed her mesmerized look.

As he took in the minister, Dre allowed his power to reach out. The minister's words faded and garbled like radio static. Had there been hair on the back of Dre's neck, it would have stood on end. To the world, Pastor Leonard Griffin appeared to be a tall, frail white male in his fifties, but under the hero's judgmental nighttime gaze, his exposed flesh looked as black as coal. He had no whites to his eyes or light pink under his fingernails. The pastor's outer appearance matched his malignant nature to a tee. He was a human shadow draped in a cheap suit. Dre wasn't sure if the preacher could be in direct league with Old Scratch, but there was no doubt which army he fought for.

The pastor radiated an amount of evil at a level usually for those weak-willed or morally corrupt enough to be seduced by dark forces. The prostitute, Rosie, had been a human engulfed by an enterprising demon. There had been no hope of her overpowering whatever darkness had invaded her. The preacher appeared to be yet another mortal willing to sell his soul to Old Scratch, like a demon familiar. Not every villain or vile creature of San Angeles served the hellspawn, but habit forced Dre to work from that basic assumption.

Dre sat back and folded his massive arms across his broad chest. He nodded at the appropriate verbal prompts; occasionally letting his gaze drift amongst the attendees.

The small church held fewer than one hundred congregants. At least three-quarters of these were women, and each hung on Griffin's every word. Like the California blonde seated in his pew, all the females seemed to be dressed in a subtly inappropriate manner, no matter their age, race, or size. An extra button undone on each blouse, high heels fit for streetwalkers, tight clothing. The make-up on many was just a touch too heavy. Bright red lipstick seemed the landslide favorite for the finishing touch.

Despite his discovery of the pastor's true nature, Dre sat and listened to the sermon for several minutes. As Pastor Griffin preached, Dre glanced around the room, allowing his attention settle on the ceiling's recessed lighting. The hero made a casual motion with his hand, and the dark shadows in the corners and under the floor-length drapes began to slide up the walls in slivers thinner than hair strands. The room dimmed slightly, and a few men looked around, not sure what had played at the edge of their peripheral visions.

Dre stared at the reverend. Griffin's fervor increased, producing a noticeable effect on the women. The thighs of the neighboring blonde, whether unconsciously or not, flexed under the fabric of her skirt. And Dre didn't need to use his heightened senses to pick up her slightly labored breathing. He brushed a fingertip across his forehead. It felt dry, but warm, as if someone had turned the heat on. It took him a moment to realize the increase in temperature wasn't emanating from Griffin, but from the women in the congregation. Dre watched as the blonde undid another button on her blouse, exposing the sunbaked swell of a breast. Several other women followed suit.

Pastor Griffin and his female flock seemed to be feeding off their mutual passion. As the preacher continued to build toward the sermon's climax, a smattering of women rose from their chairs and swayed to his words, hands reaching toward heaven.

Wrong direction, Dre thought.

He'd seen enough. Dre eased out of his seat, moving toward the chapel doors.

Griffin's fist pounded the pulpit like a fleshy gavel, drawing Dre's attention. The minister pointed a trembling finger directly at Dre. "Dweller of darkness!" he spat accusingly.

Everyone turned and looked at the chiseled black man who had disturbed their religious rites. One of the standing women shivered and collapsed to the floor. A man close by attended to her.

Orgasm, Dre thought, and then glanced up at the lighting. His hand grasped the door handle the instant the creeping slivers of shadow swallowed up the light, plunging the room into darkness. Quite a ruckus ensued as the door squeaked shut behind him. Dre checked his watch and smiled.

Midnight was coming.

Chapter Two

OLD SCRATCH

Torch flames licked along the bare cavern walls to the ceiling. Smoky shadows danced around the chamber. Noses wrinkled at the underlying stench of sulfur. The cavernous dining area had a decidedly hellish atmosphere.

"Motherfucker," a voice grumbled under its breath. Those around the dining table glanced over as The Freak slowly rose to his feet. His huge bulk dwarfed the occupants of the chairs on either side of him. "Where the fuck is he?!"

The profanity, as much as his tone, caused the room to hush. With biceps the size of basketballs, The Freak shook the ornate medieval table with a single slap of his hand. The monstrous, white-maned muscle man slowly scanned the cavern. A select number of Old Scratch's top lieutenants had been afforded seats at the long banquet-style dining table, while the rest of the crowd represented more than two dozen of San Angeles' largest and most violent street gangs, powerful crime families, and corrupt local politicians. None of the non-supervillains would meet The Freak's murderous glare.

Nervously, Ricochet, the silver-and-black costumed speedster, burst to the far end of the table. His protective googles magnified his sky-blue eyes. "Take it easy," Ricochet soothed, eyes darting between the seven-foot-tall, four-hundred pound giant, and the double-doored entrance where Old Scratch would most likely emerge.

"I'm sick of this bullshit! Waiting around for his ass like he's the fucking king of the world. Fuck him!" the giant roared, swatting his chair out of the way, and then stalking away from the table. An anxious buzz of quiet conversation filled the room. Across from the place the Freak had been seated, another voice spoke up: one of The Mob, a relatively new force operating out of the southernmost region of San Angeles, formerly known as San Diego.

"No disrespect intended, but Scratch has kept us all waiting for over an hour," the Amazonian Number One of The Mob pointed out. The Mob's quartet consisted of two men and two women, of polar-opposite physicality. Rumor had it the quartet might be siblings. The fully-masked foursome prowled about costumed in variations on a black-and-white theme. While superlative in their abilities, The Mob members lacked superhuman talents.

Number Two of The Mob, a muscular male dwarf, hopped onto the table. His bushy red Mohawk split the skull of his white mask.

"I think the question is, why are we all still here?"

"I think the real question is, why don't you shut the fuck up?" The blunt request came from Number Two's Mob mate, Number Three, a tall, reed-thin woman whose face was hidden behind a black-and-white mask. High-pitched hyena laughter came from Number Four. A hairy brute with a cement-block head and enormous hands, he looked miserable with his considerable girth squeezed into a chair several sizes too small.

"Maybe we ought to follow The Freak's lead and take off," Number Two suggested to all present.

Conversations broke out around the table. From the obscurity of the cavern's ceiling, a grotesque figure dropped onto the table, landing without a sound. The Mob's Number Two yelped and dove into the grasp of his teammate, Number Four. The gathering hushed. Spyder, one of Old Scratch's most effective defenders, had joined the party.

From her perch atop the table, Spyder's large, shiny-black, multiple eyes stared down The Mob's dwarf. The black widow/human female hybrid squatted, and, gyrating her torso like a professional lap dancer, sprayed webbing from somewhere between her muscular human legs, sealing the dwarf's mouth shut.

A geneticist's nightmare, Spyder had the head of a spider atop a strong, athletic woman's body. The tips of her fingers and toes appeared needle-sharp, but it would take a microscope to see the thousands of tiny hairs that allowed her a spider's ability to attach and move across most any surface. The red hourglass of a black widow spider displayed itself on her torso. Her outfit consisted of a few wisps of strategically placed webbing. When she spoke, her arachnid-scrambled voice hardly rose above a whisper, but tonight she seemed to have no need for words. Having made her statement, she sprang back whence she came, into the shadows of the cavern's ceiling.

Frantically, the dwarf clawed the webbing away. "Holy shit," he finally whispered, wide-eyed.

Number One stared at the table, absolutely still, listening. "He's coming."

The Freak's body exploded through the oaken-plank double doors to the dining room, the albino villain's hulk scattering some of the gathering as it landed on the floor. Old Scratch's heavy footsteps shook the room as he strode through the opening The Freak's body had created. The representative from the Tough Titties all-female gang approached the tangled heap of The Freak, then abruptly whirled and vomited.

The giant had been turned into a grotesque paper wad. Splintered bones jutted through places they shouldn't. His spine had been ripped from his back, and his body compressed so the back of his crushed head was pushed against his massive butt cheeks. His shattered legs dangled limply over his shoulders.

Once the young woman spat and cleared her throat, she screamed at the impossible sight.

The shrill scream split the face of Old Scratch into a malignant smile. His rows of jagged teeth glistened. The young woman's scream startled many of those gathered around the majestic banquet table, but no one spoke out. The demon tried to hum to match the tune of the woman's cry, but the scream stopped abruptly when the gangbanger saw the demon. The hellspawn pouted like a disappointed child and his broad, dead-gray shoulders shrugged in disappointment.

"I do miss the symphony," Old Scratch sighed. His reptilian eyes swept over the gathering. Fear and anxiety filled the large chamber like an oppressive cloud of cigar smoke. Seating himself at the head of the table in an oversized, glittering golden throne fit for the King of Kings, the demon shifted his sinewy length. Folded against his back, his leathery, bat-like wings trembled. The humanoid beast was a perfect fit for the hellish surroundings. Taking a seat to the demon's immediate left was his trusted right hand, Scarlett.

"Excellent turnout," Old Scratch teased, fully aware everyone in the room knew the dire consequences of missing a meeting or arriving late. Four chairs near the head of the table remained empty. Old Scratch nodded Scarlett, and, as his top lieutenant, and she brought the meeting to order.

"First off, I'd like to give an update on some of our missing members..." A large section of wall behind Old Scratch's throne opened to reveal a bank of monitors. All the screens flashed on, displaying images of what looked like a translucent, man-sized Amoeba. Scarlett nodded toward the four unoccupied seats.

"The gelatinous mastermind Goo is being held in a secret location by a joint world law-enforcement cartel after his last failed go-round with San Angeles' prime protector, Midnight. Our sources are still trying to ascertain his whereabouts."

The image on the screens changed to show a tall figure with more than a mild resemblance to the legendary Frankenstein monster. "Hellbent is still in a medically-induced coma as a result of his epic battle with, once again, Midnight."

"Only a psycho would attempt to go toe-to-toe with Midnight at the stroke of twelve to prove his place to the criminal underworld," Number Two blurted.

"Hellbent was lucky he was battling Midnight, and not that morally ambiguous media whore The Bat," Ricochet commented.

"That crazy sumbitch would have beaten him to death." There was several agreeing murmurs.

The screens' image changed again. A wide-shouldered, middle-aged man dressed in a natty mid-twentieth century three-piece suit appeared, his face hidden in the shadow of his matching fedora hat.

"The undead, ex-Mafia assassin Tombstone has finally been laid to rest after the Supreme Court ruled that, as a zombie, he no longer retains the civil rights of living American citizens. He was buried not-quite-alive in a monitored, seamless titanium sphere in the graveyard of America's supermax prison for the criminally insane, Lonely Boy. Our intrepid hero Midnight escorted him to his final resting place. Sadly, even Tombstone won't be able to out-exist his multiple life sentences."

Old Scratch stared toward the fourth vacant seat. Scarlett's gentle voice wafted up to him.

"The Preacher is going to be late. You were notified."

The demon turned his malignant attention to his right hand. She didn't wilt under the withering gaze. "He'll be bringing *gifts*." The smile that formed on Old Scratch's face would have killed a dove.

"That's right," he remembered with a single nod. "Gifts indeed."

Scarlett returned the nod. The bald, classical beauty re-crossed her long muscular legs and allowed herself the tiniest grin. She wore her trademark sexy outfit, a blood-red leotard with an oval cutout at the chest that displayed her ample cleavage to its best advantage. Crimson sashes cocooned her arms, and knee-high boots completed the outfit. The siren appeared relaxed, yet she remained diligent in her duties, organizing the banquet and keeping tabs on the demon's underlings. Old Scratch turned his attention back to his guests.

"Now, before dinner is served, I'd like to make an announcement. Before sunrise, the city's greatest hero, Midnight, will be dead."

The gathering erupted in celebration, though an underlying questioning murmur began at the same time. The hellion's wings unfolded and flapped reflexively. He allowed the response to continue for several seconds, and then snapped his wings closed. The loud *whomp* quieted the room.

"Now, I know what many of you must be thinking," the demon continued reassuringly, his gaze meeting the eyes of everyone around the table. "There have been numerous diabolical and ingenious plots to dispose of Midnight, but none have succeeded."

A beautiful but blank-eyed server sat a large goblet in front of Old Scratch. He dipped a talon into it, licking the soaked claw clean with a swipe of his large black tongue. "After tonight, he'll never meddle in our affairs again."

In the middle of the banquet table, a hand floated into the air. The demon recognized the respectful gesture.

"Gravel?"

Lumpy with musculature, an enormous bald man stood up. His black tee shirt appeared painted on. His worn, blood-red leather vest announced his allegiance to the outlaw biker club Lucifer's Abortions. One side of his pasty face bore multiple scars and pock marks. He squinted down the table. "What's the plan, boss?" His Russian accent was thick.

Every pointed tooth gleamed in Old Scratch's smile. "It's very simple. I dreamed his death."

Gravel couldn't help glancing around the table. "Uh, okay. But I thought Midnight was almost invincible at night?"

The hellion's wings unfolded and with a couple of quick flaps, his body had risen to levitate in the air. Seconds later, he perched atop his throne. "Almost being the key word. Tonight, nature is going to take its course."

Everyone looked around at each other, still uncertain.

"Trust me. After tonight, the whole world is going to change, starting with San Angeles."

Gravel appeared no closer to understanding, but nodded anyway. Following his boss' example, a malignant smile formed. Still perched, Old Scratch swept a clawed foot down and grabbed his goblet. He swiveled his leg at an unnatural angle and took a sip from the jewel-encrusted cup.

"And what of the lovely Catfight?" The demon's wings folded against his back, and for a moment he looked exactly like a gargoyle. "It's long been rumored the duo's heroic partnership is much more intimate in private. Too bad they never married. I would love to make her a widow."

The uncertain looks around the table turned into knowing, sinister smiles. Taunting laughter and sporadic applause filled the chamber. Gravel whooped and smacked the back of The Mob's Number Two, almost causing the little man to tumble to the floor.

A line chorus line of naked women entered the banquet hall through the opening left between the shattered chamber doors. They carried ornate trays of drinks and covered platters. As beautiful as Las Vegas showgirls, each woman wore an exaggerated smile, eyes staring blankly into space and beyond. A busty pair of ladies served the demon first, refilling his goblet with a red liquid and setting at his place a large, sterling-silver platter covered by a dome large enough to conceal a turkey. The servers placed their hands on the lid, but waited for Old Scratch's signal. As the other women filled every diner's shot glass, the demon smiled at the varied reactions. Some around the table leered at the nude women, while others paid much more attention to the crimson refreshment.

Once each guest had been served, the hellspawn raised his goblet into the air. Everyone followed suit, though some seemed more hesitant than others. "To the death of Midnight!" Old Scratch sang out before drinking deeply.

A few of the criminals glanced around the table before putting the glasses to their lips. Some winced as they swallowed the virgin blood, but knew the demon wouldn't be pleased if they refused the offering.

Old Scratch nodded to his servers and they lifted away the silver dome. On the platter beneath, a young woman's severed head, covered in squirming maggots, sat on a bed of fresh lettuce. Blood still leaked from the jagged stump of the neck. A soft retching came from somewhere in the gathering. The demon rubbed his large hands together in anticipation.

"My favorite!" His black-marble eyes shone as the edge of a talon sliced down the side of the once-beautiful face. Razor sharp, the claw cleaved a thin ribbon of flesh in the same fashion as a paring knife. As the bloody strip came off, Old Scratch flipped it into the air. The demon snapped the flesh between his jaws like a T-Rex.

The young woman from the Tough Titties gang retched again, inspiring a mixture of groans, laughter, and applause.

"I love when the meat comes right off the bone!"

Around the table, servers lifted away the silver domes waiting in front of the other guests, exposing slabs of steaming steaks. Some around the table tore into the offering, while others stared at the rare and bleeding meat. Their eyes flickered between their leader's plate and their own, less gory meals.

Old Scratch scanned the table. "Eat up, everyone. You'll want your strength for the celebration I've planned for Midnight's funeral." Even the most reluctant amongst the invited guests made motions of dining.

The Mob's leader looked sideways at the demon through her black mask. "Isn't this a little premature, Old Scratch?" the Amazonian Number One asked. "It wouldn't be the first time Midnight survived a great plan."

The dining room went suddenly quiet.

The hell demon stared venomously at his fellow villain. "Did I mention I also dreamed I killed you, put you into a meat grinder, and fed you to school children for Christmas lunch?"

The Mob's leader shook her head vigorously.

"Then shut the fuck up before I scoop out your brain and use your skull as a candy dish."

The leader of The Mob nodded, quickly cutting into her bleeding steak.

The demon's wings opened and flapped in irritation. "Such little faith. But soon, so very soon, I'll be snacking on Midnight's nut sack. It'll be like eating grapes."

"More like raisins," someone called out from down the table. An amused roar went up.

The banquet continued well into the evening. No one around the table wanted to be the first to excuse him or herself. Everyone merely waited to be dismissed.

Throughout the gathering, the demon recognized the absence of The Preacher. At one point, Scarlett leaned up to whisper to her boss, stroking the talons on his hand.

"He's never failed you before. You can be sure there's a good reason for him being a no-show."

"I really wanted something special to celebrate Midnight's death tonight." A buxom server leaned in to refill the hellspawn's goblet. Her expression remained blank as the demon appraised her wantonly. His reptilian eyes stalked her as she made her way down the table.

Scarlett's shook her head. "She wouldn't survive it."

Old Scratch turned a malignant stare to his right hand. "Who does? If The Preacher doesn't make our meeting tonight, if I don't get the *gifts* he promised, I'll leave my entertainment needs in your capable hands. Choose wisely."

"As always," Scarlett nodded, displaying a tiny, all-knowing smile.

Another statuesque beauty entered the chamber and made her way toward the head of the table. Eyes to the floor, she bowed, then spoke quietly into Scarlett's ear. The red-clad villainess nodded, dismissing the woman with a casual wave.

"Massive thunderstorms, rain, and lightning are holding course. The brunt of the system should hit after eleven tonight." She paused. "Midnight will be at the peak of his power."

The demon's smile showed all his teeth. The sight made even Scarlett rustle uncomfortably in her seat. Old Scratch noisily sucked down the warm blood in his goblet, running his massive black tongue over his lips so as not to miss a drop.

Chapter Three

GETTING SOME RELIGION

A heavy downpour had commenced by the time Pastor Leonard Griffin, a.k.a. The Preacher, stepped arm-in-arm with two of his prettiest worshipers from the rear door of the small church. By the time they all slid laughing into the back seat of the waiting black sedan, the women's thin linen dresses were plastered wetly to their bodies. Pastor Griffin leered. The second the car door shut, the rear locks clicked into place.

The Preacher closed his eyes as nimble fingers began to undo his shirt buttons and trousers zipper. He sighed in expectation.

The women went about their duties, but despite the kindling pleasure, Pastor Griffin sensed something wrong.

The car wasn't moving.

"Wellington? What the devil?!" Annoyed, The Preacher opened his eyes. The car hadn't traveled an inch from the parking lot. "Wellington?" The rest of his sentence died in his throat. The figure behind the wheel loomed much too large to be that of his regular driver and personal protector, Wellington Duke. The retired WWF wrestler had the ability to cut quite the swath with his square-shouldered bulk, but the man now squeezed in the front seat easily eclipsed him.

"Good evening," the figure said. The vocal tone sounded deep enough, dark enough, to make the women put their activities on pause. The small hairs on the back of The Preacher's neck stood to attention.

"What's going on? Where's Wellington?"

"He's on break." The baritone sighed. "Actually, more like he's broken. Aren't you late for the big Old Scratch powwow?"

Griffin caught himself before his anger got the best of him. The women didn't speak, but started fidgeting nervously. The simplest lie came out first.

"I don't know what you're talking about, and if my driver's been seriously injured, the authorities—"

The sound of the doors unlocking made everyone in the back seat jump. "Ladies, get out of the car."

The women didn't waste a moment. Griffin didn't move a muscle. After the doors slammed shut and were re-locked, the silence was deafening. Nerves got the best of the pastor. "You know who I work for. You're making a big mistake."

"I don't think so." The figure behind the wheel turned. The car's shadowy interior seemed to swirl with him. Griffin's eyes widened and his mouth dropped open.

"Mid...Midnight?" Rattled, The Preacher dove and jerked the door handle, but the door wouldn't open. He slammed a fist against the transparent partition. "Old Scratch will kill you for this!"

The shadows in the back seat started to slide toward the pastor from all angles. Some of the darkness from above his head began to drip onto his face. He screamed at its coldness.

"What do you want?!" he shrieked. He tried to dodge the black drops, and then saw the backseat slowly filling with darkness from the floorboards. He flopped around, kicking at the divider and hammering his fists against the door's bulletproof glass. Before long, the darkness rose up to his chest. Defeated, he finally sat still. He tried in vain to spit the blackness from his lips. It seemed to have a mind of its own.

"So," Midnight said, as if starting a casual conversation, "what's Old Scratch up to?"

The Preacher stared at the hero. "You're dead and don't even know it."

Midnight sighed, and the backseat continued to fill with lethal shadows.

"Fuck the clichéd villain bullshit." The hero patiently ignored the man's shrieks.

The liquid darkness rose to just under the man's lifted chin. Griffin's eyes darted to and fro.

"Last chance. What's the plan?"

"He'll kill me, damn it!"

"And I won't?" Midnight responded calmly.

"You're not like The Bat, or some of those other lawless vigilantes..." Pastor Griffin flopped and thrashed as the darkness rose to his nostrils. Midnight waited a full minute before lowering the shadow level so the man could speak.

"Okay, okay...One of the girls told me he's been ranting about a repetitive dream predicting your death. I think he believes it's supposed to happen tonight. Something about the storm. That's all I know."

Midnight stared at the man, absorbing the information. Griffin was telling the truth.

"How do I find his lair?" The Preacher's eyes got even bigger. He shook his head like a rattle.

"I don't know...I swear I don't. I meet him or Scarlett with girls in different places. He decides. I just do what I'm told." Again the truth.

"And tonight?"

"I was supposed to take the two girls downtown, to the

observation deck at Blackledge Tower." Midnight glared at his prisoner, demanding every scrap of information.

"Eleven sharp," The Preacher added.

Truth.

"Hey, I've told you what I know. I'm gonna need protection. Jesus God..."

Midnight frowned under his mask. "What did you say?"

"Old Scratch will kill me if he finds out. I don't want to die!"

Midnight pushed open the driver's door and squeezed out of the car, popping his head back in to offer his parting advice. "Use your faith as a shield."

The backseat began to fill with darkness again. Midnight listened to the frantic thumping at the blackened windows as he squinted up before looking up through the hard-driving rain. A comet streaked toward him.

His ride had arrived.

Chapter Four

WINNER TAKES ALL

The alien called Starlight swooped from the sky, her sleek form almost hidden by a streaking cocoon of white light. Midnight raised an arm above his head. Starlight grabbed him by the wrist and carried him away in a burst of energy.

"Blackledge Tower," the dark hero told her. The alien zoomed toward downtown's distant silhouette, the city flashing by Midnight's eyes almost faster than even his Ultra senses could take in.

Midnight marveled at all he could see in the micro-snapshots of his vision as he crossed the heart of San Angeles. Car thefts, assaults, burglaries. A woman being forced into a trash-strewn alley by a pair of drunken men. He wished he could help her, but Old Scratch's destruction took priority.

Midnight didn't know how fast Starlight could fly, but they reached the downtown area in less than a minute. She eased her speed as she approached the city's tallest skyscraper, gently lowering him to its rooftop observation deck. Oblivious to the high winds, the heroine floated, looking back at the approaching storm.

"If you need me to, I can swing back after a quick pass over the border. Human traffickers love harsh weather."

"Thanks for the ride," he replied. "Totally up to you if you want to swing back. By the way, there's an assault in an alley just east of the liquor store at Stanford and 24th street."

"I'll take care of it."

The access door to the roof deck burst open. From the dimly lit opening sprang a dark, somersaulting figure. The lithe, costumed woman landed in a ready crouch a few feet from Midnight. She smiled as her long tail twitched and swung. Leopard-fur trim at the wrists and neckline of a black leather jacket, paired with leopard-print tights, the sleek outfit hugged her curves. She wore her brown mane braided into a tight fishtail that hung to the dip of her lower back. A leopard eyelet mask completed the outfit.

"Starlight flies too damn fast," Catfight purred teasingly. Her Eastern European accent hinted at her birthplace. She eased to her feet, her shiny claws easing in and out of their sheaths. "Let's get ready to rumble!"

Midnight stared in awe at the heroine, his Tatiana, her heroic nature revealed in all its feline glory. Yet he frowned at the sight. He raised a hand toward Starlight, delaying her departure.

"This is between the demon and me," he growled. "If I want to end it tonight, I can't be worrying about you."

Catfight covered the ground between her and Midnight in three quick strides. She appraised him as if assessing a priceless work of art, then pouted like a small child.

Oblivious to the rain, Starlight continued to hover above the observation deck, but slowly extended the distance between herself and the two crime fighters. Their discussion appeared to be becoming personal.

"You promised I could be a part of this." Thunder boomed and grumbled, and then a burst of lightning lit up the sky. The feline heroine flinched.

"You're not at your best in this weather..." Midnight spoke softly, aware of Starlight's subtle allowance of space.

"You know Scratch won't come after you by himself. Someone needs to keep that bitch army off your back."

Midnight smiled under his mask. "Then watch from a safe distance."

"I'm not a child! And don't you dare treat me like some sidekick!"

"I found out Scratch has been having the same dream I've been having. He thinks he can take me. Don't worry. He'll be alone."

Catfight leaned in close, her tone full of concern. "This dream business is crazy." She glanced toward the angry sky. "I know you're almost invincible right now, but do you really think you can defeat him one-on-one?" Her claws retracted as she gently stroked his arm. From above, Starlight redirected her attention into the storm. The display of human emotion made her internal organs feel odd.

The dark clouds opened up and the rain started falling in huge, splattering drops. Midnight and Catfight stood so close the raindrops could hardly pass between them. "You weren't here in my dream," Midnight confided.

Catfight smirked. "It's just a dream. Since when did you become superstitious?"

Midnight's jaw flexed under his mask. He looked up at Starlight, waiting patiently, then back at Catfight, the woman he loved.

Midnight's voice rumbled. "Can you do me a favor before you head down Mexico way?"

Catfight took a cautious step back. She shook her head, dislodging a wave of drops. "Don't even think about it. I want to be here when you take down Scratch."

Midnight shook his head. "It's too dangerous. I can't risk him using you against me."

Catfight shimmered for a moment, separating into three slightly different versions of herself. Instead of just one gorgeous Catfight, a trio of catlike women faced Midnight. All three feline figures hissed and displayed their claws as they struck different fighting poses. While the original Catfight's costume was accented in leopard print, the two new versions wore outfits with tiger and black panther patterns.

Midnight signaled Starlight. "Santa Monica beach will do fine."

Before any of the Catfight trio could protest, Starlight encased all three of them in a transparent bubble of light. A split-second later, they became a fading streak across the dark sky.

"I love you Tatiana," Midnight whispered, following the alien's signature white comet trail across the heavens. Thunder continued to rumble and jagged streaks of lightning gashed the sky. The rain turned into a downpour. Midnight walked slowly to the middle of the rooftop and waited. His muscular frame rippled in anticipation. If Old Scratch actually showed up, the world would be a different place by dawn.

Midnight didn't have to see a clock to know what time it was. The special pulse in his body told him it was almost his time—midnight. At that moment he would be at his most powerful, and for the next few minutes after that, he would be all but invincible, as well.

The rain continued to come down hard, but he hadn't moved a step. The storm had blown in from the ocean and settled over the city's center. Thunder bellowed around him while the dark sky served as a backdrop for the spectacular light show. Water on the rooftop had almost swallowed the top of Midnight's boots, and the howling wind urged all living things to take shelter. The hero ignored the weather, basking in the power coursing like blood through his body.

Old Scratch was coming.

A moment later, the winged demon appeared, water splashing from the heavy two-footed landing. The beast grinned and flexed his bat-like wings, making the hellion appear even larger.

Midnight took a step forward. His mask hid his smile. He wished it didn't. "The Preacher sends his regards," the superhero said.

Old Scratch flapped his wings, and his serpentine tongue flickered out as if to catch some raindrops. His eyes never left his rival. "Wonderful weather we're having, don't you think?" The demon slurped up the water as if he'd just crawled from Mojave Desert. "It's the stuff dreams are made of."

Lightning flashed right next to the skyscraper. The demon's wings flapped against the downpour, and he started hovering a foot off the rooftop like a monstrous insect.

"I'm sorry Catfight couldn't join you. I would have liked your death seared into her mind."

Midnight's fingers curled into fists. He shook away the rain.

"Funny— my dreams had a different conclusion." Midnight took a step forward. "You've said you escaped from hell, but with your power…you could have changed the world."

The demon cocked his head slightly, surprised at the statement. He smiled as only a demon can. "How can so many believe in God and so few believe in Satan? I am one of the Dark Master's children. I grew tired of laboring under millennia-old plans. What you deem as evil is simply my nature. I am the next messiah for this pile of dirt. Your bitch Catfight will bear my spawn screaming from atop your unmarked grave."

Midnight took another step forward. The sound of the downpour surrounded him. "You know I didn't come here to take you to some specially designed prison," he said.

The demon laughed, loudly and deeply. "Of course you didn't. You came here to die."

The superhero's body twitched and he surged forward, his second step already accelerating him into a dead sprint, covering the space between Old Scratch and himself in little more than a blink. Midnight torpedoed himself into the hellspawn's chest, driving the monster hard into the water-covered rooftop.

Midnight straddled the demon, pinning his head with a hand at his throat. A series of punches blurred into Old Scratch's face with sledgehammer force. The demon slammed his talons into the superhero's back, tearing away costume and flesh. Midnight cried out at the searing pain. Old Scratch took advantage and swatted the man away, tossing him across the roof. Midnight twisted his body around in the air, but he didn't land cleanly, banging his shoulder as he somersaulted to his feet. He spun toward his enemy, the wounds on his back burning.

The demon straightened up and stared. A thought nagged at him. *Midnight had the same dream?*

But instinct took control. Midnight angled his body and settled into a defensive posture as Old Scratch launched himself like a grotesque bird of prey, wings flapping and massive hand and foot claws extended. Through the sound of the rain and thunder, the bells of a nearby church began to ring off the midnight hour.

Then the demon was on him, but San Angeles' guardian, at the zenith of his power, proved too quick. Midnight stepped to the side, grabbed Old Scratch by the wrist, and used his momentum against him, flinging the demon toward the rooftop access. Thunder grumbled as the hellspawn smashed through the reinforced security

MIDNIGHT ETERNAL

door, half-disappearing into the darkness.

Scrambling to free himself from the confining stairwell, Old Scratch had almost broken loose when Midnight exploded into him like a missile, battering him with a furious barrage of kicks and punches. The demon took the punishment, but finally twisted free. Old Scratch bolted into the air, shoving Midnight off-balance as he burst by. The superhero righted himself, searching the dark skies for the evil one.

Sudden pain lanced through Midnight's shoulders as he was whisked off the ground. Old Scratch's foot talons dug into his flesh as the demon gained altitude. The rooftop rapidly dropped away, and it took Midnight a moment to calculate his escape. But before he could jackknife his legs up into a double kick to the demon's face, an ear-splitting peal of thunder surrounded him. And even as his ears registered the rumbling boom, the accompanying flash of light snatched his vision like a master thief.

Pain devoured him. Midnight's mind froze in mid-thought as every nerve in his body disintegrated. His consciousness exploded, a million pieces of memory scattering like so many leaves on a windy day. For a blink of time he could actually see the brilliant fragments hurled out into deepest space, each tiny starburst representing a morsel of his existence from early childhood to celebrated superhero status.

And then—absolute, lifeless black.

Catfight raced through the downpour along Olympic Boulevard, toward Beverly Hills. Starlight had dropped her and her two duplicates down on an empty stretch of beach between the Santa Monica Pier and Venice Beach. As soon as the transport bubble disappeared, Catfight merged into a single figure, sprinting back toward the distant downtown landscape. The Blackledge Tower was more than ten miles from the ocean, and the traffic and the weather were far from in her favor. She started crying before she realized it, the rain hiding her tears.

At some point near the 405 freeway, the vigilante called The Bat joined her. One moment she was running alone and the next, the face-painted crimefighter appeared to her right, his supercharged Louisville Slugger strapped across his back. His outfit, grey with black pinstripes, had the look of a vintage Yankees baseball uniform, with a bold black B sewn over the heart. His worn black batting helmet jiggled slightly as he ran.

"You can tell me when we get there," he muttered, and didn't speak again until they reached Koreatown.

Catfight slowed at the intersection of Olympic and Vermont as thunder boomed, and a massive lightning bolt flashed down and appeared to strike the top of Blackledge Tower. Startled, Catfight threw a hand across her face.

The Bat spoke up. "What's wrong?"

Catfight pointed toward the top of the skyscraper. "Where the lightning struck— that's where Midnight was waiting for Old Scratch!" Catfight sprang into the traffic, dancing across car hoods and SUVs. The Bat dodged through the traffic, not nearly as agile or quick as the woman. When he cleared the traffic, she was nearly a block ahead. The vigilante grunted and sprinted to catch up.

Minutes later, the two crimefighters burst into Blackledge Tower's lobby and, ignoring the shouts of the private security force, took the first waiting elevator to the roof. Even at express speed, the trip took longer than Catfight could stand. She punched at the lit observation-deck button over and over, ignoring the obvious logic that pressing the button would not get the elevator there any faster.

When the elevator doors opened, Catfight burst into the weather, calling Midnight's name. The Bat followed, weapon in hand. He'd never faced off against Old Scratch, but he knew the demon had ended more than one vigilante's career. He didn't want his name added to that roster.

Catfight stopped running so suddenly that The Bat had to dodge to the side to avoid knocking her to the wet rooftop. As it was, a second later she crumpled to her knees, hands covering her

face. His eyes barely had a chance to take in the scene before her scream battled with the shrieking elements.

The baseball vigilante's mouth dropped open at the sight. He lost the feel of the bat in his hands.

A large man lay in the rain, rigid as a plank, his dark clothing in seared tatters. Despite the rain, smoke drifted from the smoldering body. Midnight's mask had burned away, revealing a face charred beyond recognition. The smell of electrocuted flesh caused The Bat to gag.

Catfight's keening cut through his shock. He reached out and placed a comforting hand on her shoulder. Police and emergency-vehicle sirens drifted up from the street below. The Bat looked up into the night, but the rain would never wash away the horror of the night.

Chapter Five

AWAKENING FROM DEATH'S SLUMBER

His hearing returned first. A tremendous clap of thunder boomed so loudly it felt as if it were emanating from headphones channeling maximum volume. As the rumble faded, a painful wail rose to a crescendo.

When his eyes opened, he wasn't sure what he sensed first—the warm raindrops blurring his vision, or the desperate, high-pitched plea to God. The voice belonged to a woman, but when he tried to focus, images were just fuzzy blobs.

The world had tilted off-kilter, and it took a few moments for him to realize he was down on the ground, and his line of sight included rain puddles. The desperate shrieking came from a feminine figure kneeling a few feet away. Between him and the kneeling figure, a body lay stretched out, a dark boot on its foot close enough for him to reach out and touch if he'd had the luxury of any feeling or movement in his body.

A tall figure stepped next to the kneeling one, and suddenly the kneeling woman no longer directed her screams toward the weeping skies. The woman sprang away from the sprawled body and charged toward him, but was intercepted in mid-air, caught by the taller figure. The female struggled in the arms of the other, hissing and screaming a string of profanities. Clearly the one being restrained was a woman whose pain and anger were beyond her control.

Pain came over him in a violent wave. He almost blacked out before the scream left his throat. His world whirled in an awful lopsided motion. Sickness stabbed into his midsection like a dull bayonet. A blinding explosion of agony erased his vague thoughts. This time he did black out, but like the bounce of a rubber ball, his mind jolted right back. He could feel his body lurching toward life itself. He strained against the heavy manacles of his own flesh.

Out of his sight, a door banged open, accompanied by yelling and movement. The tall figure released the woman and she darted out of sight. The tall figure drew an object from over his shoulder just in time to fend off a wave of attackers. Shouts, curses, grunts, the pounding of fists against flesh, and the crunch of bone all blended together.

Movement swarmed around him. Soothing whispers sifted into his ears as hands clawed under him, fighting for grip. He felt his body lift away from the wet ground and jostle as he was carried, his head hanging limp. He had no strength at all. Rain overflowed his open eyes, worsening his poor vision.

A small set of shiny black claws swiped past his face and tore across his upper chest. The burning pain became part of the cocoon of misery swaddling him. His mind swirled into darkness.

Nightmarish. No, more like the feverish dreams of an addict in withdrawal. Never fully awake, his mind faded in and out of consciousness. At times he could feel movement, could register passing through lighter and darker areas. Garbled voices spoke indistinct words. Between bouts of awareness, there were plenty of gaps with only darkness. Soothing and empty and relaxing, he liked those best.

In fact, his imagination devised a gently swinging hammock to cradle the wreckage of his body. He could feel himself rocking back and forth in time with his heartbeat, a cool breeze soothing his agony. Through his mind's eye he was drawn into a perfect starless sky, never once wondering where the specks of brilliance had gone. It felt peaceful here, and he was content to stay.

The constant throbbing to avenge the atrocities of Old Scratch had been quelled like a flaming match plunged under a running faucet. The jealousy and anger he'd felt since The Bat's arrival on the crimefighter scene were now healed wounds bearing no scars. Even The Bat's thinly veiled affection for Catfight seemed harmless. He experienced no unpleasant emotional uncertainty. Just an endless slide show of vivid, yet sterile, thoughts.

Fire abruptly filled his vision. A woman screamed.

The petite female fell to the floor, dropping the torch she held. Her eyes never left him. "He's awake! He's awake!" She grabbed the torch and scrambled toward a doorway. Hurried footsteps echoed as his senses fought to align.

He squinted as his sight adjusted. He lay on a huge bed in some sort of a cave. The walls were earthen and crude, as was the floor. A small torch inside the entrance lit the room. Brimstone hung in the air, with another, more cloying smell. It made him flinch as he tried to identify it. Something was burning.

His hearing was sharp enough to pick up the quiet crackling of the torch flames from across the room.

He'd been lying down, but not on a bed, he realized. It was a smooth slab of polished stone. The blanket covering him had fallen to his waist. It was some sort of patchwork quilt. It felt like velvet against his skin.

His mouth creaked open as if to speak, though he wasn't sure what he was going to say. The taste in his mouth was metallic, bitter, like copper. He smacked his lips, but the awful taste didn't diminish.

The broad double doors at the opposite end of the room pushed open, and a wave of beautiful naked women hurried into the chamber. The first few surrounded a woman who crawled hesitantly forward. He noticed some of the women wore large bandages on their forearms or thighs, while others displayed bruises and healing facial lacerations.

The females surged into the room, but didn't rush to his side. They circled where he lay, maintaining their distance. Only the crawling woman, now chattering with fear, made a sound. Finally another woman slapped her, the sound ringing in the room.

The crowd made way for a tall woman with a cleanly shaved head. The absence of hair did nothing to subtract from her beauty. She stepped clear of the others and immediately stopped in her tracks, staring at him as he regarded her. Silken black strips of fabric wound around her curves. A black gauze shawl was draped around her broad shoulders, and a slice of matching lace masked her emerald eyes. Her expression encompassed a mixture of shock and awe.

He recognized her, though his jumbled thoughts played hide-and-seek with her name.

In the silence, a sob hitched in the woman's throat. It might as well have been a gunshot. A tear streaked down the flawless skin of her face, and then she was running across the room. Startled, he could only blink, and then she was on him, smothering him with her body, her clean scent instantly vanquishing the odors of sulfur and burnt musk. She made the oddest assortment of sounds as she smothered him in hungry kisses, her lips impossibly soft. Her arms snaked around him and squeezed with python strength, her blood-red nails digging into his skin.

His arm reflexively encircled her, and he could feel her body stiffen at the contact. She pulled back, her expression unreadable, as his hand drifted toward her face. He gently traced a finger across her cheek, leaving a razor-thin streak of her blood. She trembled in orgasmic release at the contact. He couldn't take his eyes off his finger and the hand attached to it.

An exceptionally large hand, each of its dead gray fingers ending in deadly-looking talons, the first talon tipped with the crimson of the woman's blood. A hand possessing only three fingers in all; the finger next to the pinkie had been cut or chewed off at its bulbous knuckle. He studied the hand's color, its texture. The flesh appeared dead, yet it lived. A riddle. And the answer lay just beyond the reach of his jumbled mind.

"Scratch, we thought we'd lost you!"

His mouth hung open for several seconds before he found his

voice. But the deep whisper was foreign. Alien. It didn't belong to him.

"I'm...I'm sorry..." was all he could manage, and the strange world began to dissolve. The woman took his blood-tipped claw finger deep into her mouth. Her talented tongue swirled around it with practiced ease. She turned and spoke to those gathered.

"The master lives!" The chamber exploded with cheers and celebration. She smiled as she caressed the slice on her face. Her whisper was just for him. "My dark lord."

Everything swirled into a central point directly in front of him. Sights, sounds.... He felt himself lurch as he became ill, and just before the black curtains of his consciousness jerked closed, he heard the woman make one last exclamation.

"Old Scratch is eternal!"

Chapter Six

A CITY MOURNS

The stars shone with full force, but the lights of the San Angeles dulled them. In the neighboring desert or mountains, the night sky would have been an astronomer's wet dream.

Tatiana Sklovic, a.k.a. Catfight, knelt in the shadows atop the skyscraper across from the Blackledge Tower. Law-enforcement agents had removed the crime-scene tape and allowed normal traffic back through the area. Tears burned Tatiana's cheeks as she watched the steady stream of people pay their respects. The rooftop overflowed with flowers. Women and children wept out loud as they stood around the curtained-off spot where crime-scene techs had marked an outline around Midnight's body. That outline, with its distinctive broad shouldered silhouette, had become a symbol of the city's grief, photographed and artistically rendered and posted again and again in all forms of social media. Tatiana knew the lightning strike had all but destroyed her love's body. The charred remains looked far too ghastly for display at the upcoming public memorial service. Instead, per her request, the cremation process was to be completed, and the hero's ashes dumped into the Pacific Ocean.

She sniffled and swiped the moisture from her face. He'd always loved the water. She wasn't much of a fan.

The preparations were all set, except for the decision about divulging Midnight's true identity to the public. Dental records would solve that mystery for the coroner's office tomorrow. She knew she had the ability to go to the mayor and the Chief of Police to have them keep those findings private, but Tatiana felt torn. With no viewing possible, was it fair for the world not to know Andre Waters had been their beloved guardian?

Full disclosure wouldn't compromise anyone's safety. Both Dre's parents were deceased, and he didn't have any siblings. As far as Tatiana knew, Andre's only breathing relative was an uncle in the Midwest living out his last days in a cancer hospice. She didn't believe for a second even a villain as heinous as Old Scratch would seek out an elderly man with all but both feet in the grave.

The thought of the demon caused her cat claws to slide into view. A feline growl rumbled low in her throat, and fresh tears filled her eyes.

Tatiana would have given anything to have been able to rip the heart out of the hellspawn's chest that night, but there'd been too many of The Damned there. Fuck Old Scratch's army of female minions, even if they were under his hypnotic sway. And especially fuck Scarlett, the demon's partner-in-crime. That bitch was number two on her vengeance list, and Catfight wouldn't be satisfied until she was covered in her blood, and the blood of her demon boss.

Her head dropped to her chest, suddenly boulder-heavy with regret. She should have listened to Andre. She hadn't understood the transformation he'd undergone over the past couple of years from his battles with Old Scratch. When she'd first met Midnight, he'd considered himself a dark avenger for the citizens of San Angeles, and his code of conduct had been equally strict and simple: As an independent agent of law enforcement, he did not act as judge, jury, or executioner. He didn't dispense justice. He just caught the bad guys that normal enforcement ranks couldn't.

But the crimes of Old Scratch had changed that perspective. The demon was the exception to all the major supervillains. While fiends like The Freak and Goo had personal agendas against humanity, most seemed to have lines they wouldn't cross. Even human monsters like Hellbent or The Clown didn't directly target children or hospitals or the elderly.

Old Scratch, however, had no such limitations. The demon was exactly that— a being with a complete absence of moral regard for human life. While other criminals sought fame or wealth or even had delusions of ruling the world, Old Scratch used earth as his personal demented playground. While he, too, desired to take over the planet, he'd boasted too many times about wanting to turn the world into another hell. He'd been close a couple of times, but Midnight had found a way to thwart his plans.

Catfight rubbed her face with her hands, her mind whirling back to the horrible Daycare Plague. Old Scratch had found a way to infect the city's water supply with a supernatural agent, affecting only children five years of age and under. Those ingesting the water developed symptoms similar to the flu for about forty-eight hours, and then they became snarling, murderous cannibals.

Small children across Southern California attacked, maimed, and killed thousands of adults and non-carrier children. Panic and fear gripped San Angeles. The city was under siege in a matter of days. The military had sealed off the metropolis best it could, and the mayor announced martial law. The situation had been devastating to Midnight because the threat wasn't something he could confront and defeat head-on. In fact, the majority of area superheroes were forced to stand by, virtually helpless, as scientists, historians, and theologians worked around the clock to discover an antidote.

As the city's fate hung in the balance, the San Fernando

Valley's newest protector, Priest, had discovered how to reverse the process and thwart the demon's diabolical attack. Those twelve days might have been the worst period in modern American history going back to the Civil War. 9/11 had been a fall into a sandbox compared to the overall devastation wrought by Old Scratch's sick plot. It had just added even more fuel to Andre's all-consuming fire to see the end not only of Old Scratch, but the end of all hellspawn. The end of evil.

A hand gently dropped onto Tatiana's shoulder.

She had been so involved in her misery that the contact caught her completely off-guard. Her movements a whirl, she responded violently, fueled by anger and loss. Catfight grabbed the arm and tossed the unknown person over her shoulder. By the time the intruder landed on his back several feet away, she was on top of him, her gleaming claws a whisker away from an exposed throat. Nose to nose, an angry hiss escaped between her clenched teeth. Her two alternate selves appeared and flanked her protectively, one ready to extract the person's eyes, the other set to plunge her claws into the figure's groin.

"Don't," the man whispered.

It took a moment for her to recognize the voice. The three Catfights exhaled deeply, as one, their claws retracting. Slowly, all three of her stood.

The Bat didn't move until the middle Catfight reached for his hand. He took it and sprang to his feet. The feline trio took a step back.

"I'm sorry. I didn't mean to disturb you. I figured you might be around, watching..." He glanced across at the Blackledge rooftop. The procession went on, with no end in sight. "I wasn't sure if you might want some company."

The two flanking Catfights stepped close to the central one, shimmering for a moment or two, before they merged into the central body, leaving just one Catfight. The Bat blinked. The feline crimefighter collapsed to her knees. "I'm having trouble accepting his death."

The Bat exhaled deeply. "You were there. You saw the body."

She glared up into his face. "But I didn't feel him leave this plane."

"I know you say you're super sensitive, but maybe the lightning had something to do with that. Maybe that energy interfered somehow. Catfight, he's gone."

In less than the blink of an eye, Catfight got in The Bat's face, snarling.

"I know he's dead, damn you. I know he's gone." Her voice

began to quiver and break down. "I, I know...I'll never feel his touch again. I know I'll never bear his children." She burst out in tears and fell against the vigilante. His arms gathered her tight as he stared across to the spot where Midnight had died. He whispered calmly to Catfight.

"Everything is going to be all right. I'm here for you." He kissed her tenderly on the forehead.

With Catfight's survival instincts subdued, Tatiana sobbed into The Bat's chest, clinging to his sturdy frame. Flowing somewhere underneath it all, a river of hatred swelled within her. It was only a matter of time before it flooded its banks and swept along everything in her miserable path.

It wasn't fair. Dre had tried to explain his motivations for destroying the demon, but she wouldn't listen. No, she'd refused to trust the best man she'd ever known. Now he was gone, his light stolen from her because she hadn't believed strongly enough in true evil. And now she couldn't even avenge his death. Old Scratch should have been made to pay for his part in Dre's brutal demise.

With the demon also dead, where could she direct her hatred? Her jaws clenched and held. Her fury felt so perfect she wished Old Scratch were still alive so she could kill him herself. As tightly as she gripped The Bat, she wanted to dig her fingers even more deeply into the demon's throat, choking the life out of him. She'd gladly exchange her own last breath for the privilege of watching the life fade from Scratch's eyes.

Too late. Dre had already made the trade.

Chapter Seven

BAD NEWS TRAVELS FAST

This time when Dre awoke, he felt much more normal. His thoughts weren't confused and cluttered. His skull wasn't throbbing, nor did it feel like it weighed a thousand pounds. His vision was crisp, though the dark room was painted in vague hues of purple, black, and grey. His sense of smell remained sharp. The thick stench of sulfur and brimstone still hung in the air. Dying embers clung to the burnt-out torches stationed around the cave-like chamber.

He turned his head. His mouth dropped open slightly.

Scarlett— he remembered her name now— lay naked on top of the velvet-soft cover. Her beauty glowed in the darkness. Her red fingernails and toenails shone like jewels, and her low, grumbling snore almost made him laugh.

Being nude, her hairless head seemed all the more fitting. On closer inspection, it seemed Scarlett was hairless head to toe. Her skin, like milk, stretched taut over muscle and bone in the most exquisite way. Evil or not, the demon's right hand was as beautiful as any woman he'd ever seen.

If this was a dream, it was a very strange one. And if this was some kind of trick set up by Old Scratch...anger bubbled up inside him.

Andre's mind froze. The battle between him and the demon on the roof during the thunderstorm. He replayed the memory, blow by blow, and then his mind drew a total blank. Nothing. The next thing he remembered was waking up and being surrounded by Scratch's all-female army, The Damned.

He glanced over at the slumbering Scarlett, and then slowly pulled the thin cover away from his body. It didn't feel like silk, but the unknown material was soft and supple. He rolled to his feet, and slowly walked across the cavern toward a large, richly ornamented mirror. He stretched and shrugged his tight shoulder muscles. His body felt heavy and stiff, no doubt the aftermath of the fight with the hellspawn. He'd have to ask Tatiana for one of her famous full-body hot-oil massages. He smiled to himself. If he had to, he'd do her in return. Only fair.

He stepped in front of the mirror. Shock made him forget to take a breath. Confusion scrambled his thoughts.

The image of Old Scratch stared back at him.

Caught completely off guard, Midnight dropped into a fighting stance, as did his enemy in the mirror's reflection. He stared down the supervillain, Old Scratch reflecting the same mute fury.

Without thinking through his next move, Midnight quickly stepped forward and threw a hard straight right, but then pulled it just short of the mirror surface, less than an inch from Old Scratch's own loose fist. The demon's fishhook talons made it almost impossible to make a fist.

When Midnight looked down the strange, dead-flesh arm, he could feel himself begin to shake. He lifted a hand in front of his unbelieving eyes. This wasn't his hand.

The truth hit him just before he looked back into the mirror and felt a scream begin in his mind.

Old Scratch's wings suddenly burst open from their folded, at-rest position, and Midnight suddenly couldn't feel the long muscular legs beneath him. And dear God, the monstrous organ hanging between his legs…

He wanted to lash out at the reflection, but was too stunned to do anything but stare into the face of his sworn enemy.

"How can this be?" he whispered in a voice he despised. "How the fuck can this be?"

His mind searched for the solution. They had been fighting on the roof, the thunderstorm raging all around them. Rain pelted down, and thunder boomed. Scratch had snatched him up by the shoulders, and he'd been about to swing up and kick himself free, but...

He flinched at the memory of a powerful thunderclap.

The demon's reflection shook its head.

Midnight had woken up before. The Damned had filled the bed chamber.... He slowly raised the hand with the missing finger, staring at it in disbelief.

"This isn't real. It can't be. This is some sort of nightmare. Something that fucking demon dreamed up." he chuckled. "That sonbitch has quite the imagination." Midnight glanced back at the polished slab that served as his bed. Scarlett hadn't stirred.

"Does Scratch have me hooked up to some machine somewhere, or under some kind of spell? I'll play along until I can figure it out." He flapped the large, bat-like wings just enough to lift himself off the ground for a second or two. "The wings are ugly, but flying is pretty cool."

He dropped to the ground, then padded quietly back to the bed. He lay down and covered himself. Scarlett's smooth, muscular back was to him. He let his eyes close and sighed.

"Everything is going to be all right."

The darkness quickly swallowed him whole, so he never knew Scarlett had opened her eyes. She rolled toward her lover, her hand landing on the middle of his scarred chest. She cursed the lightning strike. It had changed him. To her relief, no pulse had greeted her searching fingers. She'd long grown used to Scratch's lack of a heartbeat, and the silent stillness she felt eased her back into a deep sleep. She'd think about his strange behavior tomorrow.

#

Ivy was the best fuck The Bat had ever had, but he couldn't keep Catfight out of his thoughts. He'd stayed with the heroine until she'd felt ready to go home. He'd watched her leave using the window washer's contraption he'd used to reach the roof to descend down the skyscraper's side.

With the roof access elevator shut down due to Midnight mourners trying to take pictures of the neighboring memorialized Blackledge roof, The Bat used the stairs, bounding down in record time. At the third floor, he used an office window to leap to the street, bouncing off the roof of a parked minivan as if it were a trampoline before somersaulting to the street and dashing off into the shadows. Half a block from his apartment loft, he saw someone crouched down on the fire escape outside his place.

He dropped through the building's skylight, landing lightly on his feet in the middle of his dark living area two floors below. The ample space looked more like a gymnasium than an apartment. Smelled it, too.

When he'd slid open the window, she crept in like a pale-skinned spider. She was pretty in a sleazy cheerleader way, with wild blonde hair, and feminine, yet firmly muscled curves rounding out her petite frame. He stared at the low-slung black leggings and sleeveless midriff top that showed off her ripped torso. A belly-button piercing sparkled with a small diamond. He had no doubt the jewel was real. A black headband held her hair out of her eyes. The ex-gymnast and former drug addict whispered in her little-girl voice.

"I don't have long, but I have news."

Mask and baseball uniform still on, The Bat allowed the little vixen to remove only what was necessary to free himself for both their pleasure.

She kicked out of her soft-soled boots and peeled off the leggings. The area between her legs was shaved smooth, the way he liked it. A gauze wrap circled one leg from just above her left knee, reaching to her upper thigh. She winced as she knelt in front of him and flicked the tip of her tongue against the end of his hardening flesh. She looked up into his eyes.

"The master..." she frowned, and started again. "We thought he was dead. He woke up earlier tonight. Scarlett is calling it a miracle." She spit on his length, stroking him slowly.

"Old Scratch is alive?"

Ivy nodded, then began using her mouth. The vigilante fought the urge to close his eyes, choosing to watch the young woman display her talent. "How can that be?" He put the question to the universe as well as to her. "So, what, he's been in a coma these past few days, and then all the sudden he comes out of it?"

She popped his hardness out of her mouth and pumped him vigorously.

"I don't know. He's not human. He wasn't fried like Midnight was." She plunged her mouth back down his length until pubic hair tickled her nose. Her free arm circled his hips and held him deep in her throat. The Bat grunted and moaned, and she pulled free, gasping for breath, drool slipping from her lips. She made a fist around his hardness and squeezed.

"Fuck me," she panted, turning and clutching the end of the couch. She spread her legs and arched her back. "Just you this time," she hissed, crying out as he did what she wanted.

"So...what's...the plan...?" He asked between thrusts. She

thrashed beneath him.

"There's no plan…oh God…he's weak, and still…hmmmmm ohhhh…he's resting. Scarlett is guarding him…oh shit yessssssss."

The Bat plunged in and out of her, his fingers digging into her hips. Ivy clawed at the cushions, her own passion building. She climbed to her tippy toes, calves straining, mumbling a string of profanities as her body neared its release.

His gloved hand smacked loudly against her bare ass and her head reared up at the stinging contact. A leather-covered finger slipped between her cheeks then inside her. Her body seized at the intrusion, overloading the pleasure her nervous system could manage. She cried out as her body jerked.

"God yes! Yes yes yes yes yes yesssssssssssssssssssssssss!"

Her muscles milked at him and he couldn't stave off the moment of his own explosion. He grabbed at Ivy's hair and jerked her head back as he ground himself inside her. He growled and grunted as she squirmed back against him, his orgasm shooting hot and deep.

Moments passed, and slowly their bodies and breathing relaxed. He stepped back from her, sliding exhausted to the hardwood floor. He was strong enough to flip a car, but fast, hard sex still winded him like it would a normal man. He didn't bother to put himself away.

Ivy flopped onto the couch, stretching as the sensations ebbed.

The Bat closed his eyes for a few moments, and when he opened them, Ivy crouched in the open window, fully dressed. She smiled like an evil fairy.

"You can use your bat next time," she teased with a wink, and leapt into the night.

He exhaled deeply. He'd managed to forget Catfight for a short while, but the news about Old Scratch disturbed him. He wanted Catfight for his own, but dying at the hands of that demon in order to prove himself worthy wasn't part of the plan.

A minute later he popped up to his feet, then stripped away his outfit on the way to the shower. He wondered if any of the homeless that regularly camped outside his building had enjoyed the audio portion of the Bat & Ivy show. Masked vigilantes could serve the public on more than one level.

Waking up in a dark cave didn't lend itself to determining time of day. Dre would have liked to guess it was morning, but the truth was it could have been anytime at all. He had no idea how long he'd been sleeping, or what his situation was. His nemesis had somehow captured him and done something to his mind to try and make him think he'd become Old Scratch. It seemed crazy, and the little episode in front of the mirror had been pretty messed up.

Dre woke up completely, sitting up all at once. A raging fire set in a large stone fireplace helped the torches light the spartan chamber, and there was a female guard standing at attention by the tall double doorway. As tall as Scarlett, the guard could have been a male athlete had it not been for her attractive facial features. She wore studded black fingerless gloves and a pair of low-slung gun belts over a pair of black short-shorts. Her muscular form glistened with sweat from the room's smoldering heat. Scarlett, now clothed in a red tunic and gloves, sat by his bedside. She smiled at him, her perfect white teeth as pretty as those of any Hollywood starlet.

"Good morning," she said. The salutation hung in the air. It almost felt like a test question. When he didn't answer, the wattage of her smile increased. "How do you feel?"

Dre stared at the woman, then threw back the bed cover and hopped to his feet. He rose to full height and popped his wings out to full extension. He worked the fingers of his large hands as if preparing to play the piano, clenching them into knuckle-popping fists.

The demon's lieutenant nodded and clapped her approval. "How could I have ever thought you were dead?"

"Dead?" The question escaped his lips before he realized he'd spoken. Scarlett handed him a folded newspaper. "You were unconscious for almost a week. We thought we'd lost you. The Damned mourned you so deeply they created your cover from their own skin." Andre glanced at the rumpled linen. It'd been so soft. Inside, he winced at their ghastly sacrifice. That explained all the bandages the women sported.

"And what of your sacrifice?" Hearing the demon's voice in place of his own disoriented him. Scarlett held his gaze.

"I planned to be buried with you. Skin was not enough." She traced a crimson fingernail across the specially-made linen. "Anyway, the point is moot now. You're alive, and Midnight is dead. Your dream was indeed prophecy."

Midnight is dead. The words hung in the air like a hangman's noose. Even in the greatest illusion, acting can only cover so many lies. In that moment he knew Scarlett had spoken the truth. His knees buckled. She grabbed at him as he placed a hand on the floor to steady himself. His mind spun like an amusement ride.

This is real, he thought. *This isn't a fucking trick.*

"You're not at full strength. You need more rest," she said, concerned. The guard by the door stepped forward to assist him. He lay back down and, Scarlett draped the cover back over him. He shivered at the contact, which his beautiful right hand mistook for weakness.

"You need sustenance." Scarlett signaled the guard. "Bring

him meat and drink immediately."

"Yes, mistress," the guard answered, and left the room.

Scarlett scooped the newspaper from the floor and presented it to him. "I know you're not one-hundred percent, but I thought you'd want to see this." When he didn't reach for the paper, she unfolded it for his inspection. The headline alone stunned him. He took it from her grasp.

Memorial Service For Midnight Today

Andre scanned the article. It featured several full-color photos, but none of him or his alter ego. Apparently, the graphic nature of his death prohibited the newspaper from publishing a photo. The lightning strike had done quite a number on his body. Catfight had confirmed a positive identification, the article said, but there was no mention of the name Andre Waters.

"When is this...?"

Scarlett cut him off, anticipating the question. "Five p.m. By the Santa Monica Pier."

He couldn't take his eyes off the paper. "What time is it now?"

"It's not quite five a.m." She hesitated, concern clouding her expression. "You're not seriously considering...?"

The pictures entranced him. Andre could barely hear Scarlett's voice. Photos of crying children leaving flowers and gifts on the Blackledge Tower rooftop. A picture of the mayor and the police chief consoling a grieving Catfight. Images of a barren San Angeles downtown after a special curfew had been granted the night after his death. Snapshots of various heroes paying their respects. He had never seen Starlight cry before, but in the photo she hovered over the Blackledge roof in tears. The Amphibian and Truth, standing together, heads bowed. His old friend Nighthawk.

His gaze shifted to a seemingly innocent picture of Catfight and The Bat. They were waving to a supportive crowd, their other arms around each other's waists. Tatiana's expression looked miserably brave, but The Bat's triumphant smile told of different emotions.

"I need to be there," Andre whispered, anger clearing his muddled mind.

"You're not well enough, Scratch. There will be dozens of heroes in attendance. You're not strong enough." The remainder of her thought caught in her throat. She couldn't ignore the demon's furious roar.

The demon moved faster than the human eye could follow. He leapt to his feet and grabbed Scarlett by the throat, slamming her against the rough chamber floor, her long legs kicking up into the air. Her eyes bugged out as she strained to breathe. Instincts caused her hands to reach toward his choking grasp, but they dropped away an instant later. Touching him would only inflame his anger.

He leaned in, his nose brushing hers. He barked his displeasure, spittle flying onto her face. "Has my brief absence confused you as to who is in power?"

She tried to answer, but could not get the words past his murderous grip. She wagged her head as her face took on the color of her name.

"Question my strength again and I will end you."

Her body quivered and jerked from the lack of air. Her eyes had all but rolled back in their sockets. Tears rolled down her cheeks.

Andre suddenly realized he was killing her. The demon's power equaled his own midnight-stoked strength, plus the added fuel of hellish rage.

He snatched his hand away. She strained for air, her body convulsing. He stood over her, watching silently. Scarlett sat up and pushed herself against the wall. She rubbed at her throat, eyes to the floor.

Whatever strength Andre had gained suddenly emptied through his legs into the floor. He forced himself to take steady steps to the bed. He lay back down, ignoring the custom skin linen. He closed his eyes and forced himself into control.

"You will make this happen. I will be there. Understood?"

"Yes...yes." Scarlett used the wall to stand, averting her eyes. "It will be done." She hesitated, awaiting further instructions. When none came, she moved toward the exit. Half way across the room, the doors parted. The posted guard and a woman server entered. The server carried a large, covered tray.

"In case you woke up, I wanted to surprise you," Scarlett explained over her shoulder as she left the room. The woman set the tray by the bed and excused herself. The guard closed the double doors behind them.

Andre could only stare at the mystery meal. He couldn't identify the smell wafting from under the dome-shaped metal cover, but it caused his stomach to grumble. He didn't think he could eat, but his new body disagreed. He sat up, hooked the hinged lid cover with a talon, and flipped it open. The sight startled him off the other side of the bed.

"Jesus," he murmured.

Charred and steaming remains greeted him. The famous green mask had cooked into the victim's skin. The severed head belonged to Andre's his old crime-fighting friend and mentor, The Flyer. Andre flinched at the savagery. The Flyer's eyes, nearly as green as his mask, had been gouged from his skull and placed on the platter's bed of lettuce like large grapes. The top of the hero's skull had been removed, his exposed brain ready for easy consumption.

The empty eye sockets offered a hollow, defeated stare into eternity.

The sickening sight made the demon's mouth water. Disgusted, Andre leapt across the bed and slammed the lid back down over the platter with a loud crash. He fell back on the hard bed, kicking away its skin cover. He pushed his head into his hands. There was no escaping this nightmare.

Midnight the superhero was dead. Dead to the world. Dead to his city. Dead to the woman he loved.

He might as well be dead for real.

But he wasn't.

Just his body was. He'd never patrol the streets of San Angeles in his superhero body again.

Chapter Eight

PAYING RESPECTS

The interior of the Needleman's Janitorial Services van was gloomy as it passed through the heart of San Angeles. The new Old Scratch sat in the back. Wearing the demon's skin, Andre stared past all the surrounding custodial supplies, oblivious of the vehicle's movement through the mid-morning traffic. He hadn't gotten so much as a glimpse of the sun when the van had accessed a discontinued subway maintenance conduit to pick him up. He'd climbed into the rear of the van, wings folded flat to his back. Scarlett had closed the doors behind him without a word.

Implications of his current dilemma seeped into his awareness. The obvious changes had been the toughest to absorb, but the nuances nibbled and chewed at the fringes of his mind. Even in the fantastical world of superheroes, this was a situation for the ages. He'd never heard of something so far-flung. In a reality populated by supernatural creatures and super-powered beings, he was still struggling with how he should proceed.

He felt an itch at his shoulder blades, and his bat-like wings automatically unfolded for flight. The confines of the van kept the wings from full display, forcing him to concentrate in order to flatten them back against his body. He shook his head.

Fucking bizarre.

On the plus side, he knew Old Scratch inside and out. Knew his general habits and mannerisms, though he'd already caught Scarlett looking oddly at him. The lightning strike gave him some leeway for slightly off behavior, but at some point, not having the personality of a hell demon was going to cause problems.

And he would to have to come to terms with using the demon's powers. The ability to fly was the most sought after, and Andre had envied the demon that. Old Scratch's strength rivaled his own full midnight power, but just getting used to this hell-formed body would take some time.

His human form had, at least been, well, human. The demon's body had perhaps once been human, but now it could never be mistaken for anything but a hellion shaped by the devil himself. Compared to Midnight's massive Greek-god physique, Old Scratch's frame was appeared misshapen, monstrous. Andre looked down at himself. He'd never understood why Old Scratch didn't wear clothes.

His enemy had a dead, stone-gray pallor. It felt cool to the touch, and its texture reminded him of a reptile, despite the lack of scales.

Jesus.

Andre stared down in the oversized hands. The talons matched the demon's merciless nature. They'd carved Midnight's body more times than he cared to remember, but thankfully his old body had easily mended itself, minus any ugly scars. Old Scratch wasn't quite so gifted in the healing department. The demon's hands alone told an agonizing story. Gnarled and scarred, knuckles and bones had obviously been ravaged and broken, but their aftercare had been neglected. He knew the demon felt pain; even during their last epic battle, he'd heard the creature's agonized roar amidst the deafening thunderclaps.

Maybe living in hell caused different kinds of callouses to form.

The sharp blare of a nearby car horn startled him. He blinked, and then his eyes refocused. He slowly raised his right hand, examining the amputated stump where the third finger should have been.

Christ.

He clasped his head, his upper body sagging with an invisible weight. His mind chanted a prayer, his closed eyes searching the void of darkness.

Why had this happened? Was he being punished? Why would God silence humanity's greatest threat, but play such a cosmic joke on the hero? Why not just dispatch the demon?

And as clearly as if he were sitting right next to him in the shadowy gloom, Andre heard his deceased father speak.

"Do not question His will."

Andre's head snapped from side to side, so sure his dad must be right there, but he saw no one. Just cases of cleaning solutions, paper towels, and liquid soap.

"But, I don't understand." he said to the void, the voice still sounding strange to the ugly pits where Old Scratch's ears should have been.

The van's rear doors abruptly flew open. The driver, a middle-aged man, held the left-side door open as far as it would go, while his young assistant followed suit on the other side. A puff of smoke jettisoned from the older man's smoldering cigar stub.

"We're here, sir."

The young man had blanched so pale with fear Andre couldn't believe he was conscious. The youth's mouth trembled, but no words came out. The older man frowned, speaking quickly to cover the awkward moment.

"I'll point the way whenever you're ready."

Andre moved in a crouch, dropping to the concrete with an echoing thud. He straightened to full height, and without a concentrated thought, his wings opened. The young man's eyes rolled back into his head until nothing but white showed. He crumpled to the pavement. The older man shook his head in disgust.

"Fucking pussy son-in-law." The man spat, missing the younger man's face by inches. He turned and pulled himself up on a loading dock. Andre let his wings lift him. The man pointed to his left. "Okay, the freight elevator is officially out of order, but it'll take you to the roof. This was as close as Scarlett would allow, sir." He pointed downward. "Under the van is a large grate that leads to a sub-basement. From there you can make your way into the old Santa Monica sewer system, which connects to the San Angeles subway system less than a quarter-mile away."

Andre's frown caused the man to wave his hands in surrender. "Hey, I have orders. Direct from Scarlett."

"I understand."

"She said to tell you it was just in case." The last of the man's words bounced off the demon's broad back as Andre strode toward the oversized elevator doors. "By the way, I always thought Midnight was just a Batman wannabe. Fuck 'em," the man called out.

It took Andre a second to realize he'd stopped walking. The man's words caught him by surprise.

"Most of the city's heroes are just a bunch of pricks, but I'll give Midnight high marks for his taste in women. Even the Pope whacks off to Catfight's perfect ass."

Andre started forward again. He couldn't stop his gash of a mouth from grinning. He poked the elevator call button and the tall doors parted with a mechanical rattle. His wings flattened to his back as he stepped inside. He turned and nodded to the man as the doors closed.

The guy was dead right about Catfight's ass.

At the beach, the Southern California weather had brightened into a picture-perfect postcard day. Traffic crawled into Santa Monica, flowing like hardening lava toward the coastline. Television trucks dominated the Santa Monica Pier, forcing the sea of humanity onto the beach.

Pacific Coast Highway had been closed for the memorial those handful of miles from the end of the westbound 10 freeway to the Sunset Boulevard exit. The four-lane highway was now a sea of black— local politicians, businessmen, and even Hollywood celebrities wore their more fashionable funereal clothes to mark the occasion. Even the beach-going folk showed themselves true to the day. Women strolled in black bikinis. Surfers sported black ties or arm bands.

Andre looked on from the roof of a skyscraper a little more than a long block away from the beach. He wondered if the memorial attendees' black attire was an unusual return to traditional grieving wear, or if it represented a tip of the hat to his alter ego's blue-black costume.

Not that it really mattered.

Wings flat to his back, Andre crouched at the building's edge. Helicopters swarmed the airspace like flies over spoiling fruit. The security men working the building's surveillance were already on the payroll of the Old Scratch criminal network.

Andre looked up, and couldn't help but smile.

The building's roof couldn't be seen from the sky because it was covered in large black balloons. The balloons had a glossy black sheen, and the sun gleamed off them like mirrors. Midnight had once rescued the daughter of the building's owner, a real-estate tycoon who owned more than one of the San Angeles professional sports teams. Andre knew Scarlett didn't understand why her demon boss wanted to watch the ceremony, but she'd made sure he could hide comfortably in plain sight. He'd have to remind himself to reward her brilliant execution of his wishes. There were way too many nuances to being a criminal mastermind for his tastes. He was already missing the simpler days of being an ass-kicker for justice.

Andre watched the mayor of San Angeles make his way slowly through the crowd, heading for the stage stairs built on the sand just north of the pier. The service would soon begin.

The demon's eyes enjoyed the spectacular view. Midnight's public filled the streets blocks away from the beach, but the most amazing thing to him was also the most surprising.

"Holy shit," he whispered, not believing his eyes as he scanned the stage.

Andre had never seen such a large collection of superheroes anywhere. Some he knew personally. Others he'd heard of, but had never met. Two were global icons.

His body teetered, then flopped back onto his backside. This was crazy. He'd grown up idolizing The American. The hero, wrapped in a skin-tight American flag with a short red cape, stood shaking hands with ordinary citizens and A-list celebs alike.

Just a few feet away, Titan, the most popular superhero in the world, knelt, head bent in prayer. It was strange seeing a ring of black-suited security agents ringed around the most powerful being on the planet. Titan certainly didn't need protection; he was as close to being Superman as any hero possibly could be. And he was here, paying his respects. And the effect he had— rows of people beyond the agents also prayed on bent knees.

Andre sniffled, bowing his head. This really couldn't be happening. And then a morsel of emotional clarity struck him.

As much as he'd always respected Titan, he'd also carried an underlying current of resentment toward the hero. Titan's popularity was unmatched, as were his powers, but the strict, unflagging Christian morality he wrapped himself in often clashed with Midnight's street-justice perspective.

Until very recently, Andre hadn't given serious thought to the theory of a singular deity controlling the world. While many citizens thought powers such as those Midnight had were a blessing to be used for a greater good, he'd always followed the scientific viewpoint of his parents. He and several others had simply been the beneficiary of a skip in biological evolution. Over the period of a decade, human mutations vastly superior to the current human baseline for mental and physical attributes had been born to ungifted parents all over the world. Not all of the newly gifted humans used their abilities for the world's betterment.

Titan had made it clear from his earliest introduction that he believed in truth, justice, and law. He did not kill; he'd sworn never to become a murderer in the name of those three fundamental moral pillars.

Andre did believe in killing. He wouldn't hesitate to take the life of a criminal planning to slaughter millions over some psychotic power grab. He certainly would have killed Old Scratch if he could have.

Andre wasn't sure Titan had ever fought for his life. Midnight had, and a moment always arrived where survival instincts overrode moral directives. When a man struggled to get to his hands and knees, his mind glazed over in pain, his body beaten so badly that partial sight was a gift, making sure his adversary got a fair trial by his or her peers just wasn't a priority.

Then again, Andre had never intercepted an armed nuclear missile and re-directed it out to deep space the way Titan had. So there was that.

Bottom line, there were just times when Titan acted in a manner a touch too righteous for Andre's taste, but he was glad they were playing on the same side. And it made him genuinely happy to see the superhero come pay his respects.

Along with the helicopters, several heroes circled in the sky above the memorial. Starlight flew slowly, her form covered in black. Her expression looked blank, empty. Andre didn't know if the deep-space alien could experience the full spectrum of human emotion. She certainly didn't appear happy.

The Wing was up there. Lightning Bolt. The Comet.

It suddenly occurred to him that The Flyer was nowhere to be seen, and immediately the ugly reality of his absence struck Andre like a stinging slap.

A small gathering south of the Santa Monica Pier caught his attention, and he couldn't help but smile a little. Betsy Garrett, the leader of the Mothers & Daughters for Justice, had staged a protest. Ms. Garrett had been the mother of the sinister serial rapist and murderer self-named The Coroner. Andre had tracked him to his lair and in the midst of their struggle, The Coroner had been ejected out a second-story window into the street below. Before Andre got to the window, he'd heard the squeal of the city-bus tires as the driver locked up the brakes. There'd been a sickening impact, and that had caused the demise of Benjamin Garrett.

His mother Betsy, citing her son's long history of mental illness and hospitalizations, condemned Midnight for not turning her son in to authorities and letting the criminal justice process take its course. There had been little public outcry in response to the killer's death, but Betsy was still able to gather a fanatical band of women who continued to champion the rights of the city's most notorious criminals, all along continuing to paint San Angeles' dark protector as a lawless executioner who paraded as a hero.

When Andre looked again at the beachside spectacle, the stage seating had started to fill. He recognized the dozen or so dignitaries now seated on the stage, but his eyes never left Catfight.

Tatiana sat almost directly behind the transparent podium. She wore a jet-black version of her costume, with even her fur-trimmed gloves and boots black as coal. The Chief of Police sat to her right. His wife held his hand tightly. Only her tear-reddened eyes marred the ex-actress' mature beauty. Midnight had once shielded her from a hail of bullets supplied by a street gang crazy enough to try and rob the annual policeman's ball fundraiser. His mind played over the memory.

Roaches. That was the name of the gang. The Roaches. Several of them hadn't survived the attempted robbery. Andre had been surprised by the number of tuxedo-wearing officers sporting their service weapons.

On that occasion, a 9mm slug fired by one of the Roaches had bitten deeply into Midnight's right hamstring. Another stray shot had grazed his right shoulder and his right temple. He'd completely healed before he'd arrived home. His thigh muscles had pushed the bloody bullet out into his hand. The gang's female second-in-command had turned out to be an undercover police officer, who'd since left the department and become a street minister.

Andre suspected she had also become one of the latest in a fresh wave of vigilantes, but he'd been too involved in trying to stop Old Scratch's city-wide sadism to give the matter more attention.

The rogue officer might moonlight as the tough-as-nails Truth.

He liked her style. Perhaps she would help fill the gap his absence created.

Andre blinked, then snarled as The Bat settled into the empty seat next to Tatiana.

He wore his usual Yankee pinstriped uniform. A black armband circled a bicep. He leaned in and whispered, and Tatiana leaned her head onto his broad shoulder. She sobbed softly. The Bat looked out into the crowd. Andre sensed the vigilante's expression fought back a scheming smile. That could be one reason he disliked The Bat so much. The vigilante aspired to an amoral ethical code similar to Midnight's, but he wasn't hindered by an idealistic lover.

At least, not yet.

Andre also knew jealousy was causing him to imagine things, amplifying his fears.

And feeding his rage.

Maybe that was why he and the demon had pitched such spectacular battles. Their fights weren't really about his powers against the hellspawn's abilities. They were outpourings of his real fury at Old Scratch's heinous cruelty.

Something made him switch his attention back to Titan. His prayer finished, the world's most beloved superhero slowly rose to his feet. He turned toward the stage and made eye contact with Tatiana. He nodded solemnly, and then exploded into the royal-blue sky, gone from sight in an instant. The sonic boom drew a smattering of applause, despite the sad occasion.

Andre frowned. The Bat didn't acknowledge Titan's departure at all. Asshole.

With Titan gone, the government-agent types fell back, forming a protective barrier between the stage and the VIP seating area of the gathering.

At each corner of the stage, body-armored SWAT snipers sat perched, scanning the crowd behind their red-tinted visors. Their rifles looked like science-fiction creations, no doubt the handiwork of Lyle Griggs, a.k.a. The Genius. With the recent hiring of Griggs, the city was moving forward on numerous technological fronts. Lyle had never been much of a superhero, but when it came to gadgets and gizmos, especially among the heroes who didn't have superpowers to rely on, Griggs had become the man to call on. A couple of times he'd been kidnapped by bad guys looking to upgrade their weaponry and surveillance systems, but heroes always swarmed to his immediate rescue, and the word had been put out that messing with the technological mastermind would be a bad decision. He hadn't been bothered in years.

Tatiana had mentioned using Lyle's services to aid in capturing

Old Scratch, but Andre had been too stubborn about bringing the demon to justice using only his own Ultra abilities. Maybe things would be different now if he'd listened to her solid advice.

#

Scarlett sat at the building's security panel, taking advantage of its elaborate bank of cameras. She'd waved off the audio option, choosing to only watch her superior.

Wary of the expression she wore like a tribal mask, neither of her two security guards spoke.

Scarlett stared at the video screen, analyzing the image of the demon. After all her years of servitude, she knew the escapee from hell as well as she knew herself. Through her association with him, her eyes and heart had opened to who she really was. Before becoming Scarlett, she'd been nothing more than a low-level criminal distraction. Whatever he'd seen in her during the early days, he'd been right. He'd created Scarlett, and helped transform an ex-runaway carnival performer from Decatur, Illinois, into one of the most feared people on the planet. In fact, since she'd become Scarlett, she'd stopped using her given name. She didn't need a protective alter ego. She was Scarlett, always and unafraid.

She couldn't ignore the mounting evidence. Old Scratch had been off since the night God killed Midnight. At first, she'd shielded Scratch from the villains in his employ, because they'd quickly discovered the lightning strike had severely wounded him. The subtle changes in his personality seemed all too real, and with each passing day, more permanent. It was as if part of him had died with his archenemy.

And the way he was acting on the roof right now, on the brink of his mortal enemy's memorial...the demon seemed confused, anxious, and almost distraught. She didn't understand what was going on, but she knew his insistence on witnessing the ceremony could be a dangerous mistake. She'd heard rumors that Titan and otherworldly hero X might attend the ceremony. Both beings were capable of besting the hellion, but their respect for Midnight had kept their involvement in San Angeles criminal matters to a minimum so far.

One of the security men touched his earpiece, leaned toward Scarlett, and whispered, "Titan has left our airspace."

Scarlett nodded. Her remaining concern maintained his vigil on the roof.

Silence drew out, longer and longer. Finally, one of the guards cleared his throat and spoke up. "So, what's Old Scratch's plan?'"

Scarlett sighed, not bothering to dignify his question with an answer. She stood, gloved fists on generous hips. She had no idea what Old Scratch was doing. She pressed a flat button on her right glove and tossed out a directive as she headed toward the freight elevators. "Get ready, girls. On my signal."

Neither of the security guards were stupid enough to ask a second question, but then again, neither one of them could resist watching the statuesque beauty walking away.

#

The Midnight memorial gathering continued to swell, major east/west streets clogging farther and farther from the ocean shore. Some enterprising folks started selling parking space in driveways and on front lawns for those looking to leave their cars and get as close to the beach as they could on foot.

Andre had known his alter ego was popular, but he didn't realize the whole city would turn out to say goodbye.

When he looked back to the stage, the mayor had walked halfway up the stairs, but he'd paused to have a brief conversation with a staff member. Tatiana was leaning close to The Bat.

Andre flinched.

It looked as though The Bat were staring up and out toward Andre's position on the roof. A few seconds passed, and the strange feeling crept over him. A barrage of questions peppered his mind. How could The Bat see him from that distance? How could The Bat know he was there?

Slowly, Andre stood, the demon's body unfolding to full height. He kept his wings tucked against his body. "You motherfucker," he whispered as he stared back, challenging.

The Bat continued to look up in his direction. Seemingly as a taunt, he shifted himself and gently stroked Tatiana's hair.

"Fucking kill you."

The Bat grinned, and that left no doubt in Andre's mind.

"Should I come down there and beat your ass, or should I wait right here?"

The Bat tenderly kissed to top of Catfight's head, then left his seat. He paused next to the mayor, who had ascended the stage, and whispered something to San Angeles' top official. The mayor nodded, shook The Bat's hand, and then headed toward the podium. The Bat disappeared down a set of stairs at the rear of the stage.

Andre laughed out loud, eager for the challenge. But then the truth struck him.

His anger at The Bat came from Midnight. But The Bat had seen Old Scratch goading him from the roof.

And The Bat wasn't likely to come up alone.

Shit.

Chapter Nine

A WHOLE LOTTA GOOD FIGHTING EVIL

It hadn't been a conscious thought, but whether due to a reflex or to nerves, the demon's wings unfolded, their sharp bony tips busting the nearest black balloons decorating the building's roof.

The assortment of aircraft and superheroes swarming the airspace above Santa Monica all veered in Andre's direction.

In the background, The Wing swooped up from the beach, The Bat hanging onto the flying hero's forearm in a two-handed clinch.

A fully dressed Apache helicopter dropped its nose and sped downward.

"Fuck," Andre muttered, stunned by the sudden development. Then he was hovering a few feet above the roof. His wings seemed to be taking matters into their own hands. But the real question was: now what does he do?

Behind him and out of sight at the open roof-access door, Scarlett frowned and shook her head. The shit had hit the fan. And Old Scratch seemed surprised and hesitant. Scarlett whispered into her glove communicator as she turned to the freight elevator.

"All teams go."

The Apache helicopter was just moments from the skyscraper's edge when pandemonium broke out around the stage, pier, and beach areas.

Loud automatic gunfire rang out, causing those gathered to drop to the ground. Screams filled the air. A small charge set off explosions beneath each SWAT sniper's crow's nest, causing each officer to plummet the varying heights of three to ten stories. Three of the four snipers never actually hit the ground, instead falling on panicked mourners. The entire area became bedlam.

Mixed into the crowd, Old Scratch's female army wielded weapons of all kinds. The majority pointed machine guns, but some pulled mini-rocket launchers from surfboard cases. Others had 9mm pistols duct-taped under skateboards, while a chosen few quickly assembled sophisticated rifles from pieces of single-gear beachcomber bikes.

One of the snipers was extremely lucky. He tumbled from a height of six stories, falling directly over the stage. Just feet from having his bones shatter on the metal construction, the three incarnations of Catfight interlocked their arms and caught the officer. They lowered the wide-eyed sniper to the stage to congratulatory hoots and whistles.

The trio of Catfights merged into a single figure, and with an angry hiss, leapt toward the closest gun-wielding minion.

Many of the oncoming choppers veered back toward the commotion at the beach, but the Apache merely hung in the air as if awaiting instructions. The Wing and The Bat were closing in fast.

"Come get some," Andre growled, his gargoyle-like feet touching back onto the roof. He braced himself, but quickly remembered his wicked talons made it almost impossible to make a good fist. Clipped memories of the demon slashing him and using hard backhands flashed through his mind. He quickly adjusted to a more open stance and flexed his huge hands. He'd do the best he could with what he now had.

Large-caliber ammunition carved up the edge of the roof, spraying concrete the way a lawn mower sprays grass clippings. Andre threw himself away from the Apache's gunfire at the same instant The Wing swung The Bat toward the roof. Andre rolled and sprang back to his feet, keeping his focus on The Bat's skydiving entrance.

The athletic vigilante dove headlong toward the roof, bursting through the huge black balloons, flipping and rolling with the impact. Across the roof, he popped up, magical bat in hand. He stalked toward the demon, a grim smirk on his face. His baseball bat moved into a colorful blur as he spun and flipped it between his hands. Andre didn't even try to keep up with the bat's movements, though it didn't seem to be moving all that fast.

"A little birdie told me to keep an eye out, but I didn't think you'd be crazy enough to show your ugly face at Midnight's ceremony." The bat circled his waist and flipped over his shoulders at a speed Bruce Lee would have envied.

"You have no fucking idea," Andre replied, still uncomfortable with the hellspawn's voice speaking for him.

As the Bat stepped within range, he swung a vicious uppercut. Despite being trapped in the demon's body, Andre's fighting instincts took over. His wings snapped closed against his back as he stepped into the swing. The move took the vigilante by surprise, but with the demon's large frame, the bat still clipped his shoulder as he dropped into a powerful leg sweep. Andre flinched at the blow, but executed the movement, whipping his monstrous legs through the ballplayers'. The Bat flipped into the air with a grunt, and when he landed hard on his back, Old Scratch's monster heel slammed into his solar plexus. Even with stone-hard abs, the blow forced the wind out of the vigilante. Andre pressed his advantage.

A savage series of slashes ripped The Bat's jersey into crimson tatters, followed by a pair of teeth-rattling backhands that bloodied the vigilante's nose and mouth. The Bat desperately wedged his supercharged Louisville Slugger across the demon's chest and struggled to force him back. Infuriated, Andre grabbed at the baseball bat with both hands and slammed it into the man's gore-stained shirt. Andre heard a nasty crunching sound, either the weapon's handle breaking or a rib cracking. The Bat announced the answer with a painful yelp. Andre leaned in and pressed with all his might. He had never felt this strong in the middle of the day in his entire life. The Bat's eyes widened as he struggled against Old Scratch's weight and strength. Hot drool dripped from the monster's lips onto the baseball hero's face. Andre could see The Bat fighting to breathe.

The demon's face twisted into a malignant smile. "I thought you were tougher than this."

Andre felt the slightest give, and then heard another muted

crunch. The vigilante hissed as his body surged in resistance. He had been pinned, and his amplified strength was fading. Andre watched fear flash through his rival's eyes. He ground the weapon into the man's broken torso.

"I should kill you for touching her."

Without warning he was no longer on top of The Bat, but flying across the rooftop. The Wing had swooped in and grabbed Andre by the arm. Just before reaching the roof access, the winged hero banked up and let him go. The demon's body hurtled backward into the closed freight elevator doors. Andre watched The Wing zoom back and grab up the wounded vigilante.

As he shook off the impact, Andre dismissed pursuing the pair. The demon had the power of flight, but The Wing had Ultra aerial speed. He'd never catch them.

Another round of machine-gun fire from the Apache 'copter scattered the roof's gravel, reminding Andre of a second reason why immediate pursuit would be a bad idea. He waited a few seconds, not wanting to step into a spray of large-caliber bullets. The demon was all but immortal, but that kind of ammo could still do some painful damage.

When the gunfire stopped, Old Scratch stepped out into the sunshine. News helicopters swarmed the sky. The Apache hung in the air at the west edge of the building. An arsenal of massive guns and sidewinder missiles were aimed straight at him.

Something small, about the size of a child, dropped from a hovering triangular aircraft.

The weird-looking ship sparked something in his memory. It didn't belong to a law enforcement agency.

The short, muscular figure landed on the roof in a crouch. Half Andre's height, the red-and-black armored hero stood and smiled. Fists formed on the ends of his double set of arms. One set of arms hung from the shoulder normally, while the second set of muscular arms sprouted from the middle of his elongated torso. His antennae twitched playfully.

The Ant flexed his diminutive, yet impressive, frame. The mouthpiece hidden in his full-face helmet electronically manipulated his voice into an intriguing blend of human and robot.

"Well, hello, Old Scratch. I don't believe we've had the pleasure."

"I know you," Andre said, taking a step forward. "You still working out of Dallas?"

The hero's helmet tilted. "Mostly, being a Texan born and bred. But I get around," he said. "I don't suppose you'd like to surrender?" He began to circle the demon.

"I don't want to hurt you," Andre warned, a hiss of a menace coming across in the demon's voice.

The Ant stopped in his tracks. Andre could feel the stare from behind the hero's multi-faceted visor. The Ant laughed. "No wonder Midnight had such a hard-on for you. You're quite entertaining for a soulless creature." The hero's coal-and-crimson gloves flexed before clenching into fists.

Andre listened to himself make the demon sound even more insane. "A sense of humor is a necessity in our business."

The Ant attacked.

A small hero should be quick. Andre often trained with Tatiana, and the phrase "cat-like reflexes" was exactly right. He'd gone up against the villain Ricochet and his blinding speed a couple of times, but sudden quickness was different.

The Ant was a perfect example.

He circled a few feet out of the demon's long reach, and, before Andre could process the movement, The Ant was on his chest, one pair of fists hammering at his midsection while the other pair of hands dug into his throat. The little man's strength was staggering, and Andre stumbled back against the oversized freight elevator doors, causing both men to tumble inside the elevator.

As the combatants fell to the elevator floor, The Ant pulled one hand from Andre's throat and hammered at his face. The blows worked to clear Andre's mind more than to cause damage. The demon seized the hero by the throat and bucked his body off the floor just enough to give his wings room to open. In the limited space, the demon's wings caught up The Ant and slammed him into the ceiling with a ringing clang. The Ant grunted with the impact, the metal of the ceiling dimpling as it collided with the tiny hero's body.

"Please don't force me to hurt you," Andre said.

The Ant wagged his head. "Is that what you told my friend Midnight?"

Andre's mind seized up. He knew The Ant by reputation. They'd only met once, and that encounter had been brief. The Ant considered him a friend? If there was an intrinsic loyalty amongst crime fighters, Andre hadn't ever been aware.

The elevator jolted, then started down.

The Ant raised his four hands toward Andre's face. "Let's see how you like fighting blind." The encounter had been so surreal that Andre had fought without regard to the little man's abilities. Beyond the pint-sized hero's super strength, he too possessed Ultra senses, and he equipped himself with—

Thin streams sprayed from The Ant's palms into Andre's eyes. The searing pain caused Andre to drop the hero. He clawed at his face as The Ant hit the floor. The sound echoed inside the large metal elevator.

"Now try my sting!" The Ant yelled. Suddenly, the demon's muscles seized, and his skin felt like it had caught fire. The electrical jolt scrambled his nervous system. The demon's teeth clenched in agony. The Ant pressed his advantage with a barrage of strikes and kicks. Andre tried to fend him off, hoping to regain his sight, but his vision was a blurry mess.

A powerful blow connected to Andre's chin and he pitched over, the side of his face striking the metal floor. A pair of small gloved hands grabbed his throat and pulled him up. Another punch snapped his head back.

Then came another, and another, and another. Andre's thoughts scrambled with every blow, and he still couldn't see. If this assault kept up, he would lose. The authorities would take him into custody, and he'd end up in a specialty cell the way Tombstone had, and he would never see the light of the moon again. Like dying hadn't been bad enough.

During his adventures as Midnight, he hadn't often found himself on the brink of defeat. Sure, he'd lost his share of battles, but he'd always won the wars. He knew what it was like to be down on his knees, bleeding from wounds enough to overflow the cracks of a sidewalk. He'd been blinded before, too. More than once.

And he'd been killed.

Once was enough. Instinct kicked in.

Andre screamed in desperate fury, striking out wildly, not thinking about anything other than surviving the fight.

The Ant gasped, the sound of someone getting sucker-punched in the gut. Andre knew what that sound meant; knew The Ant was hurt. The Ant made a gurgling noise. Andre recognized that awful sound, too. It was the sound people made when they'd been shot in the throat.

He heard The Ant's body fall, and then he realized the hand he'd wrenched out of his adversary dripped with something hot and wet. He wagged his head, and his vision cleared. He caught a whiff of something familiar. He couldn't mistake what was smeared on his hand, right in front of his face. His bird-of-prey talons looked as if they'd been dipped in strawberry jam. He looked over at The Ant. One pair of the small hero's hands wrapped around his helmet, while the other pair of hands clutched desperately between his legs. The hero rocked back and forth in obvious agony.

"Jesus H.," the demon whispered, catching a glimpse of the gruesome wound he'd caused.

The hero tugged his helmet off, and his screams filled the elevator.

"I'm so sorry," Andre whispered, wanting to reach down and do something to help The Ant, but knowing it would be useless. He punched the closest wall, his knuckles leaving a deep impression.

The Ant's screams preceded the elevator's ding as it arrived at the building's lower level.

Several uniformed police officers and body-armored SWAT team members waited in kneeling or standing positions, weapons aimed into the freight elevator as the doors slid open. The sight of the badly wounded, four-armed hero seemed to shock the law enforcers, and Andre used that second of confusion to launch himself into the police, scattering them like windblown leaves.

He took a flying leap off the loading dock, landing by the janitorial supply van, ignoring the surrounding commotion. Andre grabbed the van by the front bumper and flipped the vehicle, placing it between himself and the cops. Gunfire rained down, bullets riddling the van. Andre jerked the iron grating up from the driveway, remembering the driver's description of the tunnels beneath the street as an escape route. He squeezed himself into the gap and dropped into the darkness. He instinctively turned and took the tunnel back toward the city, bullets following his escape. He knew the police wouldn't dare follow, but that thought didn't slow his pace.

The going was more than a little claustrophobic. The tunnel's narrow confines caused him to hunch over as he made his way back into San Angeles. Yet despite the cramp, foul surroundings, he felt oddly comfortable. A grim smile crept onto his face. It looked like he would get away, but he couldn't help but think about The Ant's mutilated condition and the savage injuries his talons had caused. He wished he'd mortally wounded The Bat instead.

Andre could feel the blood drying on his hand as he rounded a bend and spotted a pair of his elite guard waiting with Scarlett. They stood at a junction where several tunnels spurred off in all directions. The women were armed to the teeth. Scarlett's expression was unreadable.

"With the situation at the beach and at the building, the police won't be able to cover every outlet. Orders?" she asked.

"Home." Andre shouldered past her.

Scarlett followed Old Scratch and the women into a tunnel, her gaze burning holes into the demon's back. "Was it worth it?"

The words had barely left her mouth when she was lifted off her feet and slammed against a sludge-covered wall. The smack of her body into the slime echoed down the tunnel. Stunned, the redhead flinched as the demon's fists shattered the stone to each side of her skull. She felt the razor edge of a single talon trace across the tender skin of her throat. The pointed claw stopped over her pulsing jugular. She gasped at the slight prick of the bony scalpel. The demon's wings whooshed open, then closed around her like a coffin lid. She was now an afterthought in his special darkness.

The gale force of his hot, putrid breath forced her eyes shut and scalded the skin of her face.

"Don't think I haven't noticed the change in your attitude." He leaned in, warm spittle spraying her. "Question me again, bitch, and I will jerk off to your screams as your body twirls slowly over a roasting pit." Even in the darkness she could feel the cold malignancy of his black-eyed glare.

She nodded frantically. "I'm sorry."

Andre growled and stepped away, his wings flapping open to release her, then twisting over his back like a swirling cape. Scarlet fell into the muck, buttocks and palms first. The pair of guards simply stared into the black curtain of the tunnel. Andre shoved between the women, knocking them aside and stalking ahead of them.

Scarlett pushed herself up, shaking off what filth she could. Maybe her master's mind had only been temporarily scrambled by the lightning strike. Anything powerful enough to kill Midnight had to have done some damage to her leader, but the look in his eyes. Whatever doubts she'd had about the hellion's state of mind had just been silenced.

She removed a glove, tossing it into the tunnel's obscurity. She smeared some of the demon's saliva to her mouth and let her tongue swipe it away. She smacked her lips and grinned.

Striding into the darkness, Andre laughed softly to himself. Shutting Scarlett up hadn't been hard. Pretending to be the demon might not be so difficult, after all. The fresh memory of The Bat, pinned and defenseless, flashed through his thoughts. Now that Midnight's original mission to see Old Scratch dead was complete, a new goal presented itself.

Suddenly, being reborn as the world's greatest villain offered a world of possibilities. A passage from the book of Job popped into his mind, and then the vague framework of a plan only hellspawn or a madman could conceive. A tiny smile leaked across his cruel, thin lips.

"I want everyone for a meeting tomorrow night. Everyone," he barked out.

Scarlett rushed to his side. "Name the time."

"Midnight."

Chapter Ten

THE LORD GAVE

Dead silence reigned in the torch-lit cavern. Andre sat in his throne, taking in the crowd. Unlike the exclusivity of the recent dinner meeting, he had opened this criminal gathering up to all the major crime syndicates and families, mid-level crime figures, and any parties who might be interested. He wasn't at all surprised to see a group of uniformed policemen and women in attendance. Or at least they appeared to be SAPD. The tinted shields of their riot helmets masked their faces.

As if reading his mind, Scarlett spoke up. "That's The Badges. New street gang out of Hollywood. They take their cue from that old Clint Eastwood movie about the young rogue cops..."

"*Magnum Force*," Andre said.

Scarlett smiled, a bit surprised. "Yes. And they have some pull. Most are the sons and daughters of high-ranking SAPD officers and admin. They don't consider themselves heroes or villains. When they inquired about attending, I thought it would be interesting to have them."

Andre continued to scan the crowd. "For what I have in mind, they certainly can have a part to play."

Wearing Old Scratch's skin with growing comfort, Andre unfolded from the seat of his throne and hopped up onto the massive chair's arms, his foot claws anchoring him. The simple act of unfolding his massive wings hushed the gathering.

He smiled like a hungry alligator. "I'll make this brief. Yesterday at the beach, law enforcement and superheroes at the memorial for Midnight put on a show of force when they spotted me on a neighboring building. I gave The Bat a beating he'll never forget, and The Ant is reportedly in serious but stable condition after our battle." A smattering of whistles and catcalls greeted his words. Someone called out, "That midget cocksucker," an insult Andre assumed was meant for The Ant.

"Around the world, the media is portraying my presence as an unholy showing of disrespect and some sort of betrayal of an unwritten code. The fact is, my wanting to witness Midnight's memorial is my business, and mine alone. After the show they tried to put on, I'm going to send a message back to the world that will resonate within their pathetic souls for the rest of their lives.

"And the first step is this: All disputes between rival organizations, gangs, and individuals are to be temporarily set aside. I want no acts of retaliation or aggression amongst members of my criminal network. None. Zero. Those who ignore this directive will be dealt with by me and made an example of.

"So, prepare your organizations, your foot soldiers, your arm-breakers, and every like-minded, stone-hearted felon you know, because starting at twelve midnight tomorrow night, December first, we're going to turn their war on crime into an Armageddon of biblical proportions. The citizens of San Angeles will be too busy fighting for their lives to grieve one more minute for their Midnight. The approaching holidays will quickly turn into Hellidays!"

The momentary quiet was unnatural, then a whoop came from somewhere near the back of the room, and a deafening roar erupted in the chamber. Reps from rival gangs banged forearms and slapped each other's backs. Many of the costumed villains licked their lips at the announcement. The Badges banged their metal batons against the floor in approval.

The human/arachnid hybrid Spyder sprang onto the ceiling and quickly sprayed a cinching web over one of Old Scratch's elite female guard. Scarlett moved out of the way just in time to prevent the woman arachnid from dripping venom on her. The villainess's attempt at an apologetic smile only made Scarlett shiver in a mix of disgust and flaring anger.

"Sorry," the mutant apologized in her strange, whispery voice. "Got caught up in the excitement of the moment."

Scarlett couldn't help but raise a disbelieving eyebrow. "Uh-huh. Right."

The two women held a look. The venomous sheen on the mutant spider-woman's mouth parts both disgusted and allured. Under Scarlett's gaze, Spyder began pulling the cinching web's silken strands off the entangled guard. The second the web was removed, the guard scrambled away from the villainess in a panicked crawl. Spyder looked back at the demon's right hand.

"No harm, no foul," Spyder chuckled.

Scarlett turned away without a response.

"You know how delicious you look to me?"

Scarlett froze in her tracks, then slowly turned to face the human/black widow fusion. Even in the midst of the spontaneous celebration, some of the meeting's surrounding attendees started to take notice of the two angry villainesses.

"Do you realize how fucking grotesque you are?"

Spyder smiled as only a spider mutant can. A drop of clear fluid eased from the corner of her larger mandibles.

"Someday you'll be paralyzed in one of my webs, and your imagination will be filling you with dread as I prepare to savor the taste of your liquefied organs." Another string of venom slid from the corner of her mouth.

Scarlett stepped close enough to make the spider woman rise up on her human legs, exposing the red hourglass on the underside of her torso. Spyder's mandibles yawned open, exposing the nightmare of crushing and rending mouthparts inside. Gangbangers near them stepped back and gave the dangerous women plenty of room.

"Powerful women just can't ever seem to get along," Scarlett declared. "There always has to be a Queen Bee. Problem is, you don't respect my power."

Spyder hissed angrily. Her body grew still, ready to strike. "You're not the only woman here who wears red."

The strong wind of Old Scratch's wings, flapped in displeasure, blew a strong blast of air into both their faces.

"Ladies, ladies, my directive certainly includes you both. This should be a time of celebration, not challenges."

Spyder slowly closed her mouth. The genetic nightmare seemed to forget Scarlett was even there. "My apologies, my dark lord," she hissed softly. "This was not the time nor the place."

"Cry much?" Scarlett asked the genetic anomaly.

The spider woman glared at the demon. "Never, my black-hearted sister." Coal black tears suddenly rolled from all the mutant woman's multiple eyes. Spyder quivered in startled shock.

"You fuckin' bitch!" she screeched. She shook her head, but the tears kept flowing. And harder. "I will kill you when the truce is done." Spyder leapt back up into the cavern's shadowy ceiling and scurried away. Scarlett did little to mask her contempt. Andre crossed his arms.

"What was that about?"

"She wants what I have."

"And what do you have, my dear?"

Scarlett dragged her blood-colored fingernails down the demon's mid-section until her hand found what it sought. Oblivious to everyone else in the room, she squeezed his thickening member. It quickly hardened to a width well beyond her grasp.

Andre looked into Scarlett's eyes. "There's not enough of you for me."

She smiled wickedly. "I've been preparing. Stretching my boundaries, as it were."

Andre purred like a monstrous cat, and then leaned in close enough for her to feel the cold, dead skin of his cheek. "Spyder is too useful to us to kill," he said.

Scarlett smiled like a practiced beauty pageant contestant. "I understand. And I'll be visiting you later." She wove her way back through the jubilant gathering. Red was definitely her color, and the way her outfit accentuated her feminine charms, it was difficult for Andre to look away.

The new Old Scratch stood in the middle of the raucous criminal gathering, taking in the surrounding celebration. He threw his arms up in the air and let his wings unfold, scattering a few street gang members. As the undisputed most powerful supervillain on the West Coast, he was in a position to use his vast influence on the entire region's criminal element. His word wasn't exactly law, but with Old Scratch planning criminal vengeance on something this big a scale, nearly every level of the underworld— from purse snatcher, to crime czar, to serial killer in the making— would follow his lead. Oh, the fun would soon begin. Not so much for wannabes like The Bat, but fun for the real power running San Angeles.

"Get me The Geek, now," Old Scratch's voice boomed to no one in particular. "I want the world to know what's coming." Andre was going to make The Bat rue the day he'd decided to challenge him for the protection of his city, and for the heart of his great love.

He would create a crime wave— no, a crime tsunami— of such epic proportions that both law enforcement and area heroes would be under siege as they had been at no other time in their careers. It would be a cruel, but short-lived reality for his city, but a very necessary first step in his plan to crush crime in San Angeles.

Andre yelled at the top of the demon's lungs, his proclamation echoing off the cavern walls as the crowd roared again. "Thirty-one days of hell on earth!" The demon took flight, soaring around the cavern above the rabid gathering.

Scarlett sat in his throne at the head of the table, her short blood-red outfit pushed high enough to expose her milky, muscular thighs above her matching stockings and garters. She smiled with genuine pleasure as she enjoyed her master's reveling in his followers' maniacal acceptance of his plan.

Sadly, caught up in the momentary homicidal glee of his pending revenge on The Bat, Andre ignored the tiny part of his brain screaming at him about the effect his plan would have on Tatiana's safety.

#

As the baseball vigilante stepped out onto the rooftop, he couldn't help but marvel at the glorious expanse of flowers and potted plants left by citizens paying their respects to their former protector. There wasn't an empty spot to place a step. The Blackledge Tower roof had become a sea of floral beauty backlit by a fading, shimmering sunset.

Catfight perched on the far edge of the roof. She balanced effortlessly in a squat position, her hand claws anchoring her as she leaned into the warm breeze and sunset. The Bat couldn't tell if she was watching the sun's curtain call or enjoying its last sighs of warmth. Since the chaos of Midnight's beach memorial, she'd been distant, quiet. The change had caught him off-guard.

He took a deep breath and grimaced. The punishment he'd taken at the hands of that fucking demon had taken a serious toll. He'd lain in bed the last two nights, wondering why Old Scratch hadn't finished him. And a couple of the things he'd thought he'd heard the demon say, if he didn't know better, had sounded more like Midnight than the hellspawn. His fury, the familiar tone. The demon had behaved as if he were in a jealous rage.

But there was no rhyme or reason to the freak. No one could understand why Old Scratch had been there to watch the memorial in the first place. And what he'd done to The Ant. The Bat's broken ribs felt like a good-night kiss in comparison. The diminutive hero would live, but it taken a series of major surgeries to save him. His heroic career was over; his manhood literally torn from him.

"Bat." Catfight's voice was strong enough to carry across the roof to him, but it still sounded like a bedroom whisper. Even at the distance between them, he could see she'd been crying. The sorrow of her expression tore at his heart. He glanced around, trying to figure out the best way to get to her without trampling the flowers left for Midnight.

The Bat grabbed the lip of the roof over the rooftop exit and flipped onto it, fighting back the pain in his battered midsection. He took a couple of quick steps and launched himself toward the closest edge of the skyscraper. He landed in mid-stride and kept running the building's edge until he closed in on the feline crime fighter. He drew his baseball bat from his back sheath and raised it over his head. As he reached Catfight, he dropped the bat to the roof and flipped over it and her. The vigilante landed in a seated position just to the other side of Catfight, but The Bat couldn't stop the groan of pain from the landing's impact.

"That's what you get for showing off," Catfight scolded.

The Bat rubbed at his side. "They're healing. Just not fast enough." He looked out at the fiery orange-red orb melting into the horizon. It was beautiful. "Got your message."

"Obviously," she replied. She skinned off her right glove and gently took the Bat's black-leather-clad hand. She looked into the vigilante's eyes. "I wanted to thank you...for everything."

He shook his head and squeezed her hand for reassurance. "You'd have done the same for me."

"I'm taking off. I usually spend the holidays with my parents, but with everything going on, I'm going to extend the visit." He started to protest, but she cut him off. "I need to get away for a while."

"But, the city…"

"You'll be one-hundred percent soon. The city will be fine in your hands. And there are other heroes that stuck around after the beach ceremony." Stunned at the news, The Bat found himself equally taken aback by Catfight leaning in and kissing him gently on the lips. Sadly, her soft mouth withdrew before he could kiss back.

"Thank you again for everything. I'll see you soon."

"Catfight—" was all he could get out as she leaned away from the building's edge and dropped into free-fall. He started to watch her descent, but jerked his stare back to the sunset. He'd seen her do this stunt more than once, and each time he'd found the sight unnerving. How she managed to land unhurt from such a tremendous height was beyond him. Non-lethal terminal velocity or some such bullshit. He just knew the rooftop happened to be well over one-hundred stories above the street, and Catfight didn't really have nine lives.

Not a single particle in his being had the urge to follow the wildcat beauty's fall to the pavement so far below. He forced himself to look down, anyway. Catfight was still falling. Well, it looked like his plan to seduce her would have to wait until after New Year's. In the meantime, he'd keep his bed warm with Ivy. He would need fresh info on the demon if he was going to stand any chance of bringing down Old Scratch's empire.

The Bat stood up, took a last quick peek over the edge to confirm Catfight had finally landed safely, then strode across the rooftop, no longer concerned with the number of vases or potted plants he knocked over. It wasn't like Midnight was merely missing and could pop up at any time, alive and well. And since The Bat didn't believe in heaven, he knew Midnight couldn't be watching or waiting for him. Then again, hell might be a completely different matter. Could there be a fiery pit if there wasn't a place for the good people? Shoot, a hundred years from now, he might be an escaped hell demon.

The Bat stopped to admire a particularly beautiful vase filled with roses displayed on a makeshift shrine. A card announced "The best hero for the best city in the world." The Bat scooped up the vase and casually tossed it over the side of the building.

Weird accidents happened in San Angeles all the time.

The Bat headed for the elevators, ignoring the distant sounds of impacting metal, screeching car tires, and screams from down below.

Chapter Eleven

THE HELLIDAYS

Andre hung in the air, his wings keeping him centered in the three-wall setup of color monitors. Built and maintained by The Geek, the citywide surveillance and communications room was one of the few modern-looking areas in Old Scratch's vast underground lair.

Andre had ordered the two attending women away from their posts so he could have a private viewing of the rooftop meeting at the Blackledge Tower. Alone, he'd watched the tender kiss between Catfight and The Bat, feeling the contents of his stomach curdle into a bubbling caldron. But when the vigilante stomped and kicked his way through the rooftop's floral memorial, Andre's feelings turned black and cold. The Bat's tossing of the flower arrangement down into rush-hour traffic caused Andre's oversized hands to tremble.

"Should have gutted you like a fish when I had the chance," he growled to himself. The imagined feel of his talons slicing through the vigilante's midsection and decimating his internal organs brought a cruel smile to the demon's lips. Would it feel like plunging his hands into a warm plate of spaghetti?

It was also good to know Tatiana was not only going to keep her normal holiday routine, but would extend it due to grieving. He hated to see her in such heartache, but a part of him appreciated the depth of the wound his passing had caused. He certainly didn't want her to be a part of his devilish plan for San Angeles, but like he'd once heard someone say, things were going to get a whole lot worse before they got a whole lot better.

He heard the approaching footsteps and knew Scarlett and the Geek were close. He shifted his body angle and attention to another downtown screen, turning toward the visitors as they entered the room. One of The Damned led the way. Andre was becoming familiar with the members of his elite guard, and he recognized her. A petite, wild-haired blonde with a muscular gymnast's build. Ivy.

Ivy stepped into the room, then stationed herself to the side of the doorway. Scarlett and the Geek followed, and another pair of guards stopped just outside the room's entrance.

"Scratch," the Geek said in greeting, scanning the monitors. His eyes stopped on the screen in front of the demon. "That's some hardcore shit." The slim man pushed his thick-lensed glasses back up the bridge of his oversized nose. "Then again, you are hellspawn. Must be like watching a sitcom for you, huh?"

Andre eyed the mastermind and could barely keep from laughing. The Geek appeared to be nothing more than a stereotypical high-school science-and-math aficionado. Sure, his head was a bit larger than it should be, as if housing an extra-large brain, and his complexion screamed pimply adolescent, but it was his chosen appearance of taped-together eyeglasses, bulging pocket protector, and belt/suspenders combination that effectively spelled out his talent. Andre thumbed through his mental file on the demented mastermind.

Despite his youthful appearance, unverified sources placed The Geek at well over a hundred and fifty years old. Also known as Hanson Walters, he had supposedly served in the Civil War as a young field surgeon, but there was no real accounting for why he'd never aged. Walters had fed his ravenous intellect over the decades, and had a long history of bartering his intelligence to the rich and powerful for the safety and freedom of satisfying his own perverse pleasures.

Andre casually glanced back at the monitor. A group of foot soldiers from one of the downtown gangs, a multi-race crew called the Splinters, were forcing a trio of well-dressed Asian teenagers into an abandoned trailer on a closed-down car lot. Frightened and crying, none of the teens screamed for help. Andre had to fight back his gut reaction to protest the impending gang rape. He looked at the mutant mad genius with a dead expression and didn't respond to the images on the screen.

The Geek quickly cleared his throat. "So, you rang?"

"I want to make a citywide announcement. I want you to not only patch me into all the local television stations, but—"

"Also grab all cell phones and major social media outlets. Gotcha," The Geek jumped in with an anticipatory smile that was repulsive in more ways than one. His rotten, snaggle-toothed display was offensive to dentists worldwide. The evil genius's attention wandered back to the monitors.

"I want thirty uninterrupted seconds," Andre continued.

The Geek nodded absently. "No problemo."

Andre glanced at Scarlett and smirked. "I want it for tonight at nine o'clock."

For a moment, it didn't appear as if The Geek heard the demon's last statement. The Geek's attention was riveted to the monitor with the trailer party going on. Several seconds passed. "That's like, a couple of hours away."

"I thought you were smart," Andre taunted, his tone flat.

The Geek stepped closer to the monitor. "Could you turn up the audio?"

"Can you have it ready for nine?"

The smartest being on the planet looked at the demon with such malice that Ivy's hand hovered over the throwing knives in her waistband.

"Fuck you," The Geek spat. Andre had to admire the balls on him. He could almost hear them clanging together. But the genius was being rude. An instant later, Andre snatched up the Geek, his foot talons grabbing the man by the shoulders, and flew the man topsy-turvy around the room. The pattern had no rhyme or reason, and the man started wailing like a two-year-old. The Geek's glasses were tossed from his face. Scarlett snatched them out of the air.

"Stttttttttttttttttttttttttooooooooooooooooooooooooooop!" The Geek cried out.

A few seconds later, Andre dumped Walters to the stone floor. The evil genius collapsed to his hands and knees, the contents of his stomach splashing in front of him.

"You're an asshole," The Geek gasped between heaves.

"And you should be smart enough not to fuck with me." Andre tossed an order to Ivy. "Stay with him. If he decides to use that smart mouth again, peel the skin from his face." Ivy nodded, stepping forward. The Geek pushed himself up from the floor.

"Fucking touchy for a demon."

"And someone get him a mop." Andre laughed as he flew from the room.

Nearly two hours later, Andre sat in the throne he'd requisitioned from his conference chamber and had placed in the middle of the surveillance room. He fidgeted uncomfortably in the large chair, glancing across the room at Scarlett. "Do I need make-up?"

Scarlett frowned, shaking her head. "I don't think so."

"You know I tend to have that shiny forehead thing going on." The demon suddenly smiled like a second grader. "I don't have any flesh stuck in my teeth, do I?"

"Less than a minute," The Geek called out, making last-minute adjustments on the equipment.

"What's for dinner?" Andre asked.

Scarlett did everything but roll her eyes. She forced a compliant smile onto her face. "What would you like?"

"Chaos," Andre answered. "With all the pandemonium you can give me."

"Thirty seconds," The Geek directed, gathering up the hand-sized camera. He pushed his glasses up onto his head, then checked the camera's focus.

"Would you like fries with that?" Scarlett teased.

"Actually, curly fries with virgin blood for dipping sounds really good."

The Geek was counting down from five.

Andre thought about The Bat, and his expression hardened as The Geek said, "You're on!"

The Geek had outdone himself. Across the massive San Angeles County, every radio, television, and cable program had been pre-empted. Real-time texts were being delivered to every cellular phone user in the Southland. As an added touch, The Geek dropped in a background making it look as if Old Scratch were broadcasting from Satan's living room, complete with audible wails of torment. Law enforcement was going to study the hell out of it. The Geek also mixed the real voices of ex-Prime Minister Margaret Thatcher, Captain Kangaroo, JFK, Shirley Temple, and Elvis into the hellish background accompaniment.

Andre stared into the camera, speaking slowly so that every word would be easily understood. "Due to the unprovoked attack on me at Midnight's beach memorial earlier today, I am declaring war on San Angeles. Beginning at twelve midnight, all criminal organizations and unlawful individuals will be given carte blanche to operate throughout the month of December under my protection. I will broadcast again at midnight on January first and speak to the survivors about a new San Angeles. You have three hours to flee. Or pray."

Andre smiled for the camera like a proud first-time father. "Happy hellidays!"

The Geek cut the transmission, cackling with glee. The genius did a little jig.

"That was awesome, Scratch! I'd heard rumors, but..."

The demon ignored the man. "Scarlett, contact the top crime families. I want all the area prisons under siege simultaneously at exactly one minute after midnight. Same with the local jails. See to it."

She flashed a post-orgasmic smile. "And the Allenby Asylum?"

"I'll take care of that myself," Andre answered. "Contact The Mob and tell them to stand down."

Scarlett left the room.

The Geek continued to ramble his praise. Andre ignored the man, choosing to hover in the middle of the monitors. He stayed airborne, watching throughout the three-hour grace period as the city of San Angeles gradually became panic-stricken.

Traffic jammed the freeways. Surface streets became nightmares. Within an hour, the city had sealed itself shut. Law enforcement and emergency units were quickly beleaguered. As the innocent tried to escape, the crazies came out to play. By eleven p.m., fires burned in downtown and along the Wilshire corridor.

Both the mayor and governor pleaded with citizens to remain calm, but a threat of terror coming directly from a source as powerful as Old Scratch couldn't be overcome by politicians.

Half an hour before midnight, Andre signaled The Geek, who watched the monitors, enthralled. The demon-skinned hero patted the top of his throne. "Why don't you take a seat while I'm gone to Allenby. The real fun won't start until midnight."

The Geek climbed into the oversized chair. He looked like a child. "You wouldn't happen to have some popcorn, would ya?"

Andre glanced over at Ivy, who understood the wordless command. The world's smartest man was so entertained by the myriad of calamities happening all over the city he didn't even notice Old Scratch's departure.

Chapter Twelve

ALLENBY ASYLUM

The Montgomery Foster Allenby Institution for the Criminally Insane was the closest facility in the real world to Arkham Asylum in the fictional world of Batman and his nemesis, The Joker.

Perched high in the hills north of downtown San Angeles, the exterior of the infamous Allenby Asylum had appeared in more horror films and dark television series than any other Hollywood landmark. Built to hold more than three hundred extreme inmates, the asylum now held two dozen convicted psychopaths whose crimes transcended laws and lives taken. Guests of the Allenby were true-crime Jokers— madmen whose lack of superpowers hardly handicapped their sinister and depraved attempts to murder and violate innocent victims.

Even in the dead of night, Andre could see the freshly burned halo of hillside sloping down from the asylum. Powerful floodlights lit up the surrounding grounds for a mile in every direction. As Andre broke from the clouds above and dove straight toward the facility, he could sense something wrong.

"Cut the power," he said.

His ear communicator transmitted The Geek's voice as the asylum went dark. "Power has been interrupted. You rule the darkness," The Geek reported.

"I'm headed to Ward Thirteen."

As he dropped from the sky, Andre braced himself for heavy arms fire from the nine rifle towers guarding the asylum. With an awkward-looking aerial agility, the demon descended in a dizzyingly quick, herky-jerky pattern, like a wounded moth. When no gunfire came, he scanned the central tower. He could see three uniformed officers, all armed and at their stations. Circling closer, it took him a moment to realize none of the officers were moving. Or breathing.

"Geek— the central tower guards are dead, but propped and posed as if they're on duty."

"Could be an escape attempt," the Geek responded.

"There are no alarms, no movement on the ground at all."

"Hold on a moment," The Geek said. The com line went dead for several seconds. Andre remained airborne. The nearest tower had two more dead men inside, also propped up so they looked alive at first glance.

"There are no transmissions involving law enforcement coming from the asylum. In fact, all the phone lines are operational, but none are in use."

"Going in for a closer look."

Outside the main hospital entrance, a quartet of dead guards had been tied in place by thin razor wire. The dark gloom almost masked the dried blood on their uniforms.

Andre stepped up to the oversized steel doors. It almost felt like he was about to enter an ancient temple. The doors were still locked and secure. The emergency lighting shone dully from above. He tore the left-side door off its vault-like hinges and strode into the inky darkness. The stench of savage death hung in the air.

Had he been touring the asylum as Midnight, Andre's nerves would have been jangling, waiting for the first maniac to explode out of the darkness wielding a meat cleaver. Now, wearing a demon's skin, he belonged in the hellish aftermath. The death stench didn't seem like a dire omen. Like him, it belonged there at the moment. Asylums held human nightmares. Even on the sunniest days, Allenby Asylum held some of the darkest souls on earth at bay.

Andre felt at ease. Even the craziest of the inmates would never think to attack a demon— the being most resembling them. Many of the mentally disturbed thought Old Scratch must be the devil incarnate, sent to earth to be worshiped and followed. Crazy people often cited the demon's voice as the one in their head commanding them to perform atrocities. Old Scratch's sacred mission of turning the earth into his own extension of the underworld he'd escaped seemed glorious to those who'd embraced evil like a favorite childhood doll.

Emergency lighting continued down the main administrative corridor, though the alarms stayed eerily silent. Why piss-yellow lighting had been chosen as the default was hard to fathom. Yellow never signaled emergency like red lighting did, and the yellow light's pale illumination didn't add much visibility. Old Scratch's eyes had been made to see in pitch darkness, so the lack of light didn't matter. Andre was happy that he and Old Scratch shared that ability to see in the dark.

But Andre was not happy with what he saw. The hall was a coroner's nightmare. The dead, the blood, the body pieces. The corridor was awash in gore. All that was missing from the scene were African buzzards to feast on the carcasses. With no clear path, Andre took a deep breath and started walking through the carnage. He'd have preferred to fly, but Andre knew the real Old Scratch wouldn't have hesitated to get his feet bloody. Not knowing if the security cameras were still functioning, best to continue the charade. The Geek could be watching him.

When the administrative corridor ended, Andre took a sharp right into another long hallway. This one was lined with doors that presumably led to the inmates' rooms. He explored the hallway, and none too quietly. The floors echoed and squished with each heavy step he took, but no noteworthy psychopaths sprinted out of dark doorways, screaming like banshees, butcher knives raised and ready. As far as he could tell, the inmates had been equally victimized by whatever had happened.

An observation struck him. Andre stopped walking.

Outside of his own movement, the place was graveyard quiet.

At the end of this hallway, Andre reached a bank of elevators. All three sat open, reset by the interruption in power. They were all oversized to accommodate gurneys, and equipped with special equipment for transporting dangerous patients.

Heavy-duty leather-and-metal restraints had been fitted into the center of each elevator's rear wall. An S&M image passed through Andre's mind as he stepped inside. The compartment was actually taller than he had anticipated, and he was able to stand upright, though the tips of his wings scraped against the ceiling's metal light housing. As the elevator door closed, a woman's high-pitched scream reached him. The sound was desperate, but muted, as if some distance away. Wherever she was, the victim wasn't close enough for Andre to help. Besides, he really couldn't afford to get caught acting out of character. He could only hope she wouldn't suffer long.

Andre thought about the asylum's layout and started to press the button for the ward he was looking for, but then he noticed the blood-splattered access card inserted in the elevator's electronic reader. He smiled at the simple gift. Instead of going up to Ward Thirteen, he pushed the restricted access "B" button, which stood for basement, and the asylum's central operations center. That's where he'd find whoever was behind the asylum's hostile takeover. He had a couple of strong guesses. As Midnight, he'd put his share of Allenby maniacs away.

As the elevator settled to a stop, an oddly pitched voice spoke from a hidden speaker, a voice blending human male and underworld being. Its unholy timbre held a signature like no other. Beginning as a gravelly baritone, by the end of every sentence the tone reached a high, inhuman squeal. Its duality was unnerving. "Welcome to Allenby, my old friend. We were hoping our sacrifice would be worthy of your attention."

Andre smirked as the door opened to a well-lit corridor. One of the words piqued his curiosity— "we." Psychopaths didn't tend to play well with others. And he knew the owner of that distinct voice was no exception.

Tatiana sat in the first-class section of the Air France airbus. Across the aisle, the CEO-type gentleman's glances were getting bolder. Tatiana's short skirt barely reached mid-thigh, and it had crept up even more upon sitting. If the gentleman offered her a drink, she'd accept it politely.

She'd been staring at a slide show of photos of Andre and herself on her cell phone when the news feed alarm went off. She quickly scanned the news summary, shocked at its contents: an update of the earlier breaking story involving Old Scratch. She'd been on a massage table, phone turned off, in the Air France executive lounge prior to boarding. In the meantime, Old Scratch had pronounced an epic crime wave against San Angeles. And for one of the rare times in her life, Catfight wasn't sure what to do.

The declaration of an all-out offensive against the city's citizens and law-enforcement agencies during the holiday season was totally insane, and so typical of the hellspawn's demented thought process.

Tatiana knew that some of the heroes who had come to San Angeles for Midnight's memorial had stuck around after the rooftop melee between the demon, The Bat, and The Ant.

The Bat.

Her thoughts flirted around the rugged vigilante. It seemed like he'd never left her side since Andre died. And as a woman, she didn't have to possess special abilities to realize he wanted her. Just the way he looked her. It reminded her all too much of the way she'd always looked at Andre, especially when he wore his Midnight costume. As Midnight, Andre was truly himself, and when he was himself, he was the sexiest man on the planet. *People* magazine had thought so, too, two years running.

Tatiana rocked in her seat. Just that tiny spark of memory had been enough to awaken her body's desires. But this wasn't the time. She grinned. She could almost hear Andre telling her that. Not that they hadn't become members of the mile-high club long ago. The first time had been when they'd been recruited to escort Tombstone to Washington D.C. in a private, specially equipped containment jet. She'd packed a bag and surprised Dre with an old-fashioned stewardess uniform mid-flight.

If she kept down this path, she'd have to excuse herself to the restroom and take the edge off.

Her mind jumped back to The Bat. She was sure he could help her smooth that edge off, and it wasn't like the thought hadn't crossed her mind. She could only imagine the rough-and-tumble ride they'd create. No doubt The Bat got plenty of practice. Tatiana had caught the very strong scent of a woman simmering on his skin beneath his own musk.

Her body ached for Andre, but the time would come when another man would step into his role, albeit temporarily.

She shook her head, trying to clear the jumble of swirling thoughts. She ignored the captain's voice as he did the departure speech. They would be backing away from the gate shortly.

What should she do? Should she get off the plane and prepare to join The Bat, Starlight, The Wing, and a few others in a citywide crime war? Old Scratch's declaration would have a ripple effect. Some of the heroes had their own cities to protect. Once word got out that The Amphibian was fighting crime in San Angeles, what was going to happen in New Orleans? It would be open season for crime there, as well.

And what about San Angeles? What about her city?

But it wasn't really her city, was it? And the place she'd called home didn't exist anymore. Her family had been lucky to escape the true horrors of the past conflicts in her country and start again in Sweden, while she'd moved to the States to pursue her dreams. But her heart had never belonged to San Angeles the way Midnight's had. San Angeles had been his city, his mistress.

Tatiana had fallen in love with Andre as she'd begun to climb the ladder as a model/spokesperson/hostess, and she'd stayed because Andre and her work were there. She'd always known that because of Hollywood, San Angeles would forever be a cesspool ringed in palm trees, attracting the best and worst people from all over the world. Dreamers weren't just actors and singers and writers and kind-hearted foreigners looking to escape the cruel hardships of their birth countries. Some dreamers imagined pitch-black pits with innocent people waist-deep in gasoline, burning alive while the dark dreamer danced to the jagged melody of their screams.

There weren't as many of those types of dreamers, but they existed just the same. Andre had been happy to be their nemesis. She realized Andre knew his own dark brand of justice wouldn't exist without their evil perspectives.

The "Fasten Your Seatbelts" signs flashed on in first class.

Tatiana looked at her fingernails. A manicure and pedicure junkie, her nails were normally professionally trimmed, painted and polished. They hadn't been touched since Andre's death, and she'd taken up her childhood habit of chewing on her nails during times of extreme stress. They looked ragged, to say the least.

She felt the rock of the plane pushing away from the gate. An attendant walked by and smiled at her. She wouldn't get off the plane. She didn't want to. She didn't have a strong enough reason to. She wanted to go home and curl up against her mother's lap and cry and grieve for Andre. She wanted to feel safe in her father's big mechanic's arms.

Andre needed to be Midnight, but Catfight was just another wardrobe change for Tatiana. She could give up fighting crime at any time. She loved the thrill and the physicality of capturing criminals, but protecting the public from felons and lunatics wasn't her calling. And for the past few years she'd mainly suited up to be with the man she hoped someday would be the father of her children.

Tatiana burst into tears, covering her face with her hands. Someone gently placed a hand on her shoulder, but she shrugged it away with a mumbled apology. Probably the CEO taking the opportunity to grope.

Maybe she'd never return to San Angeles. There was really nothing there for her. Her career was going well; she could work anywhere. And there were men like The Bat all over Europe.

#

Andre passed through a pair of thick plexiglass and wire-mesh doors, and turned into the basement's central operations room.

Central operations was a slaughterhouse. Blood soaked the room. Any staff unlucky enough to be on duty had been broken and mangled. Some had been carved open and disemboweled. Down here, the bright institutional lighting had stayed on, which only made the carnage stand out more vividly.

Andre stepped forward, then ducked back as blood dripped from the ceiling. Looking up, Andre saw a severed head hanging to drain. An expensive ink pen had been plunged through an ear and into the ceiling tile.

"Really? A little blood never hurt anyone." The voice came from the open director's office across the space.

A spark of recognition lit in Andre's mind. It was the same voice that had greeted him in the elevator, but now it sounded much more familiar. The voice had an intellectual, academic quality to it.

With nowhere clean to step, Andre took flight, landing just outside the director's office. His left foot squished into a large blood puddle. He cursed under his breath.

"I've never seen a hell demon so averse to blood," the odd voice growled from the office.

"I like it better when I do the spilling." Possibility turned into stark recognition. Midnight's blood would have chilled at the hellish portrait before him.

Three men and a teenage girl lounged in the blood-splattered room. Andre knew them all. To the left, perched shoeless on the far end of the office couch, was Irwin Carp, a.k.a. Roach. Hands and face smeared with dark blood, he gnawed on the remains of a human brain.

As Midnight, Andre had actually debated taking Roach into custody because of his extremely violent impulses and psychotic proclivity for consuming brains for sustenance, but the problem was, just like his namesake, Roach was very hard to kill. As invulnerable as he was insane, Roach could sustain a sniper shot to the head and a few days later be eating someone's brain as if he'd never had his own skull ventilated. Andre had determined vivisection and cremation to be the only viable combination to permanently dispose of Roach, but there were lines he wasn't willing to cross in his earlier crime-fighting days.

Roach stared across his meal at the demon, his chewing deliberate and noisy.

Seated in the director's high-backed leather chair in front of the broad desk, the asylum's director, Bob Robertson, was barely contained in an inmate's gray jumpsuit.

Standing a few feet to the right was an exact duplicate of the director, staring into the empty space before him, a bloody meat cleaver holstered in the front hip pocket of his jumpsuit and a second cleaver hanging from his hand. The standing Robertson giggled softly like a young girl with a naughty secret, rhythmically raising up on his bare toes like a ballerina. Something was insanely wrong with the seated version of Bob, and the truth became apparent an instant later.

The seated Bob unzipped his jumpsuit. The guts and blood inside glittered under the bright lights. As Andre watched, another, smaller man emerged from the viscera. A man who, despite the gore surrounding him, wore the expression and manner of a college professor. His build was slim, and he was shirtless. At some point he'd taken the time to re-insert his quarter-sized platinum nipple rings. The crude pentagram scar on his forehead made his identity a dead giveaway, but it was his red eyes that reflected the truth of his situation. Starting at the very top of his shaved skull, the Lord's Prayer was tattooed on his head, backward, in blood-red ink. Casually, he held a dog leash in his hand.

Andre was too stunned to blink.

Former psychiatrist Dr. Wilton Sabastian Reese, also known as the spirit-possessed Straitjacket, was seated inside the carved and spread-open torso of Director Bob Robertson. Robertson had been an exceptionally large man, and Straitjacket seemed a comfortable fit inside his mutilated body.

"With only the emergency power on, the place got chilly," Straitjacket explained with an impish grin.

On the other end of the leash pouted the deceased Director Robertson's teenage daughter. Wearing only a blood-smeared pair of sheer white panties, filthy white socks, and a spiked leather dog collar, she lay curled up at Straitjacket's feet like a house cat. On one side of her head, straight black hair grew to shoulder length, while the other side of her head had been shaved down to dark stubble. The tips of her long hair had been dyed a startling safety-first yellow-green. She looked up at Old Scratch, and her malignant, bloody smile might have been the most horrifying sight in the room.

Before he could stop himself, the question popped out of the demon's mouth.

"Courtney?" he asked.

Years ago, Midnight had met Bob Robertson, the then-Gulf war veteran and Deputy Chief of Police, and his family at a Hollywood police fundraiser. Courtney had caused quite the stir when she'd torn open her shirt and displayed a white Midnight tee shirt underneath she'd worn for the hero to autograph. The fundraiser attendees had laughed it off, and the press made light of the incident, but there had been something about Courtney even then that made Andre uncomfortable. Since growing into young womanhood, the asylum director's daughter had been kicked out of a series of local private schools on charges ranging from prostitution to extortion to drug use to the sexual assault of a teacher.

Sometimes kids were just bad. So far, Courtney had been a poster girl for birth control.

"Ahhhhhh, you must be quite the bad girl if Scratch knows you," Straitjacket mused.

She stretched, as much an erotic exercise as anything else. "We met before I had pussy hair."

Between bites of brain, Roach laughed at the crude remark. The standing, cleaver-wielding double of Robertson grinned.

Courtney smiled flirtatiously. "Maybe the demon will take me under his wing like he did that whore Scarlett."

Straitjacket gave the leash a corrective tug. It was hard enough to lift the girl off the floor. The asylum inmate smiled apologetically at Old Scratch as he reprimanded his pet. "Now, darling, we must be respectful of our elders and betters."

She rubbed at her throat. "So Scarlett isn't a devil-worshipping whore?" Courtney stared at the demon, letting her eyes drop to Old Scratch's massive member. "You ought to give me a try at what's hanging."

"America's young people," Straitjacket laughed, without an ounce of humor. "So outspoken, given their limited real-world experience."

The noted serial killer, the first convicted psychopath to have legally been found to be possessed by another entity of unknown origin, pushed himself up and out of the human cocoon he'd fashioned for himself. The moist sucking sound he made when he pulled free of Robertson's insides made Andre queasy. Straitjacket dropped the leash.

"Stay," he commanded. Courtney didn't move, but she licked her lips teasingly as she stared between the demon's legs.

"So good to see you again, brother," the inmate said, his fluctuating voice beginning as a low gravelly tone, but ending as a high-pitched squeal. "Let me congratulate you on slaughtering that tick-turd Midnight. His death made me shit a fucking rainbow."

"It was overdue," Andre replied, his eyes darting between Straitjacket and the murderous Robertson double. Straitjacket caught the double-take.

"That's Match," he announced. "He wanted to try the director on for size when we took the place." He gestured to indicate the blood on the walls and floor. "I think he and Roach did a fabulous job redecorating, don't you agree?"

"Crimson does go with your eyes."

"Being a man sucks shit-crusted ass," Match whined. "I miss wearing high heels."

Andre stared at the director's duplicate with hatred and disgust. Straitjacket glanced at his associate, cleared his throat, and changed the subject.

"We'd been planning to do the asylum for a while, but when you made the announcement earlier, and Robertson's family just happened to be visiting, we thought it was the perfect time to execute."

"I'm sure your prior time as director here served you well. Did you say family?" Andre questioned.

The former criminal psychiatrist smiled like a choirboy."Ahhh, yes. Courtney accompanied her mother Suzette here earlier this evening." The possessed serial killer and the demon stood looking at each other. Moments passed and the silence stretched out.

"And?" Andre was forced to ask.

"When mama made it quite clear she didn't want to join her daughter at my feet, I was a complete gentleman and gave her a choice. Roach could cut her throat and then eat her brain while she died…"

Across the room, Roach grinned as brain squished through his fingers.

"Or she could take her chances with a mystery inmate. She chose the mystery inmate. Turned out to be Hatchet Man."

Hatchet Man. Andre hadn't heard that name for years. Hatchet Man had actually been captured by police a couple of years before Andre had begun patrolling the streets as Midnight. Andre couldn't remember Hatchet Man's real name, but he did know the killer had once been a pro football defensive end who'd had a psychotic break after losing a playoff game. A couple of nights after the loss, he'd attacked his ex-wife, raping her multiple times between various limb amputations. He'd evaded police long enough to savage several more young women before he was brought to justice. His instrument of choice was a razor-sharp camping hatchet. Andre imagined the sound the blade made as it struck bone. And then he remembered the faint scream he'd heard at the elevator. Jesus.

"I have a feeling the old boy is going to take his time with her. Rumor is he hasn't been in the same room with a flesh-and-blood woman in years."

"Does he fuck the stumps, or what?" Courtney piped in. Both Andre and Straitjacket stared at the young woman. The serial killer sighed.

"Quite the prize, isn't she?"

"You always had an eye for talent..." Andre suddenly found his mind blank. Which demon had possessed Dr. Wilton Sabastian Reese, twisting him from the inside out until he became the depraved Straitjacket?

The serial killer raised an eyebrow. "Don't tell me you can't remember my given name, back from when I had true flesh and form, and didn't need to pour myself into lesser vessels."

Andre stared at the bloody inmate. He had no idea. The killer tilted his head as he appraised the demon. "I've heard a story or two, you know..." he began. "Lightning is nothing to play with. It can scramble a memory's capacity for minor details..."

"Lucius," Andre said, pulling the name from thin air.

Straitjacket clapped. "Then again, one spawned directly from the Dark Father himself can laugh off a petty little thing like lightning."

"I have transportation for all of you," Andre announced, unwilling to continue the conversation. "San Angeles is your hunting ground for the next thirty-one days."

"And then?"

"And then you'll do whatever I tell you to do," Andre growled, wings unfolding impressively. Roach fell back off the couch. Match's version of Bob Robertson flinched so hard he dropped his cleaver. Straitjacket took an intimidated step back.

"Hey, can we stop by my house?" Courtney piped up from the floor. "The nanny is there with my little sister. She's very pretty. You'll like her." She sang "you'll like her" like a soft-drink jingle.

Straitjacket thought about it for a moment. "Sounds promising. And what about your little sister?"

Courtney frowned. "Duuuhhh— I meant my little sister."

Roach screeched with laughter. Match smiled as he bent over and retrieved the meat cleaver.

Straitjacket shrugged as he picked up the girl's leash. "America's youth."

"They are the future," Andre joked drily. He turned and took flight out of the room, the trio of infamous serial killers and Courtney following him. Andre hoped Hatchet Man had finished with Suzette Robertson.

Chapter Thirteen

A SIMPLE QUESTION

Scarlett stood in the doorway of the surveillance center. Old Scratch hovered in the middle of the room, lit only by the monitors, studying the chaos portrayed on every screen. The city had become a living nightmare. There just weren't enough police, National Guard, and emergency personnel to handle all the major crimes. Banks all over the Southland were getting robbed. Major fires had been set. Robberies, rapes, and assaults occurred unchecked.

Andre fought the pounding headache. Leaving the asylum director's wife in the hands of that hatchet-slinging lunatic had probably been the hardest thing he'd ever done. And thinking of all the other innocent people whose lives would be ruined...

He fought the urge to bury his horned head in his hands. Knowing Tatiana would be out of the city made the consequences of his plan easier to bear, but even he hadn't expected the explosive nature of the plague he'd allowed to descend upon his city. It was hard to watch. Very, very hard.

He'd sensed Scarlett's presence in the doorway, but he ignored her for a bit. She finally stepped into the room. It was obvious she had something on her mind.

"Just say it," he told her, remaining focused on the monitors. He could feel her gaze.

"So, what happens come New Year's Day?"

Part of him wanted to swoop down and strangle the life out of her. For a split second he imagined the demon's right hand at the mercy of Spyder. Talk about a horrible way to die.

Instead, he remained focused on the monitors. One screen showed a number of school buses from what was once the South Central part of Los Angeles parking in the small downtown area of affluent Pacific Palisades. The buses' doors opened and armed members of the Bloods and Crips poured out into the dark, quiet streets. They swarmed the area like army ants. Attempts from private citizens to protect or defend their homes or lives were met with overwhelming firepower. When SAPD officers finally arrived in the only three squad cars available, they found themselves quickly overpowered by the sheer numbers of hardened gang members. Similar scenarios were playing out all over the city.

Andre finally answered Scarlett's question. "A show of power unlike the world has ever seen."

When it became obvious the demon wasn't going to elaborate, Scarlett turned and left the room, closing the door behind her. Andre continued to hover, watching, absorbing the horror he'd unleashed as a precursor to the endgame he'd always wanted to execute in his city, but, as Midnight, had never dared to attempt.

As the unstable demon Old Scratch, he'd be able to clean up and protect San Angeles. Or at least whatever parts of the city survived the holidays.

It was going to be a long month for the innocent.

And a major test of Andre's sanity.

Chapter Fourteen

BUT FEAR ITSELF

The Bat was in the midst of wrapping up a botched smash-and-grab at a downtown jewelry mart when his earpiece scanner picked up an emergency call from St. Luke's, a smaller midtown hospital.

There were no police cruisers available to respond, but when the 911 operator acknowledged children were involved, The Bat used his namesake Louisville Slugger to bash the remaining would-be jewel thieves into unconsciousness before racing to catch the rear of an express city bus headed in the hospital's direction.

He was almost back to full strength, but the near-continuous crime fighting since the clock struck twelve was taking a toll on his energy level. He'd been lucky that none of his encounters had involved gifted villains. Eventually, his luck would run out.

The wind whipped around the bus, forcing him to squint. The sounds of sirens and gunshots and screams and screeching tires filled the air. It was like a crime festival had opened to a packed house. The city was being shredded, and this was just night number one.

For a fleeting moment, he wondered if Titan might return and help quell the craziness. "Fuck that righteous bastard," The Bat cursed.

As the bus rolled by the Orpheum movie theatre, moviegoers burst out of the lobby doors onto the street, yelling and screaming as they scattered in every direction. He couldn't understand what they were saying, but he wasn't going to concern himself. He'd committed to helping the hospital children.

In the few minutes it took the bus to near the medical center, the vigilante watched a city in complete chaos. Police fought gun battles, struggling to stop multiple crimes being committed in the same short blocks. Looting had begun. Public safety was the top concern, but The Bat could only guess at the approximate number of reported dead there would be by sunrise. Hundreds? Thousands?

And again, this was just the first night. He let out a weary sigh. At least his shattered ribs had healed.

A couple of blocks from St. Luke's, The Bat sprang from the bus and hit the street, running hard. He burst through an alley as a short cut, leaping over the grunting tangle of two men's arms and legs. The Bat hardly batted an eye. He put his head down and ran as hard as he could. He might be a lot of things, but when it came to little kids, well, every second could mean a child's life.

A fleeting memory flashed by: the face of his own baby brother from the funeral. Joey would have been eight years old in another month.

The Bat dodged through an adjacent parking lot and headed for the hospital's emergency entrance. A small crowd had gathered outside. Most appeared to be medical staff, but with them stood plenty of patients and interested civilians. A steady flow of people hurried out of the entrance and the fire exits. The Bat nearly ran over a frantic security guard barking into his shoulder mike. The vigilante kept the man from hitting the pavement, but didn't have time for polite chit-chat.

"Heard...the emergency call," he explained, breathing hard.

The wide-eyed, moon-faced guard was drenched in sweat. He pointed back toward the entrance. His voice had gone ragged from his own yelling.

"...Eating the fucking babies!"

The Bat flinched, not completely sure he'd heard the man right. He grabbed the front of the guard's uniform. "What'd you say? Slow down!"

"The report from Clyde on the fourth floor is that the NICU is completely sealed up and there's a woman, or something, inside, eating the babies!"

The Bat glanced up at the building toward the fourth-floor NICU— the Neonatal Intensive Care Unit. He shook the uniformed guard. "And why the fuck aren't you up there?!"

"Dwayne and Josie went up, and then radioed me to start evacuating the rest of the fourth floor and emergency." The chunky officer bent and grabbed at his knees as he fought for the breath. "There were gunshots a few minutes ago. Then their radios cut off."

The Bat pushed away from the guard and started toward the hospital. Avoiding the clogged emergency entrance, he sprinted instead to the stairway exit. He bolted between a couple of people and burst up the wide cement stairway, bounding up several steps at a time.

When he reached the door with the brightly painted number four on it, he paused. Not sure what to expect, The Bat reached back and drew his weapon from its sheath. The wood gleamed in his hands, and he felt stronger just holding it.

He took a deep breath. For a second he wished Midnight were there. As much as The Bat loathed the city's ex-night time protector and wanted to assume his standing, there was no arguing his adversary's talent as a fighter. No, not just a fighter. An ass-kicker.

The Bat chuckled. What had he heard someone say once?

Midnight had whipped more ass than a donkey trainer. And Midnight never needed a weapon beyond his body to have an edge.

The Bat grasped the fourth-floor door handle, and all the humor flowed right out of him. He jerked the door toward him. With the strength he applied, the door should have been pulled from its hinges, but it merely creaked open, giving entrance reluctantly. Strands of white webbing coated everything, including the door.

The hospital's nighttime lighting fought unsuccessfully to pierce the fog of silken threads. A few feet away, the webbing swirled into a small tunnel. The Bat stood frozen at the sight. This was not what he'd expected. What a fucking cosmic joke.

That fucked-up bitch Spyder and her legion of arachnids had come to feed upon the newborns.

He stared into the webbed vortex. He still hadn't stepped out of the stairwell onto the hospital floor. Somewhere beyond where the webbing allowed him to see, infants wailed. At least some were still alive.

A bead of sweat streaked down from his hairline and dropped into his eye, half blinding him. He yelped, swinging his bat wildly. Wisps of webbing caught and then sizzled as the bat's energy vaporized the strands.

He stumbled back against the stairway railing, wiping at his eye and blinking it clear. Now both eyes began to moisten, and not just from the intrusive drop of sweat. He leaned against the door, his body weight forcing it shut. He let himself slide to the landing, grasping his head in his black-leather-gloved hands. It felt like a twenty-pound greased rat were squirming in his gut. He could feel his heart pounding, and soon its sound filled his ears. One sob, followed by another, and another, quickly escaped him.

The fire door almost shut out the infants' cries, but not quite. The vigilante dropped his bat and clapped his hands over his ears, too late. Just as he could conjure up the memory of the last time he saw his little brother's face, his mind would recreate the infants' desperate wailing, and the sound would haunt him for the rest of his miserable, worthless life.

The vigilante couldn't save those innocent babies.

The Bat, the man looking to fill the big shoes of the city's protector Midnight, was deathly afraid of spiders.

He sat there for he wasn't sure how long, but staying well after the crying on the other side of the door had gone quiet. At some point, he pushed himself to his feet and slid the bat into its sheath. He walked down the stairs on autopilot, tear-reddened eyes cast down. His mind was a total blank. Each foot found the next step, one after another. If any people passed him going either direction, he neither saw nor acknowledged them.

He just kept drifting downward until he bumped blindly into the ground-floor exit door. He shouldered it open, and was immediately met with a series of photo flashes. Microphones were thrust into his face. Camera lights made him squint and turn his head from their glare. Shouted questions surrounded him. He batted the microphones away, hearing himself growl a series of profanities.

The chubby-faced security guard from earlier got in his face. He acted just as frantic as before. "What about the children? Did you save any of them?"

The Bat brought his eyes up to meet the hospital guard's. "They're all fucking dead."

Chatter exploded around him, followed by a bombardment of questions. As The Bat tried to put the media swarm to his back, he noticed the fire truck. Its long extension ladder had been hooked just below a fourth-floor window. The ladder was being retracted.

The hospital guard grabbed The Bat's arm and twisted him around. "All dead?" He pointed toward the receding ladder. "The firemen just reported there were babies still alive."

The Bat rattled his head as if a small piece had broken off inside.

The guard went on. "And then they got attacked by that thing, Spyder. That was just a couple of minutes ago. What are you talking about?"

The Bat shouldered past the man and started jogging toward the downtown skyscrapers.

"Did you even go up there?" The guard yelled at his back. "Midnight would have!"

It was the last thing the vigilante heard clearly as he burst into a sprint down a narrow alley that ran between Sunset and Fountain. The guard was right. Midnight would have squeezed through the eye of a needle and straight into the devil's ass to save children.

But Midnight had been a hero with a violent, winner-take-all attitude. The Bat was just a garden-variety vigilante, and the city had been doing just fine before he'd donned his uniform and started swinging the bat for justice.

The Bat headed out onto Santa Monica Boulevard and ran down the broad avenue's double center-line. As his eyes teared up, he pushed himself harder and faster. The cries of the babies echoed in his head. He should have saved those kids. He was supposed to be a hero. He was supposed to protect those who couldn't protect themselves. Like Joey.

The moisture in his eyes and his total disregard for his own safety completely tuned out the rumble of the bus speeding through the intersection. The impact was so great it blasted him out of his cleats. The world careened into a swirling blur, parts of him burning as if seared with a torch.

When The Bat tried to sit up, he screamed at the flash of white pain. He lifted his head and tried to look himself over, but he could only manage a peek. He could hear the approaching footsteps of bystanders running to his aid.

He started to hyperventilate, and his body started to tremble. He could feel consciousness slipping away.

Both of his legs and one of his arms were bent and twisted in ways only dolls could be forced to imitate. Bloody, shattered bone glistened under the nearby streetlamp. The Bat's eyes rolled back into his head as the first person arrived to render assistance.

#

Andre lounged in his throne, enjoying the early outcome of his very simple plan. He ignored the fact that the rising number of casualties didn't seem to bother him as much as he thought it would. Ultimately, he knew loss of life was inevitable in a war against crime of this magnitude.

Heroes and civilians would die. Hell, he already had. And he'd done it for them. And many of them hadn't even liked him.

He frowned. He hadn't died for the citizens of San Angeles, or the heroes either. He'd died because of his own ego.

The sacrifice would be worth it once his plan worked. San Angeles would be umpteen times better. But innocent people would have to die. At least Tatiana wouldn't be among them.

And, with any luck, The Bat wouldn't survive.

Then, as if the major networks had been listening to his thoughts, one channel after another switched to breaking news. Andre could only watch and hope. A local news broadcast was on the monitor directly in front of him. One of the drive-time anchors sat behind the desk with an expression that indicated he was genuinely disturbed.

"Early tragedy has struck in what many around the world are calling the San Angeles Crime War." A grin started to grow at the media term. Projected behind the anchor were the photos of three masked males. Andre knew all three. "High-level sources in the law-enforcement community have reported the deaths of two costumed heroes."

Andre's grin wavered as the news footage started.

"Local superhero The Wing lost his life less than an hour after midnight as a gang of thieves attempted to rob the San Angeles Federal Reserve Depository. A powerful laser being used to cut through the vault door was turned into a weapon against the winged hero. Authorities on the scene said the robbers' counterattack was totally unexpected, and The Wing died instantly. The following footage from a police-cruiser camera is gruesome and young children and viewers with weak constitutions should turn away for the next thirty seconds."

The video showed The Wing flying from around the dark brick depository. He pulled up, hovering about twenty feet above the street. As he started to encouraging the robbers to surrender, a white-blue beam swept across the sky from outside the camera frame, slicing vertically through the crimefighter. The two halves of The Wing dropped to the asphalt like sacks of raw meat. Seconds later, a pair of ski-masked robbers ran over to the hero and fired their handguns point-blank into his head. Police then fired on the robbers. The clip ended.

Andre's imagination concocted the familiar stench of burned fresh.

"And, in a bizarre sequence of events," the commentator continued as a split screen displayed photos of The Ant and The Bat, "Still recovering from surgery for injuries caused in the Midnight Memorial Day rooftop battle, The Ant, whose alter ego is not being released until next of kin are notified, had secretly been transferred from the San Angles Clinic to the smaller, lower-profile midtown St. Luke's Hospital. Early this morning, the hospital was attacked by the villainess Spyder and what some emergency personnel are calling a "plague" of arachnids.

"Details are sketchy at this time, and reports are unclear as to whether Spyder's attack was originally aimed at The Ant or at the St. Luke's hospital's Neonatal Intensive Care Unit, but sadly, The Ant was among the many casualties. The investigation is ongoing, but early sources estimate that more than twenty adults and nearly three dozen infants lost their lives."

The anchor paused for effect, then turned to face into a second camera. "And in a related story, Channel 6 reporter Amelia Rodriguez is on the scene of another breaking story. Amelia?"

An attractive Hispanic woman held a microphone by a Santa Monica Avenue street sign. Her expression was subdued. "Good evening, everyone. I'm in mid-city, reporting the latest on a developing situation involving the street vigilante called The Bat. Earlier this evening, The Bat arrived at St. Luke's prior to police and emergency personnel in response to an all-units involving an attack on the hospital."

News footage began. "Here, the vigilante is shown exiting the building, obviously affected by the tragedy inside. But when questioned about his involvement in a rescue attempt on the fourth floor's NICU wing, he fled from reporters. Less than a mile away, The Bat was struck by a cross-town Metro double-decker bus as it sped southbound through the intersection of Santa Monica Boulevard and Vermont. Witnesses and city surveillance footage confirm The Bat was sprinting down the middle of Santa Monica toward downtown and didn't look or slow, ignoring the red traffic signals. The Bat is said to be in critical condition at an undisclosed medical facility."

The screen then split between the news anchor and the reporter at the scene.

"Amelia, is there any more information about the attack at St. Luke's?"

"The only thing I can verify is that the mutant villainess Spyder was involved. Authorities have yet to make a statement about the situation."

"Thank you, Amelia. We'll be right here to bring you the latest developments. The staff here at Channel 6 send their condolences to the families of those fallen heroes and citizens, and prayers go out to The Bat, whom some saw as the successor to the fallen hero Midnight as protector of the city of San Angeles." The anchor let out a deep, mournful sigh, then continued. "In other news..."

Andre scanned the other monitor screens. Several other stations relayed similar reports, including national channels Fox News and CNN.

Just a few hours in, and the city was already down three heroes. Four, counting the absent Catfight. And five without Midnight.

Out of reflex, Andre pressed the heel of one palm into his forehead. He felt genuinely sorry for The Wing, and his heart went out to The Ant. His direct actions had practically killed The Ant, and now The Ant was dead.

He quickly tried to calculate which heroes might still be out there. Probably Starlight, and Nighthawk. Maybe The Amphibian. And Truth. But without Ultra abilities, Truth would be in serious danger during this type of crime-war escalation.

With only the first night of destruction close to being in the books, how would San Angeles survive the entire month of December?

"Titan better keep his fucking ass out of here," Andre muttered under his breath.

"What?" Scarlett stood in the doorway, flanked by Ivy.

"Nothing."

"Ivy has a source with a line on where The Bat is being treated. She's volunteering to follow it up and get an eyes-only update, then report back."

Andre waved his hand dismissively. "Fine. Go."

Ivy nodded, disappearing from sight. Scarlett sauntered over to the throne. Her smile beamed through the shadowy gloom. "You should savor this first-night victory, and prepare for thirty more just like it."

He nodded, but didn't answer.

"Are you ready for bed?" she asked.

"I want to see this through until sunrise."

Scarlett's expression flirted with disappointment. "As you wish. Also, Straitjacket and the others have been made comfortable. If I might speak candidly."

Andre looked at his right hand.

Scarlett forged ahead. "I completely understand you wanting to set Hatchet Man loose upon the city, but I'm not sure bringing him here…is good for your army's morale."

The comment caught Andre off-guard. He hadn't given his earlier on-the-fly decision a second thought. And he certainly didn't see any of his female warriors as potential victims for the vicious psychopath. But Scarlett had a reasonable point. He also needed to be careful. These were the types of decisions and reactions that made Scarlett doubt his stability. He'd have to guess at how the real demon would respond to such a situation.

"Any of my soldiers weak enough to fall prey to one of my guests' urges is meant to be a victim," he answered, "but your point is well-taken. None of our current guests be with us long, but feel free to check on them."

Scarlett nodded. "Thank you. I will do so. Good night."

Andre continued to focus on the collection of wall monitors and the overall destruction level across the city. He'd committed to a plan. He couldn't back out after a single night. He needed to see it through.

But as the monitors continued to blare news of continuing mayhem and murder, he decided not to make a habit of spending the night in the surveillance room. It was all too much to take in. He needed to keep the war at arm's length for everything to work out in the end.

The sun would be rising soon, and he was calling it a night. Perhaps he ought to take Scarlett up on her offer. Since he didn't know the true depth of the relationship between the demon and his beautiful right hand, this was just another avenue where suspicion lurked at every turn.

#

Scarlett strode through the maze-like bunker comprised of a former water treatment facility, a derelict subway station, and a secret government laboratory. She often used an electric golf cart to travel between the trio of constructs, but tonight she wanted to take a more silent approach. Her long legs carried her quickly from the demon's operations center to the area used to house the women warriors, and then onto the section used for recreation and guest quarters.

The larger offices had been turned into a half-dozen comfortable suites. The accommodations were seldom used, but worthy of five-star status. Housing a quartet of homicidal maniacs there seemed unthinkable. Not many villains didn't have some type of disorder, but Straitjacket, Match, Roach, and Hatchet Man...the last two had the stench of filthy street people when they'd arrived.

Unlike Straitjacket, who was crusted with gore from head to toe, and requested the hottest shower with the best water pressure, Roach hadn't seemed to be in a big hurry to clean up. Hatchet Man had been filthy, but he'd also been covered in fresh blood and other fluids. He'd seemed semi-catatonic when he'd shuffled in from the helicopter pad. Scarlett had noticed a slight change in his body language whenever his group passed any of The Damned. She did not want any of these "guests" to get too close to Scratch's female guards.

She turned down a short hallway, dimly lit to simulate late night. Dawn was close, and the lighting in the entire facility would soon brighten to mirror daytime brightness.

Roach occupied Suite A, while Straitjacket and the teenage girl were using Suite B. It was obvious that the girl was with Straitjacket of her own free will, but the arrangement still made Scarlett feel uneasy.

The girl looked just a little younger than Scarlett had been when she'd left home with the carnival passing through her small Midwestern town so many summers ago. When the third murder had occurred that summer, the town had forced the carnival to pack up and leave early, taking the young redheaded murderer with them. She'd never looked back, but she'd grown to be much more cunning when it came to unleashing her power.

The hallway teed to the left and right. She took the right-handed spur, but slowed as she reached suites E and F. The serial rapist and torturer known as Hatchet Man had been placed in Suite E.

Suite E's open door offered only pitch blackness.

Scarlett stared into the darkness. She didn't hesitate out of fear as much as out of not having a clear understanding of Hatchet Man's importance to Scratch's master plan. Insane or not, armed or not, he was still just a human male. How much could he do?

A sob sounded so softly Scarlett almost missed it. The crack of an open-handed slap, however, was impossible to ignore. The quiet that followed lingered like death.

"Come in, pretty bitch." The man spoke in a low, hushed voice.

"This is not how a guest should act in the house of Old Scratch."

"A demon should know better than to bring a rabid fox to a chicken coop."

"I don't want to hurt you," Scarlett sighed. "But I will." The darkness was impenetrable to her eyes. She couldn't get a read on the man's location in the room. At some point, she was going to have to go in blind and play it by ear.

"I'll take my chances," the man said. "And I wish I could promise it won't hurt, or that you'll die quickly. Neither are going to happen once you step in here."

"And what if I simply call Scratch to deal with you?"

The man's burst of high-pitched hyena laughter sounded both silly and sinister. "Oh, I doubt the great Scarlett needs help with a common hatchet-wielding, escaped mental patient."

The goal of the taunt slipped past her ego, but she understood the implication. Word would leak out that the frightful right hand of Old Scratch couldn't handle a lone, armed man, infamous serial killer or not. Once Spyder heard the story, the challenge from the mutant arachnid would come. And Scratch had already warned her.

"I want to know the mysterious power of the lethal Lady Scarlett."

She stared into the darkness, anger blushing her face. Self-defense would be her alibi. If she survived the encounter.

Scarlett walked into the dark. The room's air felt at least twenty degrees cooler than that of the hallway, but it didn't help stifle the stunning funk of an asylum inmate's total lack of personal hygiene. It was a potent mix of bad breath, sweaty balls, and unwashed ass, . Hatchet Man's scent matched the image of human garbage Scarlett considered him to be. She drew her power like a sword.

The space got graveyard-quiet. Familiar with the suite's layout, she walked a path that would take her through the middle of the combination living room/study. Hatchet Man's voice hadn't been obstructed, so she knew he wasn't in the bedroom or in the opposite-end bath. As she reached the middle of the chamber, she expected his attack. Instead, the lights of the short connecting hallway flashed on, exposing a captured female soldier.

She was on the floor, knees bunched to her chest. Her ankles were tied, and the way her arms were pulled back suggested her wrists were also secured. Something had been stuffed in her mouth. It took Scarlett half an instant to recognize it as a worn-out pair of men's underwear. Part of the torn waistband drooped from the captive's bottom lip. Her mascara had been cried down her face. Her tunic had been torn so badly it appeared to be a ruined vest.

The woman's weapons had been placed neatly on the counter above her head.

Her name popped into Scarlett's mind at the same instant the woman's eyes widened and her scream was strangled behind the cloth.

Josslyn. Her name was Josslyn. She was once a junkie single mom with an innate talent for knives. She'd joined The Damned, kicked the heroin, and become a scary little bitch. Calling her lanky would be an understatement. She was whip-thin, but her muscle was piano-wire hard. She liked to quote lines from Bugs Bunny cartoons. She was one of the select few in the demon's army he allowed to address him by a name other than Sir, Master, or Lord. At their first introduction, she'd smiled and said, "What's up Doc?" Old Scratch had been so amused he'd assigned her to his personal guard, and she'd done nothing to prove him wrong in his choice. She also had her daughter's name tattooed on the inside of her right wrist. A "J" name, like hers.

Jenny.

Scarlett spun and dropped to one knee, throwing her gloved hand up in the anticipated direction of the assault.

Hatchet Man exploded out of the darkness, a small camping axe raised high. His clenched teeth were all but rotted down to his gums.

Scarlett smiled, clenching her hand into a fist.

Hatchet Man's expression went from savage to crippling pain in a flash. He grunted as his legs buckled, and he dropped like a sack of potatoes in mid-stride. The small camping axe flipped from his hand as he clutched his chest.

His momentum almost carried his seizing body to within arm's reach of Scarlett. Hatchet Man couldn't breathe.

Scarlett smiled as she walked over to Josslyn. "Do you know what a heart attack is? A heart attack occurs if the flow of oxygen-rich blood to a section of heart muscle suddenly becomes blocked. If blood flow isn't restored quickly, that section of the heart muscle begins to die." She worked at the expert knots he'd tied on Josslyn.

"How's that elephant sitting on your chest?" she asked him. "Is it comfortable? Good." Almost casually, Scarlett reached back with her right hand and made a twisting motion. The serial rapist's body clenched and arched off the floor as if he'd received an electrical shock. Scarlett freed the woman, then walked back to stand over the killer.

"You've heard of a stroke, haven't you? It's a condition in which the brain cells suddenly die because of a lack of oxygen. It can be caused by an obstruction in the blood flow, or the rupture of an artery. A person may suddenly lose the ability to speak, there may be memory problems, or one side of the body can become paralyzed."

She nudged the man's blockish head with the pointy toe of her glistening red boot. His eyes had all but rolled back into his head. "And then there's the aneurysm…"

Josslyn's growl served as a warning, but Scarlett wouldn't have stopped the woman from doing what she needed to do. The guard slammed her butterfly knives into each of Hatchet Man's eyes, plunging them through his skull and into his brain. Hatchet Man flopped like a dying fish in a fisherman's cooler.

The suite's main lights turned on. Andre stepped in. Straitjacket and Match were a step behind.

Josslyn screamed into the killer's face, grinding the blades against his eye sockets. She quickly pulled the blades out, and then turned her focus on the rapist's groin. She plunged the pair of knives in and out of his manhood like a lethal sewing machine. She left both blades sticking out of the bloody mess she'd made.

The room stayed quiet for several moments. Josslyn finally looked to Scarlett, who merely smiled her approval.

Josslyn stood, surprised by the small audience that had gathered. "That's all, folks." Her bleary gaze dropped to the floor, reason fighting through the rawness of the moment. "I'm sorry, my dark lord," she said, her voice trembling with fear and emotion.

Andre stepped forward, conscious that he must not act too caring. "Survival usually means death for someone or something. I'd prefer he die, rather than you." He gestured to Scarlett. "Escort her to her quarters."

Scarlett nodded, putting a hand gently on the woman's back. The two of them left the room. Andre noticed Match watching the exiting pair, Josslyn in particular.

"Just plain rude," Straitjacket cursed, spitting on Hatchet Man's body. "Even a maniac ought to know how to be a house guest for one fucking night."

Match eased back to the threshold.

"Don't even think it," Andre warned the asylum-director duplicate. Match pouted.

"But she has so much potential for mayhem," he pleaded. "Her heart is darker than a nigger's ass."

Andre's temper flashed and he'd backhanded the evil mutant before he realized what he'd done. Match smashed into the wall and crumpled to the floor. Andre pointed a jagged talon at the freakish chameleon. "Look at any of my army and I will feast on your steaming entrails while the rest of you flops on a red-hot skillet!"

Match cringed into a ball. His hands shot up in surrender. "I'm sorry— I've just been locked up so long. I don't want to be anyone's meal."

It was Straitjacket's turn to pout. "Too bad. What a dinner that would have been."

"I've never eaten human meat before. At least not that I know of," Courtney remarked as she walked into the room. Her lack of clothing surprised no one. She wore her bare skin like a tee shirt and a favorite pair of jeans. The dog collar was still around her neck, with the leash dragging on the floor. "I wonder if people taste like chicken?" Answered with derisive silence, she seemed perplexed. "What? Everything else seems to."

Even Straitjacket didn't have an off-the-cuff response.

Chapter Fifteen

GOOD NEWS AND BAD NEWS

Ivy stood in the visitors' waiting room, rattling the quarters in her fist like a pair of dice. She hadn't eaten a candy bar in so long. She was torn between the choices. She peeked at her reflection in the vending-machine glass. The scrub pants and top hid her cute figure, and her short hair gave her a pixie look that befit a young intern. The authentic hospital name tag read "Jennifer Block," and her recent photo displayed a bleary-eyed med student.

Amazing what a thousand dollars in cash and quarter-kilo of weed bartered for. The blowjob she'd thrown in for free. The human resources guy was cute, and might come in handy down the road.

Finally choosing a candy bar and placing the quarters in the machine, she waited as a mechanism pushed the candy outward until it dropped. Seizing her prize, she skinned the wrapper and took a bite of Snickers. She took a step back as she chewed, glancing up at the waiting-room clock, and then peeking through the door's reinforced glass. The matronly charge nurse was still manning the nurse's station, but the end of her shift was coming.

A husky, salt-and-pepper-bearded gentlemen in purple scrubs stepped around the nurse's station. He conversed with his matronly colleague for a couple of minutes, and then the night-shift charge nurse took the sweater from the back of her chair and headed toward the elevators.

Ivy left the waiting room and skipped down the corridor like a happy kindergartener. The newly arrived male nurse smiled as she approached. She returned the smile as she continued to chew on the Snickers bar.

"Eleven-fourteen. It'll be on the left. You don't have long. Leave the scrubs under the bed."

"Gracias," she replied with a wink. A few more skips got her where she wanted to go.

Ivy slipped into the dimly lit room. The first bed was empty. The room's dividing curtain was drawn. She stepped through it and was shocked by the sight. Despite the rumors of The Bat being in grave condition, a part of her had ignored the intel, believing the media was trumping up his injuries to make his triumphant return all the more newsworthy. When she'd become aware he was in a regular room with no guards, the knowledge had eased her anxiety about his condition. But she'd been seriously mistaken.

Her mouth dropped open as she approached the bed. This was the first time she'd ever seen him without his mask, but the tubes and bandages still hid his identity. A casted arm and leg were suspended. Where there wasn't padded gauze, there were bruises and ointment-covered scrapes. His skull was covered, along with one eye. One of the machines peeped quietly.

She lifted the electronic tablet from its padded sleeve at the end of the bed, reading attending doctor's concise notes.

"Oh my God," was all she could manage, occasionally glancing at the battered hero. He had a long list of serious injuries. Fractured skull, compound fractures, broken neck, eye and spinal injuries... His ability to walk was in serious jeopardy. Swelling of his brain had necessitated an induced coma.

Her eyes teared up. She wanted to call him by his name, but she didn't know his real identity. During her many trips to his downtown loft, she'd never seen a piece of mail or any form of identification. Research on the loft had yielded a dead-end loop of corporate ownership and a long-term lease signed by a University of Southern California engineering student who had died in an alcohol-related drowning almost two years earlier. Even running his photo through facial recognition databanks served up a big fat blank. The Bat was an off-the-grid loner. A ghost.

And by far the best fuck Ivy had ever enjoyed.

Tubes ran from his nostrils, the elbow bend of an arm, and from underneath the covers, where she assumed a catheter had been inserted. To him, the catheter alone would have made being put in a coma worth the hassle.

The prognosis was cautionary, predicting a need for long-term care. The Bat hadn't been diagnosed as an Ultra, but his ability to survive an accident that would have surely killed any human man or woman had his doctor calling his physicality an "anomaly."

More surgeries had been scheduled. And even with his enhanced genetics, his recovery was going to be lengthy and painful.

For once, the media wasn't pissing in the wind. The Bat was seriously fucked up and out of the game, perhaps permanently. Ivy dropped the tablet back into its sheath and backed away from the bed toward the bathroom. Absently, she began to strip off the scrubs. It was hard to wrap her mind around what she had just seen. She pushed her scrubs under the bed and pulled a lumpy garbage bag from the small closet.

Ivy didn't skip when she left the room. She ignored the male nurse still sitting behind the nurse's station as she wheeled the bucket and mop down the hall. The blue custodial jumper was even less flattering than the scrubs, not counting the fat suit it came with. Adding in her fake rotten teeth and the pair of thick-lensed eyeglasses, and she was night and day from the intern who'd entered the room. Even her work boots added three inches to her height.

The elevator doors had barely closed when the first tear streaked down her face. Ivy couldn't stop the heartfelt sob, either.

#

Tatiana slept through the plane's descent into Stockholm's Arlanda Airport and had to be awakened by a weary, peroxide-blonde flight attendant. "Welcome to Stockholm."

Tatiana felt exhausted. Her body ached, and her mind was foggy. When she looked out the window, the plane was all but to the gate. Her family would be waiting down in the baggage area. She'd had terrible, fractured dreams. Many included Andre and Old Scratch. Some featured herself and Scarlett. The Bat popped in and out without rhyme or reason.

None of it made sense. There was just a never-ending battle between Andre and Scratch, a death match where neither would die despite the mortal wounds they suffered. Each kept getting up, blood drooling from their mouths, dislocated arms dangling, broken legs dragging.

Every time The Bat became involved he was dispatched with relative ease by both superhero and supervillain. Near the end of one nightmare, The Bat lay in the intensive care unit of a hospital, and both Andre and the demon crashed through the room's windows and tore out all the tubes and wires keeping him alive. The Bat flopped around on the hospital bed like a fish thrown on a river bank until he lay still and died.

Andre and Old Scratch laughed like bar buddies, and then started fighting again.

At one point, she was in the middle of the fray, battling Scarlett as Catfight. Old Scratch briefly got the upper hand on Andre, and then spun blindly in her direction. His razor-sharp talons made a whistling sound as they sliced the air. She saw the strike coming, knew the blow would catch her in the midsection and cleave her in half. She was frozen, caught in the headlights of her own doomed mortality. There was nothing left to do but die.

At the very last instant, she closed her eyes and tensed.

But the blow never came.

Slowly, she opened her eyes. She felt a series of slight stings in her midsection. Old Scratch had paused, his swing stopped the split second his claws bit through the fabric of her costume and touched the flesh beneath. He looked at her, almost as if he was seeing her for the first time. She looked down at the claws poised to puncture her skin. The world paused, and the two of them stood like statues.

"I love you," the demon had whispered. Her eyes grew as she recognized the voice as Andre's, but the next instant brought Scarlett's kick into the small of her back. The explosive power impaled the feline crime fighter onto the demon's wicked claws. She coughed up bloody spittle as shock dulled the first few moments of the pain.

She screamed like a birthing mother when the demon withdrew his claws. Her dream exaggerated the wound and her death scream, and it was that, along with the flight's attendant's gentle shoulder shake, that woke her up.

Her mind still hazy, areas of the airport flowed past. She didn't remember leaving the plane. She made eye contact with a heavily armed security guard and his flat, ambiguous look almost convinced her he was a statue, not a real man.

She stood on a slow moving sidewalk headed for the baggage area. Many of her fellow passengers, including the staring CEO, passed her by without even walking briskly. She suddenly wondered if she'd been drugged on the flight.

Something was wrong.

As she descended on an escalator, she could see her family bunched together at the far end of the baggage area, by the rental-car kiosk.

When she reached the floor, she ignored the luggage carousel for her flight and moved through the crowd toward her people. She caught the eyes of her parents, and the joy on their faces quickly faltered and then slipped away. Totally unaware, her younger sister ran into her arms, hugging her with a ferocity only youth and unbridled emotion could generate.

As her parents stepped forward, Tatiana could feel the hot tears running down her face.

Her mother's bottom lip began to tremble as she reached out for her firstborn daughter. "My baby," her mother whispered, already knowing what was in her daughter's heart.

"We have seen the news," her father said, emotion underlying his deep, matter-of-fact tone.

"I have to go back," Tatiana sobbed into her mother's shoulder. Her mom smelled of fresh flowers and honey, and Tatiana suddenly became sure this would be the last time she'd see her family outside of heaven.

#

It was still very early morning, but Andre lay in the dark cavern of the demon's bedroom, the flames of the torches burning low.

He looked down at himself. He was naked. Wearing Old Scratch's body meant he was always naked. The demon wore no costume and never made an excuse for the continual exposure of his huge genitalia. It was kinda funny that over the years, seeing and fighting Old Scratch so many times, the demon's freakish nudity had sort of become his costume.

These minor quirks of existence only seemed to bother Andre in the quiet moments like this. The fact that he didn't have to undress to go to bed. Hell, there was no process involving hygiene at all. As had happened when he was Midnight, when the night sky slowly brightened turned into day, he grew tired and sleep called to him like a seductive siren that refused to be ignored.

It was the little details that were so strange. Every day meant a new discovery, something odd he'd notice. When he was lying on his back like he was now, lying on his wings wasn't uncomfortable. Actually, he didn't seem to feel them at all. How could that be? They were incredibly strong and flexible, and considering they folded flat against his body, impossible to ignore. Maybe the lack of irritation had more to do with the fact that with all the unbelievable miseries of hell, the demon's body simply didn't recognize the relatively trivial discomfort of the wings.

Who knew?

The demon's taste buds were also unusual. There was never a doubt about Old Scratch being a carnivore, but his draw to human flesh actually paled in comparison to his craving for sweets. Andre found himself eating lemon cookies and vanilla wafers by the box. Of course, with a demon's constitution, unwanted weight gain or diabetes wasn't a concern. And that was another detail he'd learned. He never felt full, no matter how much he ate or drank. And he didn't drink much, either.

He kept expecting his eyes to water due to the torch smoke and the horrible stench of brimstone and sulfur his body generated, but his old personal sensibilities didn't really translate to his new existence. Not that every time he shut his eyes a little part of him didn't expect to finally wake from this really detailed nightmare. Each morning began with resounding disappointment and heart-wrenching loss.

Like most on the planet, Andre had taken his wonderful life for granted and now would do anything to return to it.

The bottomless ache he felt for Tatiana. He didn't have the Harvard vocabulary to adequately describe the daily heartbreak of knowing he'd never be with his love again. As he lay there, he couldn't help but think of all the days and nights he'd made love to her and watched her fall asleep, and then had lain awake trying to solve the greatest riddles of his life— how to destroy Old Scratch and make San Angeles safer. How many nights had he silently pledged he'd do anything to fulfill those missions?

Now, trapped in the ultimate prison, he might be on the verge of both. What had been that old movie line about being the hero long enough until you became the villain?

Welcome to his new world.

There was movement outside his chamber. And in that next

instant the emotional and mental weight of the last twenty-four hours crashed down upon him. He was wrecked. He closed his eyes and wondered if Old Scratch had ever felt so tired in his centuries-old existence.

One of the doors to his private quarters opened. Soft footsteps entered, and then stopped. The door closed again.

He didn't bother to open his eyes. He figured it was Ivy with a report. Neither of the guards at the door had introduced his visitor. He somehow felt that his version of Old Scratch was a bit less formal.

Seconds passed, and there wasn't a sound. He felt too tired to lift his head.

"Yes?"

When there wasn't an answer, alarms went off in his head. His Midnight instincts wanted to leap up and confront whoever was there, but that wasn't what Old Scratch would do. Not at all.

These were his private quarters, his innermost sanctuary. There wasn't an enemy alive or dead with the ability to penetrate this deeply into his empire without setting off alarms.

"Scarlett," he said, not moving a muscle, in fact allowing himself to relax even more. If he was wrong, so be it. He should be dead anyway.

Several seconds passed before she responded.

"My lord." Her voice was husky and dripped with desire. Andre didn't need the demon's senses to hear that.

Andre let out a deep breath, opened his eyes, and sat up.

Scarlett was dancing. Slowly, sensuously, gyrating to music that existed inside her own head. Dressed in a black fishnet body stocking, she corkscrewed her body down into a squat, turning to show off an ass that rivaled Tatiana's. She swayed her way back to full height, her bare feet carrying her with effortless grace. Muscles stretched and rippled beneath her milky skin. She wore a wig of flowing red locks that had been pulled up in a ponytail on top of her head, its flaming strands spraying from the top. The look was an exciting blend of exotic and punk. Even through the haze of exhaustion, Andre liked it. And the demon's body also noticed.

Scarlett grinned like a barn cat who'd caught a rat. Her eyes locked on his, then slowly drifted down to the prize she sought. There was no mistaking her intent, and when Andre felt the demon's hard organ jerk between his legs, he knew he'd have to think fast, despite the heavy blood flow away from his brain.

The tip of her tongue flicked out like a serpent's, and she continued to gyrate closer and closer to the bed.

"You asked me what would happen when the month ended," he

said, closing his eyes and laying back down. "I will lay claim to San Angeles as my own sovereign territory until the sun dies."

"And for me?" she panted, her hands sliding down between her shapely thighs.

"If you've prepared correctly, I will fuck you to death. On this bed. You will scream to be released from my promise but you'll be forced to endure my unrelenting..." He paused for a moment, searching for the right words. "Focus on satisfaction."

Andre imagined Scarlett throwing her head back, her fingers working frantically at the shaven crease between her legs.

"Pleeeeeeeeaaaaassssssssssssssssse," she panted and hissed. In his mind's eye, he could see her hips rotating and pushing and thrusting against her invading fingers. He imagined her having trouble standing, her legs wanting to buckle as the waves of pleasure continued to build inside her.

Andre allowed himself the tiniest grin.

"Good night, my bitch," he whispered just loudly enough for her to hear. He never opened his eyes to see what she did, and the truth was, he didn't care. There were times like these where being the demon wasn't hard at all. He was asleep less than a minute later.

"My lord," Scarlett's voice floated over his mind like mist over a Scottish moor. It didn't interrupt his dream, but somehow became a part of it. He was Midnight again, wearing his dark midnight-hued costume. He was lying in a casket, propped up so he was nearly standing. Eyes open, he was able to watch an endless stream of mourners pass and pay their respects. Most were faceless San Angeles citizens, but on occasion there'd be a familiar face, such as The Flyer or Starlight or the mayor. Some Hollywood celebrities were sprinkled in. He kept trying to speak, but he was unable to.

"My lord." Scarlett nudged at him again, reluctant but firm.

A lot of the mourners were crying, which was a little surprising. Tatiana finally appeared, tearing streaming. Her parents comforted her, and then moved on. His own parents followed, his father splitting time between consoling Tatiana and commiserating with his mother. This was no easy feat as the ex-three time Olympic heavyweight weightlifter struggled to keep his own emotions from overwhelming him. Tatiana stayed at the casket as the line continued past. Sometime later the last people paid their respects and left Tatiana alone with him.

She stood there, sobbing and trembling.

Tatiana was reaching out to Andre's cheek when The Bat rolled up in his custom wheelchair, still in costume and all smiles.

Tatiana smiled at him, dabbing the latest tears from her eyes.

The Bat grabbed her around the waist and pulled her onto his lap. She wrapped an arm around his neck and smiled as he rolled them both away.

"Scratch!"

"What?!" he blurted out, sitting up. Scarlett was at the end of the bed. Across the room in the doorway stood Ivy.

"Sorry to disturb you, but the Police Chief is holding a press conference. I thought you'd be interested."

"I already know the police are getting their asses kicked. The last two nights were worse for the city than the first."

"Word is a hero is going to speak. Could be Titan."

Andre snorted as he moved from the bed. "If I wanted to hear a sermon, I'd go back to hell and pull a seat up next to my father's throne." For a moment, he felt discombobulated, as if he were supposed to pull some clothes on before leaving his private chamber. Some things weren't as easy to adjust to.

"Ivy is also requesting to check back in on The Bat's status."

Andre stopped at the doorway and eyed both women. "The Bat is a tick turd when he's healthy. Now that he's out of the game, he's of no concern."

Ivy's eyes dropped to the floor for a moment, and when she looked back up, Andre was staring through her. "I don't need an update on his condition. Go during your off time, but report to Scarlett about what you learn. Just too bad a bus got to have all the fucking fun."

Ivy nodded and led Scarlett and the demon toward the communication center.

One of his female army was stationed in the control room. She acknowledged her leaders, quickly manipulating her computer keyboard. "Replaying the press conference on all screens," she reported.

When Andre moved to stand in the middle of the viewing area, Scarlett slipped into his oversized throne. Her boots dangled above the floor.

All the screens displayed a simple podium with the SAPD logo. The Chief of Police stepped up behind the microphone. Normally in his dress uniform, today he wore a tactical officer's outfit, complete with heavy vest, secondary weapons strapped to each lower thigh, and ear mic. The one-time street cop looked impressive for a man in his sixties.

Andre noticed the chief had no prepared written statement in hand. He was really intrigued now.

"Good afternoon, everyone. We apologize to our citizens for the short notice. As everyone knows, our city has been under siege for the past three nights. The lives of many innocent people have been taken or destroyed. Ordinary and extraordinary heroes have fought, and some have perished.

"Early this morning, one hero reached out to city hall and requested a meeting with city officials and law enforcement. Afterwards, she requested an opportunity to speak not only to the citizens of greater San Angeles, but also to the vermin attempting to overrun and devastate our city.

"With that, I'll proudly give way to Catfight."

Andre's gasp was loud enough to cause the control-center operator to turn around. He tried to cover with a quick clearing of his throat.

In another surprising move, Tatiana appeared behind the podium neither masked nor in costume. She was dressed like she was heading out to do errands: double-layered tank tops and jeans. Her hair was pulled up off her neck. When she looked up into the cameras, her expression was a blend of exhaustion and fury.

"My name is Tatiana Sklovic. Some of you know me as a professional sports model and spokesperson, but I'm here to share with you today that I'm also the costumed crime fighter known as Catfight." She paused as the media-packed room exploded with questions and camera flashes. Tatiana had to wait a full minute for the room to settle down enough for her to continue.

"Three nights ago, when Old Scratch declared war on the city, I was on an airplane to Europe to spend time with my family and to continue to grieve for the love of my life, whom you all knew as the hero Midnight. Once I saw a replay of the demon Old Scratch's threats, I had to make a decision on what to do. My heart told me to go home and be with my family, but it would be very difficult to leave San Angeles under these extreme circumstances.

"During the long flight, I decided to return and to fight for the city Midnight loved so much, very much aware that it might cost my life. But I feel I owe it to the citizens, and even more so to my beloved, who was right in his obsession to protect the city from Old Scratch at any cost." Her voice began to waver, and her eyes moistened, but she never looked away from the gathering.

"So, tonight I have a message for Old Scratch. I will have my revenge for your taking the life of Midnight, but I also issue a challenge. I do not have the power to challenge you one on one or even three on one, but I challenge any of the women under your command, including Scarlett, to a fight to the death, anywhere and anytime of your choosing, with the stakes being the city. I win, and the war is over and you and your army leave forever. And if your fighter wins, the city is yours."

"The city is already ours," Scarlett whispered as the Police

Chief dashed back to the podium. Both he and Tatiana struggled to speak over the other. "Catfight has not been authorized to make such a deal—"

"Do you have the guts to bet your empire on Scarlett or Spyder or one of the women from The Mob? Do you?"

"Thank you, Ms. Sklovic. This press conference is over." The press room was in total chaos.

"You know where to find me." Tatiana challenged, pointing at the news cameras. "You know where to find me!" The Police Chief and a pair of uniformed officers helped usher Tatiana quickly from the podium and off the small stage.

Tatiana was beaming when she reached the ready room. "That went well."

The Police Chief was fuming. "That wasn't what we'd discussed–"

"Something has to be done before this city burns to the ground. My challenge will mess with his ego. Scarlett is an extension of him. And she's not afraid of me. It's worth it if I can save the city." She moved toward the exit.

"But what if you lose?" he shouted. "You can't just offer up the city like a Dairy Queen dessert!"

Tatiana stopped at the door. "The city is already lost. You know that. This just gives us a chance. I'm offering the people some hope."

"Scarlett or Spyder will kill you," the top cop called after her, taunting.

"Not if I kill them first," she mumbled under her breath as she banged open the door to the emergency stairway and headed for the roof. But it was true— defeating Scarlett or whoever Scratch chose would mean murder. Tatiana was all in, and finally understood the level of commitment Andre had in his quest to defeat Old Scratch.

Andre continued to stare at the dark screens after the operator turned off the broadcast.

Scarlett was standing next to him before he realized it. "That bitch," she spat. "Let me kill her and then present her severed head for the world to see."

Andre heard her, but her words were like the buzz of a dying mosquito. Had he still been human, he would have sighed. His Tatiana had stirred up a serious shit storm, and he wasn't sure how to deal with it. She was supposed to be in Europe, out of harm's way, while he pushed forward with his plans.

He didn't want to see her dead. But Old Scratch couldn't appear weak.

What would Old Scratch do? Andre had no fucking idea.

"Don't even think about giving Spyder the chance," Scarlett said venomously.

The statement got Old Scratch's attention. He looked at his right hand with disdain. Silence fell between them for several seconds. "Don't forget your place."

"I've never forgotten my place. But since the lightning strike…" Her voice trailed away.

When he didn't answer, an odd look passed over her face. "You don't think I can defeat her."

"I don't want to create a martyr."

"The citizens of San Angeles don't give a shit about her."

"They didn't before Midnight died. They didn't before the airwaves were filled with images of her from the debacle at the beach. Grieving widows have power." Before she could respond, he continued. "How many times did I underestimate Midnight? How many times did he find a way to rise to the occasion and thwart plan after plan? I won't allow him to do it after his death! You're so confident you can kill her, yet you've never managed to do it. How so?"

Scarlett had no ready answer.

"Suddenly you're so confident. People, police, other heroes are going to rally behind her willingness to die for the city. So we can't have her go and die quite yet. Put the word out that Catfight is untouchable. No one is to engage or harm her in any way, shape, or form."

Scarlett's face pinched in anger.

"Catfight dies, and a city on the brink of disaster suddenly pulls together, rallying behind their slain protectors. Be patient, Scarlett. Trust my plan."

"But I don't know what your plan is."

"You think I don't notice you looking at me strangely since Midnight's death? You think I don't know about your second-guessing my decisions, wondering if the lightning might have done something to me? My plan is simple— I'm going to send this city to hell and then show everyone, and I mean everyone, a demonstration of power never seen in the history of man. So either serve me or get out of my sight. Forever."

Scarlett averted her gaze to the dark monitors. "My faith in you is absolute. Please forgive me." When he didn't speak, Scarlett dropped to her knees in front of him and pressed her palms and forearms to the floor. Ivy and the control-room operator quickly joined her.

And for just a moment, Andre felt like a god. The part of him that felt like a soulless traitor.

A soulless traitor who had a very important meeting that night.

Chapter Sixteen

CHOOSING SIDES

Tatiana, dressed in full Catfight garb, sat on the Blackledge Tower rooftop, watching the sunset, perhaps for the last time. Many of the remembrance plants and flowers blanketing the roof were dead or dying slow deaths dealt by the strong Southern California sun. Parts of San Angeles looked the same way after the recent crime wave.

As expected, a virtual media circus had camped outside the old garment factory where she rented her loft. Anticipating the response to her press conference, Tatiana dyed her platinum mane a rich black at her small studio off Hollywood boulevard, then walked down the block and got herself a deep spray-on tan. She wanted to get a tattoo, but that would have to wait until after the demon had been defeated. She was actually surprised she didn't find one of the demon's elite lady guards already waiting for her at the roof shrine. But no one was there, not even a mourner changing out a gift of flowers, or the Blackledge Tower's security force doing their rounds.

Close to sunset, Tatiana chose the most westerly corner of the roof and just sat, taking it all in. Emotionally, she was riding a rollercoaster. Unlike Andre, whose hatred for Old Scratch had grown into obsession, her anger had limits. Challenging the demon had probably not been the best idea. Even if she defeated whomever he sent, Old Scratch was not going to give up his empire. Hell, he might be willing to sacrifice Scarlett or Spyder, call them weak in their defeat, and then come after her himself. No way would she last a minute with him unless he toyed with her. She didn't have the strength or weapons to hurt him. Even Andre, in all his glory, at the stroke of midnight, could barely hold his own against the demon, fighting at one-hundred percent, with absolutely zero holding back.

So now, for better or worse, Tatiana could only wait for her fate to reveal itself. She wasn't sure how Old Scratch would play it.

And what about The Bat? She hadn't seen him, but the Chief of Police seemed sure the vigilante's condition was such that even if he did recover, it wouldn't be during this hell month. His body was healing on its own, but though physically exceptional, The Bat wasn't an Ultra.

But equally serious were the facts surrounding the hospital incident. Confirmed facts had The Bat entering the hospital to save the newborns in the NICU, but ultimately doing nothing to stop Spyder and her arachnid horde from feeding on many of the children and stealing several others to dine on later. Tatiana couldn't fathom The Bat allowing that to happen without a fight, but the Police Chief had eyewitness accounts, along with hospital security footage of The Bat never venturing farther than a stairwell exit on the neonatal unit floor.

And to think she'd entertained the notion of sharing a bed with that coward. Again, she couldn't help but think about all the times she'd defended The Bat to Dre. He had obviously seen the truth about the baseball hero, and she'd been too stubborn to listen. Somewhere, Dre was laughing at how gullible she'd been.

In the distance, something was streaking toward her at jet-fighter speed. Too small to be a plane, it took her a moment to realize the blazing white trail belonged to Starlight. Seconds later, the alien crimefighter was floating to the roof like a feather on the wind. Catfight smiled, despite the small twinge of jealousy she always experienced when she saw the flying heroes in action. The heroine's neutral, androgynous beauty projected a calming presence.

"Good evening, Catfight." The alien's gentle voice made the greeting equally soothing.

"Hi," was all Tatiana could manage, relieved to have company.

Despite The Bat's attempts to console, Tatiana had been lonely to her soul from the moment she'd found Andre's charred remains. Her mind flashed to the recent embrace at the airport with her mother, and in the next second she fell sobbing into Starlight's arms.

When she finally pulled back from her friend, night had all but fallen. As she blinked her eyes clear, Tatiana realized she and Starlight were no longer alone.

Hardly more than an arm's length away waited a gathering of local heroes. There was the non-super powered, black leather-costumed, human lie detector called Truth. Crawling over the building's edge onto the roof was the marine mutant called The Amphibian. Surprisingly handsome, the genetic blend of man and bullfrog had beautiful smooth skin and a broad-shouldered surfer's physique. A smile also seemed eternally plastered across The Amphibian's broad head. Catfight couldn't understand how his black Speedos never needed re-adjusting.

Gliding down to the roof was the after-dark hero named Nighthawk. Upon landing, he struck one of a half-dozen classic superhero poses, grinning ear to ear. He reeked of a comic-book geek given a chance to play hero, but there was no questioning his heart and loyalty. The dark-tinted visor of his metal helmet concealed his identity all too well. Tatiana had always thought he must be on the younger side. Tall and thin, he had just a touch of youthful gawkiness. Or he could be a mildly retarded, computer game-playing college dropout. Hard to say.

Completing the group were three relatively new players on the crime-fighting scene who spent the majority of their time in the San Fernando Valley area of old Los Angeles. They worked together in a variety of combinations, but didn't promote themselves as a team. There was ex-Shayetet 13 agent and professional cage fighter Babydoll, who sported a white silk baby doll slip over military fatigues.

Shoulder to shoulder with her was Gunn, a known Ultra whose talents lay in the utilization and deadeye aim of every handheld weapon with a trigger. Having shrugged back his floor-length black duster, Gunn drew the handguns from each hip with impossible speed. He tossed the weapons from one hand to the other, and holstered them in a blink. Catfight had seen him execute that trick at crime scenes, but now she wasn't sure if he did it out of showmanship or anxious boredom.

And finally, there was Priest, a mysterious Latino man of God tasked with protecting the innocent. Priest had quite the formidable reputation in the heavily populated sections of the Valley. He'd pledged he would not kill, but he sure kicked serious ass on a near-nightly basis.

Of all the costume details amongst the collective, it was the Priest's collar that caught and held Catfight's eye. Murder, of course, was a sin.

It was Priest who stepped forward and first took her hand, giving her a comforting hug. She could feel his powerful essence; it was almost a vibration.

"I am so sorry for your loss. Midnight was a warrior who gave his life in the war against evil. Old Scratch is certainly a child of the devil. My beliefs, too, would be tested where that abomination is concerned."

Catfight fought back emotions welling up inside her, and merely nodded at the sentiment.

"We're here to stand with you," Truth added. She stepped forward for a brief embrace. "If it weren't for you and Midnight, I wouldn't have put on this mask. I owe my life to Midnight, and I intend to repay every cent of that debt."

Nighthawk pointed into the northern sky. "Mother Mary and Joseph."

Everyone turned to see the large figure dropping toward the building.

Andre knew Tatiana would be camped out on the Blackledge roof, but he didn't expect a cadre of heroes to be with her. He shook his head at the gross miscalculation. Of course the other heroes were going to rally around Catfight. She was the living embodiment of everything the city and the heroes were feeling in the wake of Midnight's death.

Even at a distance, the demon's vision enabled him to recognize all the players. Priest and Gunn stepped up to protect her. Nighthawk took to the air, as did Starlight. The others fanned out across the roof.

Andre's only other choice was to veer away, but it was too late. He could only hope this didn't turn into a battle royal. Hurting more heroes was not in his plans, but he had come too close to executing a master plan worthy of the ego-fueled insanity of a Napoleon or a Hitler to quit now.

Had he just associated himself with Hitler? He was losing it. But in the next moment he'd reassured himself that only those crazy enough to think they can change the world are crazy enough to attempt it.

He dropped from the dark sky, wings shadowing the rooftop as he landed.

Without thinking, he raised his hands in a peaceful gesture, which startled more than one hero. Gunn's gloved hands flinched over his holsters, but Tatiana gently touched his arm, stopping him, before stepping in front.

"I didn't come here for a battle," Andre said, hearing how fearsome the demon's voice sounded. "I came here to speak to Catfight."

Priest stepped forward to stand next to the feline crimefighter. "Be gone, unclean spirit. You are not welcome here." His hand slid inside his black suit coat.

Andre slowly moved forward, hands still held out in peace. "Of course I'm not, but I need to speak with Catfight." He looked at his ex-lover and tried his best to project sincerity. "You have my word I will not harm you or anyone here."

An odd expression wrinkled across Catfight's face. She started forward, each step finding a small clear spot amongst the sea of flowers and gifts. Andre continued his slow progress toward her.

When they stood about ten yards apart, they each stopped walking. Andre attempted another step, but Catfight raised a hand. "Close enough."

Andre nodded respectfully, dropping his hands to his sides. He looked at the heroes standing at the ready behind her, and then spoke to her in a whisper. "Can you hear me?"

She nodded.

He took a deep breath. He had to get this right. "You understand it was the lightning that killed Midnight, not me," he began, hardly using any breath.

"What do you want?" Her tone barely contained her fury, impatience, and fear.

"I'm surprised you flew back."

The statement clearly surprised her. Warily, she shifted her stance. "What are you talking about?"

"Tatiana, we live in a world far beyond the normal, in the realm of the fantastic."

"Don't use my real name, Scratch," she warned him, her body tensing. Andre knew she was on the verge of splitting into triplicate.

"I'm Andre. It's Old Scratch who's dead," he told her, his anxiety making his voice a little louder than he would have liked. It was obvious the other heroes were trying to listen, but only Starlight had drifted within range and had the ability to hear him. And in fact, the alien drifted a little closer, focusing hard on the demon.

Catfight stood quietly for several seconds. Even her tail didn't twitch. "You're a liar. What do you want from me?"

"I've put out an order of protection on you."

"What are you talking about?" she yelled. "Your declaring open season has caused the loss of countless lives. You are the plague Midnight always thought you were."

"I'm going to do what I always said I would. I'm going to end major crime in San Angeles."

"You're insane, and I'm going to find a way to stop you."

"I know there's no way to convince you about what happened the night of the storm, but listen to me carefully," his voice dropped back, hushed. "Things are going to get confusing very soon. Just remember, I tried to tell you the truth, but I understand why you can't believe it. At least, not now." His feet left the rooftop as his wings pulled him upward by a subconscious command. "By the way, I am sleeping better."

Catfight ignored Andre's statements, and a cocky smirk flashed across her face. "I've reached out to Titan," she announced.

"You won't need him," Andre responded, rising out of whispering range. As he started to fly back the way he came, Starlight moved toward him. She reached in his direction with an open palm. He hung in the air, unafraid. She traced the air around him, her expression neutral. When he veered away, Starlight looked at her right palm carefully, and then drifted down next to Catfight. Priest remained at her side. Tatiana didn't take her eyes off the demon until he was little more than a distant speck in the sky.

"He knew personal shit about me," Catfight complained.

"I scanned his aura," Starlight offered, as the other heroes moved forward. "It used to be a perfect black. Predictable for a creature capable of such evil."

"And?" Priest asked.

"Now it's a familiar shade of gray."

Catfight looked at the alien.

"Midnight's aura used to read that way," Starlight said.

Catfight laughed. "It's a trick. Scratch tried to tell me he was Midnight. It's just a sick lie."

"Auras don't lie," Starlight pressed.

"It's Old Scratch. His father is supposed to be the devil himself. I doubt his aura is beyond his ability to distort." Catfight walked back to join the other heroes.

Priest looked at Starlight, then followed Catfight to the others. Starlight's gaze tracked the tiny speck that was Old Scratch until it dropped out of sight somewhere in the Hollywood area. Her curiosity piqued, she wondered if she should have followed the creature, but she knew another opportunity would come.

Starlight also knew this hadn't been the time and place to explain the aura scan to Catfight. The demon's aura had always been a perfect black because his talent for mayhem stemmed from his lack of a soul. There was no way to go from the absence of a soul to having one stained by hatred, revenge, and violence, quite fitting for a hell-bent hero.

The lightning strike had done something startling to the demon. Starlight was going to find out what.

#

Truth and Babydoll stepped away from the men. Priest raised an eyebrow, but kept walking with Catfight.

"Tough night?" Babydoll asked.

"She's had a string of tough days and nights," Truth stated.

"I want this war over. And I want Midnight in the ground, buried so deep none of these vultures can get to him."

"Actually," Starlight offered, "I have an idea about Midnight's final resting place." She gazed up into the sky. The other women followed her lead. Catfight was the first to catch on, and her smile felt good. "Oh, Starlight..."

"It seems fitting, and his remains will not be disturbed. No villain has that kind of reach, including the demon."

"The moon?" Truth whispered. "That's perfect."

"When the time comes, I would be honored to transport him." The alien bowed.

As she straightened up, Catfight hugged her tightly. "Thank you so much," she said, fighting back a happy sob. "He'll finally have peace again."

"Even more so if we could neutralize the demon," Babydoll growled.

"Neutralize?" Starlight asked. The three heroines looked at her.

"You want to kill Old Scratch?" the alien asked. "I'm not sure that's a good idea."

"I don't want to hear any more about the demon's latest trick, Starlight," Catfight said. "Old Scratch's greatest power is his ability to deceive. Look at his army of women, for Christ's sake."

"Speaking of women," Truth broke in, "Catfight, Babydoll and I were thinking you needed something to take your mind off... everything."

"Uh, I think the crime war will keep me distracted enough."

Truth smiled. "Why not both? And have a girls' night out at the same time?"

"Do a little girl-power bonding," Babydoll grinned. "I've been a fan of yours for quite a while. It would be an honor to fight beside you, and as much as I enjoy being around my Valley boys—" she tipped her head in Priest's and Gunn's direction— "It'd be a nice change to hang with some super girls."

Catfight looked at the women and shrugged. "Okay. You have something specific in mind?"

Truth chuckled. "Oh, yeah. I could probably handle it myself, but I thought this would be a perfect mission for us ladies of justice."

"Does justice recognize neutralizing?" Starlight asked.

"Mine does," Babydoll answered.

"Chill out, Babydoll," Truth whispered. She smiled at the alien. "Neutralizing the demon is a discussion for another night. You're invited for this mission too, Starlight."

"Thank you, but I have another matter to investigate." Starlight turned to Catfight. "I'll speak to you soon."

"Looking forward to it. And thank you," Catfight replied.

"Ladies." Starlight floated into the sky for a short distance, then burst into flight toward Hollywood. She looked like a human comet.

"I wish I could fly," Catfight whispered.

"And what's your damage?" Truth demanded of Babydoll.

The streetfighter just shrugged. "I don't know. She always comes off like she's better than us..."

"Better?" Truth asked.

"You know," Catfight explained, "faster, more powerful, and

exotically beautiful in a Star Trek kinda way."

"Yeah," Babydoll agreed. "That's it."

"She is better than us," Catfight said with a chuckle. The other two heroines couldn't keep from laughing at the true statement.

As they walked to rejoin the men, Babydoll stole a last glance into the sky. "Man, I wish I could fly, too."

Across town, at Old Scratch's basement in the bowels of the city, Scarlett grimaced at the bank of monitors locked onto images of the Blackledge Tower rooftop. Everything was falling apart. Since the lightning strike, Old Scratch hadn't been the same malignant being. Always her confidante until that night, Satan's son had become secretive and unreadable. And then this...there was no plausible explanation for what he had done on that roof. She knew the fact she felt like he needed to be watched was equal to treason. Old Scratch had forced her into playing the role of Mr. Christian to his unstable Captain Bly.

Deep inside, she'd known the day might come where the demon's defeat would put her in a position to seize the reins of his dark empire. She'd been a major key to its creation, and she'd certainly been very hands-on in structuring the organization to suit the demon's vision. And Scarlett had become the recruiter of talent for the demon's Inner Circle, the empire's executive branch, reserved for mafia godfathers and the deadliest and most dedicated supervillains in the city.

But now, things were spiraling out of control. The rooftop camera view was at Old Scratch's back, so Scarlett only had the demon's body language to tell her what had been said. The fact he'd shown up at a gathering of heroes with his hands in a peaceful gesture, and had left minutes later without a hint of violence...

Scarlett had not believed her eyes as she'd watched Catfight walk up to the demon with little hesitation. He could have killed her easily, yet he'd done nothing. His excuse of not wanting to make her a martyr was too reasonable. Something was terribly wrong. And since the demon had not chosen to divulge his plans, she had no choice but to protect the empire she'd helped him build, at least until the demon fully returned to his senses. If he ever did.

The control-console technician smacked her keyboard, shaking her head in frustration. "There are no audio feeds for the Blackledge surveillance system. Microphones on neighboring structures weren't strong enough to pick up the conversation."

Scarlett snorted angrily. "Contact the Inner Circle on back channels and convene an emergency meeting at Ground Zero immediately. No absences will be tolerated."

Scarlett headed for the exit, but the tech asked another question, this time with a nervous waver to her voice. "Including Old Scratch?"

Scarlett didn't break stride. "Our leader does not need to know of this meeting. Do not disturb him."

"Yes, Scarlett." The villainess' echoing footsteps faded down the hallway as the tech followed her orders.

#

"We're here, mistress," the driver's voice announced politely from a hidden speaker in the rear cargo compartment of the Needleman Janitorial Supplies van. Scarlett chose to sit in the dark for the hour drive out into the desert north of San Angeles. It gave her time to think, and the cool darkness soothed her. The rear of the van still held the scent of her master.

She heard a door from the front cab close; then the rear doors were unlocked and opened. The driver reached in and assisted her as she stepped down from the van. A handful of black sedans and limos had already parked, facing the abandoned gravel processing-plant office. Grand Zero. Two helicopters rested not far away from each side of the building. Mafia security types were stationed around the vehicles and property. As she strode toward the building's office, a vehicle threw up dust as it sped down the access road. As it neared, she could see it was a taxi. Bodyguards readied themselves, but she waved them back.

The meet spot was too secluded, and its location known by only a dozen or so top-level criminals. And what major threat would arrive in a cab?

The taxi sped into the overgrown parking lot, leaving smoking skid marks as its driver hit the brakes hard. The sedan rocked on its suspension as an intrigued Scarlett stepped toward it, passing henchmen with automatic weapons at the ready.

The rear driver's side door opened, and out stepped Straitjacket, dressed in Dr. Wilton Sabastian Reese's renowned classic tuxedo attire. He grinned and held up his hands innocently. "Good evening, Scarlett." He looked around. "I certainly feel secure."

A shot rang out, and in the momentary firing flash, Scarlett watched the taxi driver's head explode and spray the inside of the windshield as the bullet passed right on through, cracking the glass around the bullet hole. The car horn blared, presumably from the weight of the murdered cabbie.

"Just tipping the driver," Straitjacket explained. A gun-toting Courtney Robertson quickly joined them after reaching into the front seat and shoving the driver off the steering wheel. The resulting abrupt desert silence sounded almost as loud as the gunshot. Dressed in a black party dress with a crotch-level hem, Courtney stood barefoot next to Straitjacket on the dirty pavement.

Her leash hung from her black leather collar. Straitjacket casually took the gun from her hand, then picked up the leash.

"Uh, I didn't mean to crash the party, but prior to my incarceration at Allenby's fine facility, I was an honored member of the round table. Please forgive my preemptive assumption of reinstatement to the Inner Circle."

"How'd you know where the meeting was being held?" Scarlett demanded.

The doctor smiled. "The woman manning the operations center was very helpful." Seeing the flash of anger in Scarlett's eyes, he quickly continued. "Once I mesmerized her, of course. We both know how fiercely loyal Scratch's army is to him, don't we?"

Scarlett turned away a split second too late.

Straitjacket caught a glimpse of her odd expression. "With everything going on, this must be quite the emergency gathering," Straitjacket fished, following the bald villainess toward the office.

Passing through the small office space, Scarlett stepped into a conference room. No one was seated. The only conversations were on cell phones. When she entered, those conversations quickly concluded, and the phones were turned off and put away.

There were fewer than a dozen seats around the table. The top bosses of the Japanese, Russian, Black, and Chinese crime organizations were represented, as were the two largest street gangs, the Bloody Crips and the Harem. Gravel, of Lucifer's Abortions, represented all the motorcycle gangs in the Scratch's empire. Number One, immediately recognizable in her black-and-white costume, represented The Mob. Also in attendance was a nervous Ricochet. He moved in a blur from one end of the table to the other. Spyder had nestled up in a far corner of the ceiling.

"Good evening, ladies and gentlemen," Scarlett began without introductions. She gave Spyder the briefest of acknowledgements. "There's not much time, so I'll keep this very brief. Old Scratch was observed tonight meeting with a group of San Angeles heroes. The reasoning behind the meeting involves Catfight, but nothing else is known. We're all aware of the recent lightning strike that killed Midnight. Scratch has not been the same since awakening from his coma. He has stopped confiding in me, and I fear he's set to put the empire in extreme jeopardy. For these reasons, I'm calling on the Inner Circle to prepare for Plan B."

Murmurs filled the room. The head of the Russian Mafia spoke up first in his KGB I-will-bury-you accent. "And what about the demon? If we go to Plan B with him still alive, we'll all be in extreme jeopardy."

Scarlett pressed her fists into the table. "Not if we're able to convince him that he's still confused from the lightning strike and needs more time to recover."

"How do we know this isn't a power grab for you?" The leader of the Black Fist organization questioned.

"Nobody's that stupid. We need to be very careful…" Straitjacket said.

"I thought you were a fellow evil spirit or something?" the leader of The Mob asked Straitjacket accusingly. "I thought you and Old Scratch were tight?"

Straitjacket glanced at Scarlett. "Scarlett is correct in her assessment of Old Scratch. He wasn't right at the asylum. The change is subtle, but noticeable." He looked around the room. "But if we're wrong, we'll all die screaming." The word "screaming" ended in a high pitch screech.

From the ceiling corner, Spyder whispered menacingly. "For the record, I don't trust Scarlett, and I don't know the dandy with the pet, so I'll take no part in a mutiny. When Scratch finds out about this meeting, and he *will*—"

Shouting and loud voices could be heard from outside. Something heavy landed on the roof. Strangely, no guns fired. Scarlett's eyes snapped to the ceiling.

Straitjacket chuckled and leaned against the doorframe. "Daddy's home."

"Scratch," Spyder hissed, darting along the ceiling and out of the room. The Mafia fathers all looked sick. Despite the mask hiding her facial expressions, Number One of The Mob showed distinctly tense body language. Profanity filled the room. The head of the San Angeles Yakuza pulled a short sword from under his long coat. The Russian mobster got up and moved away. After a few seconds, the Yakuza boss seemed to realize his folly, replacing the weapon.

There was a crash at the building's entrance, followed by slow, heavy footsteps. Straitjacket casually stepped out of the doorway an instant before the front door that had been torn off the hinges sliced through the air and smashed into the rep from the Harem, the largest organized female street gang on the West Coast. She was dead before her body touched the floor.

"Shit," spat the goggled Ricochet. He rocketed out the room, a blur.

Seconds later, Old Scratch squeezed through the doorway. He held the speedster by the neck. Ricochet hung from the demon's grip, his expression one of defeat and fear. Once Old Scratch had fitted himself in the room, he tossed Ricochet into the closest unoccupied seat. "What's your hurry, Ricochet?"

Absolute terror caused the speedster to start talking so fast no one could comprehend what he was saying.

"Shut up," Andre commanded.

The man closed his mouth with equal speed.

"So, the gang's all here," Andre spoke softly, sizing up the room. Most of the Inner Circle could not meet his look. Only the Russian mobster, Scarlett, and Straitjacket were capable of making eye contact. Straitjacket even managed a smile. "Glad you could make it, boss."

The demon ignored the serial killer's greeting. His hard stare fell on Scarlett. When her gaze dropped to the floor, Andre spoke his mind. "I can guess why you're gathered here, but whatever the point, it's now officially moot. The month of December was supposed to be both a gift to my empire and a demonstration of my power over the city. But because of this display of treachery, my plan has just changed."

"This isn't about treachery," Scarlett began, but Andre's backhand tossed her across the room and into a wall with bone-crunching force. She crumpled to the floor in an unconscious heap. No one lifted a finger to help her.

"Tonight will be the last night of carte blanche for crime in San Angeles. Starting at six a.m. tomorrow morning, all criminal endeavors originating from within my empire will cease."

The silence in the room changed from frightened obedience to shock. Straitjacket's smile slipped from his face.

"In what will be a much truer display of my power, there will be no more crime for the foreseeable future."

The small conference room went dead silent until Courtney spoke up. "Does that include murder? Doctor Reese had this really fucked-up murder spree planned out at this posh beach hotel."

Everyone looked at the teenager like she was a smashed, yet still living, cockroach. Straitjacket patted the top of her head, then growled into her ear.

"Shut up." The force and inhuman tone of his words held unquestionable power.

No one cared when she pissed herself and the floor.

"I will tell you when the crime embargo will cease. If any of you or your subordinates decide to ignore my order, and someone will, I will personally make an ugly example of you. Do I make myself clear?"

Silence continued to dominate the room.

"I'm sure Scarlett called this meeting after watching me meet with Catfight. Catfight told me she has contacted Titan." Mentioning possibly the most powerful being on earth re-focused everyone's attention. "If Titan comes to San Angeles, everyone in this room will end up dead, exiled, or imprisoned."

"Including you?" Straitjacket asked.

Andre looked at Scratch's old acquaintance. Andre chose his words carefully before making his tone low and menacing. "Everyone loses if Titan becomes a major player in this town. I can return to hell. Do you think Titan will follow me, or clean up the city?"

The leaders of San Angeles criminal underground looked around at each other, but no one spoke.

"Tell Scarlett the next time I see her, I'll kill her very, very slowly." The demon started out of the room, but paused for a parting word with the possessed criminal psychiatrist. "The same goes for you. Brother."

"See you in hell," Straitjacket answered evenly.

Ricochet burst out of the building as soon as Old Scratch passed through the front door.

It was impossible to ignore the sounds of rending metal, busted glass, and heavy crashes that followed. Once it got quiet outside, terse conversations broke out. Gravel moved to see about Scarlett, scooping her up and placing the unconscious villainess in the middle of the table.

Straitjacket took in the evil beauty, a gleam in his eyes. "Well, I thought that went well," he said.

"I don't know if Scarlett is right or not," Gravel, the biker, commented, "but Scratch is acting crazy."

"What do you expect? He's a demon!" Straitjacket said. "All of you are nothing but pawns for his use, and you've known this all along. He'll do whatever he pleases, when he pleases."

"Then maybe Titan being here wouldn't be such a bad idea. At least he wouldn't torture us like Scratch does," Number One said.

"I'm not going back to prison," the Russian crime boss declared, rising from his seat angrily. "I'd rather be cooked on a spit."

"Dramatic, but unnecessary," Straitjacket responded.

"We're not even sure if Titan can take Old Scratch out," Gravel said.

"Well, I don't think anyone denies that Scratch was telling the truth about Titan, and his coming to San Angeles being bad news for all of us," Straitjacket responded.

"Then what's the alternative? Do nothing and watch our organizations wither and die?" the Yakuza crime boss barked, first in Japanese, and then in English.

"I'm suggesting we all do what Scratch ordered while I look into advice from a higher power," Straitjacket said.

The room got quiet. Scarlett groaned softly from the table.

"What are you talking about?" Gravel asked.

Straitjacket shrugged, and he turned to leave the room, Courtney in tow. "I'm going to try to reach out to Satan."

The Russian crime boss frowned. "The devil himself?"

"I don't mean Ronald McDonald," the possessed serial killer called back.

The Russian Mafia leader crossed himself and scurried from the room. The other Mafia bosses were right behind him. Number One and Gravel stayed long enough to help a recovering Scarlett down from the table.

"I'm thinkin' San Angeles is getting ready be to a fuckin' dangerous place for everybody," Gravel proclaimed. "Might be a good time for Lucifer's Abortions to take a major road trip. Maybe Miami."

Number One shrugged. "This is our home." The Amazon looked at Scarlett. "You all know the old song— to live and die in L.A...."

"Good luck with that," Gravel replied. "See you when I see you."

Though Scarlett could now stand up, it was another full minute before she could lift her chin from her chest. Her expression was bleak. "I've created a shit storm of epic proportions," Scarlett moaned.

Number One shrugged and sighed. "Like Straitjacket said, I think we've all forgotten what we were dealing with. Evil is a word to us. Just bad shit we do. Old Scratch IS evil. We've all been playing with fire."

"Hellfire," Scarlett whispered. She looked at the black-masked leader of The Mob. Her eyes began to moisten. Number One grasped her arm, gently helping her walk out of the building.

The pair stopped at the front door.

"Fuck," Scarlett said softly.

It was a war zone. Most of the vehicles had been crushed or smashed into each another. Both of the helicopters were fiery heaps. The janitorial van was on its side, a small fire throwing smoke up from under its hood. The driver stood by watching helplessly. Across Mojave's flatness, emergency lights and sirens headed their way.

"Need a ride?" Number One offered.

"Yes, thank you," Scarlett accepted. The Mob leader spoke into a metallic wrist band. Seconds later, a 'copter appeared over the small mountain range to the east.

"Never hurts to be cautious," Number One explained.

Scarlett placed a hand against her head and closed her eyes. The pounding pain was the least of her worries. She was dead. She just didn't know the details yet.

Chapter Seventeen

WHILE THE CITY SLEEPS

Andre left the desert wearing a huge crocodile smile. It had felt good to destroy all those cars and helicopters. Felt even better to finally lay out Scarlett. Which opened the door to an eventual endgame he'd have to give some serious thought to.

As he flew toward the lights of the San Fernando Valley, everything became vividly clear. His simple plan, the world, and his future became a blender swirl of the past, the present, who he was before he became Midnight, who he was when he was Midnight, and most importantly, who he was the instant before the lightning ended his life.

He remembered a time when he'd appeared in a hospital parade and children cheered for him, sharing drawings they'd made of him. A tiny little girl, bald from her chemo treatments, clung to his leg the entire time he visited the children's wing like she was on a carnival ride, smiling and whooping. She'd cried when the nurses finally pried her off him an hour later.

He'd carried elderly women from burning buildings. Pets, too.

He'd spoken at schools. Church programs. His parents had always taught him to believe in himself, and to accept the responsibility of the power he'd been blessed with.

Andre had been a hero, and then something had happened, and he'd become the dark-of-night avenging vigilante.

Not something. He knew exactly what had caused him to become someone else. When he'd been stained.

Before Old Scratch and Straitjacket, there had been the serial killer Benjamin Garrett, The Coroner.

The Coroner case had gotten under his skin like no other. Dealing with The Coroner had made him realize he wasn't much of an investigator, watching helplessly as victim after victim was discovered all over San Angeles. Lonely rooftops, deserted beaches, the underbellies of piers, back alleys, and abandoned churches all became shrines for the victims. The Coroner gained the grisly status of infamous killers like Jack the Ripper, Jeffery Dahmer, and Ted Bundy.

It wasn't until he killed a young single mother...Andre's mind ground to a halt as his wings continued to carry him. What was her name? She'd been a pretty Southern Californian blonde from the Midwest. Iowa? Indiana? Maybe it had been Illinois. A beauty who hadn't moved to San Angeles to be an actress, but had left a small-minded, blink-or-you'll-miss-it town to mold a better future for herself and her then-unborn biracial child.

Theresa Hibbert. That was her name. She'd been the eleventh victim.

Andre became suddenly aware of wind whistling by.

The demon's body slammed into the rocky edge of the low-lying mountain range that separated the desert from northern San Angeles County, sliding to a ledge below. At some point, he'd quit flying. Crazy. He'd been jarred, but he wasn't hurt. The rough terrain prickled unpleasantly under him, but he didn't feel an urgency to get up.

Instead, Andre stared into the star-filled sky.

He'd found a distant spot to watch the young mother's funeral. It'd been a simple ceremony with just a handful of mourners present. Then came the moment when Theresa's five-year-old daughter stepped forward and dropped a single white rose into her mother's grave, planting the seed of vengeance within Andre for the little girl, instead of justice for all the victims.

The night when Andre tracked The Coroner to his abattoir, he could have easily captured Garrett. The murderer had put up a weak struggle, waving a scalpel with a desperate ineptitude. Andre had taken it from him and for a moment had every intention of cutting his heart out. Instead, he'd slapped the killer around, taunting and playing with him the way a cat toys with a half-dead mouse. Garrett had continued to mock and run his mouth until Andre's anger flashed white-hot. In that moment, he'd totally forgotten what floor they were on. He'd simply thrown the man through the large loft window. The commuter bus had taken care of the rest.

In many ways, the killer's mother, Betsy Garrett, was correct. Real heroes didn't allow those kinds of things to happen. But he had, and it wasn't long before Straitjacket became the next media-hyped killing machine, while the demon Old Scratch slowly pieced together his criminal empire. Maybe Midnight could have slowed Scratch down some if he hadn't had to deal with Straitjacket, but everything happened for a reason. Past events had led him to where he was right now.

The Coroner had awakened Andre to the fact that although he'd begun as a crimefighter, he'd become a warrior not just against crime, but against evil. Sometimes he was the only solution to certain criminals. The police, the FBI, and other organizations could contend with organized crime, gang violence, bank robbers, serial rapists, and race wars, but The Coroner had been more than a serial killer or serial rapist, or mutilator of women. The crimes he'd committed, the atrocities, had burrowed into Andre's gut and beyond. He'd had nightmares about the serial killer never getting caught, and of the killing continuing without end. The women were assaulted, tortured, and killed in ways that grew more perverse, more hellish. More children were left motherless. Graves overflowed with blood. Severed body parts squirmed like earthworms after a spring rain. More little girls with more white roses...

Andre couldn't ignore it. He'd seen enough death and destruction to fill a dozen lifetimes, but The Coroner had been the force that changed him.

Corrupted him. Stained him. Stained his heart and soul for the rest of his life. Crimefighter became avenger. Avenger became vigilante. And the majority of the people in the city still wept like orphaned children at his passing.

He owed Theresa Hibbert's daughter better than that. He still had an opportunity to make the city a safer place. He still had a chance to defeat the bad guys. He'd once said he'd trade his happiness for the power to help make San Angeles a better place. God had taken him at his word and concluded the deal in His own time. Now to take that opportunity and use the power correctly.

And now here he was, soon to be an outcast amongst the demon's evil breed. He'd already lit the first bundles of explosives that would eventually destroy the foundation of the demon's empire. If he followed through with the rest of his plan, he had to accept the fact that the people of San Angeles would never accept him, as Old Scratch, as a hero.

Lying on the desert floor in the dead of night, trapped inside the grotesque body of the mortal enemy he'd sworn to destroy. Classic. This was the most peace and quiet he'd probably enjoy during these last days.

Andre pushed himself up, taking wing again. He'd try to keep himself airborne this time.

And what would he do if Titan came to San Angeles to destroy him?

Just another variant he'd have to deal with when the time came.

Like the now-constant mental and emotional struggle of how he could still be a hero while being trapped inside a monster's body.

And he suddenly remembered something someone told him a long, long time ago. So long ago he couldn't really remember who said it. It might have been his tough-guy, man's-man father, but he didn't think so. It might have been a line in a movie, but usually the fictional stuff never stuck with him.

Following Lankershim Boulevard south from the air, he strained to remember where the line had come from. It seemed the fringes of his memory were becoming hazier. Odd little bits of information seemed harder and harder to retrieve. Did that mean he was losing his mind? Did it mean his mind was struggling to maintain itself in the demon's brain?

Father Macaroni had said it.

Father Macaroni was the nickname he'd given his parish priest when he was a little boy.

Maccarelli had been the man's family name, but Andre hadn't called him that until after graduating college. Father Maccarelli had become a great friend and confidante, especially after the death of Andre's parents.

After Andre confided in Father Maccarelli about his identity as the superhero Midnight, the two of them had a long and very thought-provoking discussion. At some point, the priest had said, "Once a hero, always a hero." That once a man found the courage and fortitude to put the lives of others before himself, the hero part of him would never die, even when it wasn't nourished. It would just lie dormant, patiently at rest until called upon again.

The Coroner had almost made Andre forget the heroic part of himself. His ability to conceal himself inside the skin of a hell demon for this long was the ultimate testimony to how far he'd fallen from his father's dream for him to be a pediatric surgeon or head up the Pope's security detail.

Leave the white gloves and biblical scriptures to Titan. He probably flossed after every single meal, too.

But Andre was a different kind of man. And Midnight was a different kind of hero. Thriving during the same dark nights criminals used as a security blanket was a part of his personality. Beyond his understanding, there was a reason why he was most comfortable at night, why his powers were at their greatest at the stroke of twelve. Picking a name for himself had been easy. Nighttime was when evil things, like Old Scratch, used the darkness to hide their cowardice. Midnight was when Ander choose to stand and protect the innocent.

And now he'd turn the night against the predators. He smiled so hard he could feel the skin stretch at the corners of his mouth.

What was scarier to criminals than an obsessed nighttime-only superhero?

The same hero inhabiting a demon's body.

When he reached downtown, Andre flew directly to the Blackledge Tower and landed on the westward-facing ledge, the talons on his feet anchoring him as surely as if he'd hammered himself in with iron rivets.

He'd sat on that ledge so many nights, looking out over his city, searching for the next potential victim or evildoer. Now he was like a gargoyle, looks and all. And soon, very soon, he'd know exactly where to look for the villains.

He glanced back over the rooftop. Most of the flower tributes were dead. He hadn't noticed that earlier. All he'd been able to see was Tatiana.

The flowers and Tatiana had one thing in common. Even the prettiest things died. And he knew with what was coming, the order of protection he'd given wouldn't last long. But he couldn't save the city and completely protect her, too.

So he sat and watched the last hell night the city would have to endure. It wasn't easy to block out the wailing sirens and not react to the fires and dark smoke in the distance. Women's screams were the hardest to ignore. He winced more than once, absorbing the sounds of pain and suffering as they blew over him like a hot Santa Ana wind.

Chapter Eighteen

THE BEGINNING OF THE END

Andre sat motionless for hours. As Midnight, he would have known the exact time of night based on his energy level. Now, the demon's affinity for nighttime was much more a residual comfort with darkness from his time in hell.

As the night had passed, the mayhem had eased. An hour prior to dawn, Andre still watched as the city he loved suffered. He wasn't sure if he'd blinked even once.

He sensed, more than saw or heard, someone approaching. He looked up to see Starlight blazing through the sky. She was moving at a great clip, but suddenly veered in the direction of the rooftop. As he'd seen her do so many times before, one moment she was a missile, a blur of motion. In the next instant she was there, hovering in the wind over him as if she'd just performed a magic trick.

Andre couldn't help but tense, unsure of her intent.

She smiled, slowly drifting down to the rooftop. "Hello, Midnight."

Andre was so shocked he couldn't speak.

For a moment, Starlight's expression flexed from welcoming to concern. She landed on the roof just a few feet away from him. "Please say something that confirms my suspicion."

"Hello, N'eve." Her native name sounded strange in the demon's voice, but it made her smile brighten. He was one of the very few people on earth she had trusted with her alien name.

Andre stood up, and she stepped in front of him. Her large yellow eyes glowed with emotion. She placed a palm against the middle of the demon's chest. "I'm so happy your essence survived the lightning strike."

"You have no idea how happy I am that someone knows it's actually me."

"We have to figure out how to transfer you into another body. Maybe something synthetic. An android, maybe."

"I'm not sure it's doable."

"Of course it is. It's already happened once."

Andre chuckled. "True. But this isn't as horrible as I initially thought. I'm coming to terms with it. And I have a plan to use Old Scratch's power to wipe out a shitload of the major crime."

Starlight started to speak, but Andre beat her to it. "You'll be wasting your time. Tatiana will never believe it. And she needs to focus on staying alive, just like you do."

"She needs to know," Starlight argued.

"And maybe someday she will. But she's not ready or open to the truth. Her hatred is blinding her, though if this situation was reversed, I'd have a very hard time believing she was alive in Scarlett's body."

"I'll try to reason with her, Midnight."

"I'm sure you will," Andre chuckled.

"So strange," Starlight pondered. She placed her hand gently on the side of the demon's face. "Beauty truly is only skin deep."

There was a whistling in the air, and Andre couldn't place it immediately. Then he saw the missiles approaching, and he yelled a warning. "Incoming!" He tossed himself over the side of the skyscraper, momentarily forgetting the demon's ability to fly.

Starlight turned, and with less than a second to react, flared her stored solar energy and screamed. The first missile impacted her energy and exploded, shearing off a good chunk of the top of the tower.

Andre plummeted toward the street. "Noooooooooooooooooo," he wailed.

A second and third missile exploded right after the first, throwing rubble everywhere. The glow of Starlight's protective energy globe flashed and disappeared.

The demon's wings started flapping, and Andre was flew back up to the remains of the roof, smashing through the debris he couldn't avoid. What remained of the roof was a smoldering ruin. Areas of the top dozen floors had been decimated. Andre could only hope all the floors had been vacant because of the early hour.

#

As he drifted above the wreckage, the high-altitude fighter jets broke the sound barrier as they headed toward the ocean. Their sonic booms angered him.

Then he saw Starlight's remains, and he screamed in rage. Devoid of any sign of power, her half-buried body looked like an empty, withered husk. Her large eyes no longer glowed with life. He could only imagine what he looked like, the demon howling in rage over the dead body of a fallen hero. The media was going to have another field day pinning Starlight's death on him.

Then the truth struck him hard. The missiles had been aimed at him. Starlight had just gotten in the way.

And the only person in the world who knew who he really was dead because of him. Dead before she could try to convince Tatiana who he really was.

He reflexively started to move toward his friend's body, but approaching news choppers startled him back to reality. "I'm so sorry, N'eve," he told her, darting into the dark sky toward Hollywood. He swooped under one helicopter and so wanted to grab it and make it crash, but he kept flying, controlling his anger. He wasn't surprised that the choppers didn't attempt to follow him.

He perched on top of the Hollywood Bowl until the break of dawn, and then headed into the Hollywood Hills and his ex-alter ego's home. It had been a long night of losing friends and gaining enemies.

Even though the sunrise weakened him psychologically, his determination had never been greater. No more waiting. His plan would shift into high gear at sundown.

#

The Bat's hospital room was cool and quiet. Dawn was breaking the horizon, but with the shades drawn, the room still reflected nighttime.

Ivy pulled her chair to the bed, meaning to rest her head for a moment. The soft glow from the machines, and the quiet beeps, began to tug at her tired eyes. The last few days hadn't brought much sleep. As her head touched the blanket, she closed her eyes, and she was out.

She didn't dream. Her mind didn't take her on any mythic journeys. There was no vivid night terror. No blood-sucking monster, no inescapable quicksand, no Arctic-cold shadow creature steadily closing the distance. She wasn't a soaring bird, flying free in a cloudless sky, carried by love and hope and faith.

One moment she was conscious, and the next, she was unconscious. That was the way it happened for her. And Ivy never remembered any of her dreams. If anything, all she ever brought back from her sleep was the inky blackness she sank into whenever she had the chance to rest.

The one thought that clung to her as her head nestled against The Bat's thigh was that she didn't love this man in the hospital bed who was fighting for his life.

She didn't love him—

Ivy jolted awake, instantly recognizing the feel of the gun muzzle pressed against the back of her head.

"Easy, little lady."

The voice had substance, yet sounded young. She didn't recognize it.

"If I wanted you dead, I could have killed you from eight blocks away."

Gunn. Some of The Damned had encountered the sharpshooter before.

"We need your help, young lady." Second man. Heavy Hispanic

accent. The voice spoke firmly, but gently. Like a teacher, or...

"I know who you are, and I know the sins you've committed, but I can see inside you, and I see the good. The seeds of love have blossomed. That can't happen without the fertile soil of goodness."

Priest. She'd heard of him.

"If something happens to me, Old Scratch will avenge me a thousand-fold."

"The worst has already happened to you," Priest said, stepping around the bed. He looked at The Bat. "He'll live, by the way."

"How do you know?"

"God has blessed me in many ways. There are plans for this young man far beyond this bed."

Ivy smiled at the news. She couldn't help but believe him. She wanted to believe him.

Gunn removed the automatic's muzzle from her skull. "The city is at a crossroads. It won't survive much longer. We need to know where the demon's base of operations is."

Ivy's eyes got wide. She shook her head. "I can't do that. I can't betray him that way."

"He is a demon. An abomination. His very nature is evil. You owe him nothing," Priest charged.

"I'd be dead if it weren't for him!"

"When the city burns, we'll all burn," Gunn said.

"Scratch will protect us."

"Spoken like a true believer. But I know you have doubts, Ivy."

Ivy dropped her gaze to The Bat, and shook her head again. "Scratch gave me a purpose, an identity. I'm nothing without him!"

"You've been kneeling before the wrong 'him'." Priest nodded to the vigilante. "You have a purpose now. You have love. You don't need the demon."

Ivy started to whimper. Fear and confusion were swallowing her up.

The clergyman stepped closer and placed a gentle hand on her head. "For the first time in a long time, follow your heart."

Ivy burst into tears and clutched at the leg of the slumbering Bat. She cried for quite some time, but when she finally raised her head, she nodded her agreement to Priest.

Chapter Nineteen
AND NOTHING BUT THE TRUTH

"Think of this as a little warmup," Truth said, holding out the small telescope.

Catfight ignored the offer, staring across the distance to the closed-down car lot's sales trailer. A faint glow emulated from a couple of windows. Her feline eyesight had no trouble taking in the dark area.

Babydoll also refused the scope, adjusting her own dark-tinted goggles.

Nothing unusual to see, other than an older white-paneled van parked by the front door. The front cab was unoccupied. Catfight didn't pick up any unusual sounds, though at this distance, hearing distinct interior sounds would have been too much to ask. Once she covered some of the parking lot toward the trailer, her hearing would be much more valuable. "So what's the plan?" Catfight asked.

"Intel says The Splinters have at least a half-dozen underage girls held captive. Sexual assaults, brutality, kidnapping…and now possible white-slavery charges if that van is there for transport," Babydoll informed her.

"I've heard about a bad place just south of Tijuana for women," Truth whispered. "Freaks come from all over the world to pay top dollar for anything and everything, including snuff."

"Screw that, then," Babydoll declared, stepping out of the shadows and striding straight toward the car lot.

Truth chuckled. "I had a feeling she might get a little fired up."

"You think?" Catfight smiled.

The two women jogged across the empty street to catch up to the street commando. Truth signaled to the two other female crime fighters, and they responded. Babydoll sprinted full-out around the perimeter of the lot, while Catfight split into triplicate, the trio spreading out.

Truth moved quickly toward the sales trailer's front door. One Catfight followed. The second Catfight leapt onto the roof of the white van, while the third stationed herself by the van's rear doors.

Truth quietly tried the trailer's front door. It felt unlocked, but she didn't open it. Instead, she waited another thirty seconds, then signaled up to the Catfight accompanying her. The feline triplet sprang up, gripped the edge of the roof, and swung herself up. As she did so, Truth pounded on the trailer's front door, then reached into the pouch she wore at her waist.

Movement and voices inside. The front door swept open. "What the fuck?" cursed a baby-faced Splinters gang member.

Truth threw a perfect straight right, and the brass knuckles she'd slipped on shattered the young man's nose. Catfight swung herself down from the roof, blasting a two-footed kick into the gangbanger's chest, tossing him back into the double-wide. Truth was a split-second behind.

The scene before them was equal parts bad prison film and infamous ancient Rome. A Biggie Smalls song played in the background. Not steps from the front door, a naked teenager, bent at the waist, was tied stomach-down to a sawhorse. A Splinters gang member violated her from the rear. Another gang member stroked himself, at the ready. Yet another man wearing Splinters colors straddled the other end of the sawhorse, forcing himself mercilessly into the young woman's mouth.

A few feet away, another young woman struggled in a swarm of Splinters, every available orifice filled to capacity. Her eyes were like saucers. She appeared to be screaming, but the large manhood between her lips stifled the sound to a muffled whimper.

There were men and women sitting and standing around the former office space, and everyone looked shocked by the surprise arrival. Truth heard the back door get kicked in, and before she knew it, Catfight had blasted the door man there, sprung to her feet, and flashed her cat claws. She jumped up into a backflip, kicking out the ceiling light. Shattered glass showered the room.

"Kill these bitches!" someone shouted, and the place exploded into a whirlwind of violence.

Catfight leapt at the man straddling the sawhorse. Eyes closed, he was smiling and singing to the rap song. He was too absorbed in the pleasure of the Asian girl's mouth to see the claws flash across his midsection. His pain-filled cry was startling, and he fell to the floor, clutching at his shredded flesh.

Catfight leapt onto the spine of the sawhorse and stared down at the girl's other rapist. He didn't have time to react as the feline crime fighter forced her claws in and out of his face. He was still in shock a second later when she kicked him under the chin, tossing him backward into the man waiting behind him.

Truth flashed into the room, throwing herself knees-first into the chest of a huge gang member trying to get up off a worn, floral-patterned couch. She hammered his face bloody with a series of brutal blows, bounced off him, and backhanded his coke-snorting companion. A stream of blood arched through the air, following a jettisoned tooth.

At the rear of the office, Babydoll was attacking in her own amplified style, which blended Krav Maga and aikido.

Across the room, a small-caliber gunshot rang out. Then Catfight realized it wasn't a gun, but a bone breaking. And that particular "gun" went off several more times as the combat continued.

A couple of non-gang members, who had been there to party, grabbed a couple of the victims and scrambled out the front door. One guy went straight to the driver's door of the van, while the other, waving a handgun, forced the captive girls toward back of the vehicle. As the gun-toting kidnapper grabbed at the door handle, he was suddenly snatched straight up. When the teenage girls looked up for him, all they heard was a blood-curdling scream.

As the driver jumped behind the wheel, he turned on the car's headlights and cranked the ignition. His partner's wail filled the air as he flew from over the roof and out in front of the van. The driver watched his associate crash into the pavement with an audible crunch. Once the man's momentum stopped, he didn't move again.

"Fuck me!" the driver shouted, the van catching, then dying.

"Yes, fuck you," Catfight mocked, standing outside the driver's side door.

The man cranked the key again, bouncing in his seat like a sugar-filled two-year-old. Catfight used her forefinger claw to calmly trace a fist-sized circle in the window glass.

The van's engine cranked and almost caught, but didn't. The driver punched the steering wheel in panic and frustration.

"Don't flood it," Catfight warned, almost completing the circle on the window.

The man jerked a gun from his waistband.

"I'll fuckin' blow your tits off, bitch!" he threatened. Something landed on the roof above the driver's head. He looked up, listening, brandishing the weapon, but not firing. When he looked back out his window, Catfight had vanished. When he looked back out through his headlights, his partner's body had disappeared, too.

"Shit shit shit!" he cursed, dropping the gun on the seat and cranking the key again.

Out of the corner of his eye, he saw Catfight at his window again, already in mid-punch. The blow caught him on the temple and sent him sprawling into the passenger side seat. The passenger-side door jerked open and two sets of claws snatched at the sex trafficker and slung him roughly out of the van.

He started begging for his life before he landed on the asphalt.

"Oh Jesus, please, please. I never touched the girls. I'm just the driver."

Catfight's second self stood over him. The third Catfight joined her.

"I swear to God, I never touched them. I have a ten-year-old daughter." He didn't see the elbow strike that knocked him out.

The two Catfights meowed to each other, then darted toward the trailer.

#

Water splashed into the driver's face, startling him into consciousness. He sputtered and coughed and wiped at the wet intrusion. When he raised his head, the back of his skull bounced off the wall of the van's reinforced rear compartment. He grabbed at the back of his head, trying to focus on the sight at the door of the van.

A dim streetlight threw out just enough light for the groggy man to see a small group of teenage girls looking at him. Some of their faces were roughed up. He blinked several times. Only one or two of them were fully dressed. Then he realized just behind them were two, no, three versions of Catfight, and two other costumed women. One was Truth, fuck. He knew who she was. The other, the other was fucking beautiful, and wore a weird outfit too. Her legs were covered in army pants, but over those she wore a lacy lingerie top. Jesus.

"Rise and shine," Truth said, and some of the teenage girls giggled and laughed.

"Here," said the beauty in the sexy top. She pulled a pair of black cylinders from her waist, snapping her wrists. Telescoping batons. Their shiny black metal gleamed even in the low light. The driver flinched.

Truth shared her blood-stained brass knuckles with two of the girls. They slipped them on their fists. In the distance, sirens wailed. All three of the Catfights smiled.

"I don't think those police cars are headed here, but you never know," Truth said. She nodded at the driver. "So, I wouldn't waste a second."

"Wait a minute," the driver protested, waving a hand in surrender. He noticed another of the girls holding a baseball bat, while another clutched a large butcher knife in white-knuckled grip.

And then he noticed there were bodies of Splinters gang members in the van with him. None were moving. He wasn't even sure any were breathing. Even in the gloom, he recognized one of the bodies as that of his partner-in-crime. The guy was staring back at him, even though he should have been lying face down. God-darn neck was twisted around like the top of a soda bottle.

The driver remembered the awful crunch he'd heard when the man had landed after being thrown over the van.

Fuck.

"Girl power," Babydoll sang out, and high-fived a couple of the young women. They slowly climbed into the rear of the van.

The driver struggled to get to his feet, but his balance had been short-circuited. He fell back into the corner, begging, reaching out into the air as if mercy were something he could grab onto. "Please, please don't do this. I never hurt any one of you. I've got a daughter not much younger than you."

The girls slowly stalked toward him, savoring the fear they were causing. The man started to sob, but none of the teenagers, or crimefighters, reacted to it, at least not in the way he might have wanted.

Truth hopped into the van, moving toward the man. She skinned off one of her black gloves and grabbed the man's hand. She stared into his eyes as she held it in a death grip. After a few moments, Truth chuckled, and then tossed the man's hand away like a piece of trash. She climbed back out of the van as the teenagers closed in.

"He's a liar," was all she said, and walked away. The man's screams were hard to hear over the girls' taunts and mean-spirited laughter.

Catfight merged from three into one as she followed Truth. Babydoll stayed at the rear of the van, watching, for a full minute, listening as the man's cries of pain turned into agonized whimpering, gradually fading to a telltale silence.

She left the young women to complete their revenge while she followed the same path as her two costumed companions. As the three heroines crossed the downtown avenue, an SAPD police car zoomed by, sirens blaring. The two officers inside didn't even glance their way.

Babydoll smiled. Sometimes, street justice was the best justice a woman could get.

Or give.

#

It was a dark night, which meant it was not difficult for Andre to swoop down close to his Hollywood Hills house and move unseen through the deep shadows to the secret entrance. A large slab of rock lay embedded in the hillside less than a quarter of a mile from his home. Somewhere in the distance, a coyote howled to a hidden moon, setting off a smattering of answering domestic dog barks.

Andre stepped up to the rock slab and sighed. This probably wasn't the smartest thing he'd ever done, but with the way things were going, it was probably the last night he'd have the opportunity to sleep under his own roof, much less in his own bed. Who knew what was going to happen in the next day or two?

Demons were obviously not immortal. A being such as Titan could take his life, though the hero's religion-based moral code would probably prevent it. Andre had already decided he'd rather die than be sentenced to life in a specially designed cell like the one imprisoning Tombstone. He also wouldn't allow himself to be transported back to hell, or wherever Old Scratch originated from.

No way. No how.

So, with time definitely not on his side, why not spend a few hours in a home he'd never be able to enjoy again?

To the left of the large stone sat a trio of bowling ball-sized rocks. Andre pressed against each of them, then stepped around to the right side of the large rock and pulled. The disguised doorway swung open like a bank vault: silent, but heavy. Too heavy to open by accident.

His demon wings flattened to his back and he stepped into the blackness of a circular tunnel. He touched a small press-pad to his right, which reset the entrance, scrambling the order of the trio of rocks that needed to be pressed to unlock the slab. A small screen flashed on under the press-pad, displaying the new press-pattern for a few seconds. Then the screen went dark.

Andre followed the tunnel, in no particular hurry. It wasn't long before he emerged into his basement wine cellar. At his larger demon size, he had to squeeze a bit to go up the spiral staircase. He didn't bother to turn on any lights. As Midnight, he'd rarely turned on any lights. His night vision was better than his excellent daytime sight, and the demon's rivaled that.

When he reached the main floor, he stood in the open living area, trying to appreciate its quiet comfort. Tatiana loved it there, loved the peaceful quiet. He loved the hustle and bustle of the city, but there were times he really needed to decompress from all the annoyances that had a way of getting under one's skin and building up.

Despite the money he'd inherited after his parents' deaths, his home was spartan. The decorations were simple and clean, with few luxuries, other than the wine, which was really for Tatiana, and a living room that doubled as a home theater.

So many memories made in this house. Hardly any worth remembering prior to Tatiana. Most of the house had been redecorated with her. They'd made an unspoken promise that they would live in this house when they were married, and there was land to expand when they decided to start a family.

And, of course, Tatiana knew about the secret entrance. She was the only one he trusted enough.

She was The One.

Andre stood in the dark, the room stale from the central air being off and the windows being closed for so long. Compared to Old Scratch' lair, his stuffy home felt like the beach on a nice breezy day.

Andre finally turned toward the wide stairway and headed upstairs to his master suite. The stairs groaned under the demon's weight.

The pedestal bed protested, but didn't collapse under his added poundage. His pillows felt almost too soft.

The sheets smelled of Tatiana. In fact, her scent was everywhere. The demon's manhood rose like a king cobra.

He'd have to settle for keeping Tatiana out of harm's way for as long as he could. Their future together had ended with the lightning strike. He felt as if he were floating above the soft king-size mattress. It felt good to be back home, even if only for a few precious hours.

He glanced toward the master bath, wishing he could take a long, hot shower, but knowing he'd never fit into the glass enclosure he'd installed for himself and Tatiana. He stared at the open doorway to the bath, almost expecting her to walk out, a small towel wrapped around her torso and another piled on top of her head.

They loved fucking in the shower. It was a better-than-even bet that their first child would have been conceived there.

Andre closed his eyes, searching for a quiet place in his mind. Ignoring his raging hard-on wasn't easy, but as soon as his mind replayed the last moments he'd spent with Starlight, any excitement vanished. She had been so unique and beautiful, yet that missile had stolen her life like a thief— *one moment you're smiling and fine, and the next...* —making her into something so foreign and ugly. A sob caught in his throat. The final sight of her remains was branded into his mind forever, and now that he was bound in a demon's body, forever was a lot longer than he really wanted it to be.

He concentrated on the musk of the sheets and pillows, trying to remember the last night he and Tatiana had lain there together. She'd spooned her body against his, wrapping her arms around him. Tatiana's smaller body was a tiny furnace next to his. He used to tease her about purring in her sleep. And that was all he had left of her. Remembrances that would fade until he wouldn't be able to recall her scent, or her laughter, or the color of her eyes.

He was asleep less than a minute later, trying to burn every tiny detail of her into his mind.

He awoke with a start, immediately looking to the edges of the bedroom curtains for a hint of the time. The room was still dark, and the bedside clock told him he had less than an hour before sunrise. He really couldn't take a chance on being seen in the vicinity of his old place. It was extra trouble he just didn't need. He rose to his feet and made his way back out of the house.

After what had happened in the desert, had going back underground been the best idea? Scarlett could have set a trap for him in the hours he'd been away. He didn't figure her to be the type to go away quietly. Scarlett would strike at him, but from what direction? This might be the best time to lay the foundation for one of several possible scenarios. There wasn't really time to do much else. Whatever damage had been done to San Angeles was beyond his remedy at the moment.

Andre entered the wine cellar escape tunnel. He felt like a rat scrambling along the beam of a burning, sinking ship. The end had already come, and all that was left was death. His own. The others around him. Hopefully not Tatiana's, though he couldn't even be sure she'd survived the night. He still felt numb from Starlight's demise.

Chapter Twenty
ROME IS BURNING

The burnt-orange sun forced its way from the horizon, brightening the cloudless Southern California sky. Across the area, pillars of black smoke continued to snake toward heaven, marring the postcard blue. The all-night orchestra of mayhem blared into the day. Emergency-vehicle sirens pierced the air throughout every neighborhood from Silverlake, to Watts, to Long Beach. Tens of thousands of car alarms shrieked. Tens of thousands of house and business alarms activated to little or no response. Countless dogs barked and yelped and howled. And then there were the people sounds. Screams, shouts, curses, groans, moans, whimpering, cries for help, pleas for mercy. Hundreds. Thousands. Tens of thousands. Men. Women. Children. Infants. Seniors.

San Angeles and its surrounding area were crying out for help like wounded soldiers caught behind enemy lines. Faith was being tested on every level.

Hospitals had triages set up on their lawns and in the surrounding streets. Police stations and firehouses were under siege, with greater numbers of citizens seeking help and safe shelter. 911 was a wasted call.

The National Guard was stretched so thin, its impact was minimized.

Traffic was snarled throughout the county after another night of perilous evacuations. San Angeles' mayor had closed schools, and asked citizens to stay home unless a life-or-death emergency occurred. Public transportation had been canceled because of violent hijacking. Cabs had all but stopped running due to safety issues.

Every area airport had been shut down due to the massive overcrowding and unlawful behavior of those desperate to escape the city. The unauthorized departure of a small private plane from Van Nuys airport shortly after midnight resulted in a fiery crash and the death of all its passengers when the plane was sprayed with heavy automatic-weapon fire from unknown sources. Law-enforcement agencies could only speculate as to who the culprits might be, with hundreds of murders committed over the past seventy-two hours.

News helicopters were being fired on.

Even peace demonstrations and prayer vigils did not escape attack and ravaging.

Looting had begun.

The city was teetering on the brink of an abyss even Rome hadn't been able to survive.

Andre flew over and through it all. He'd helped create this near-apocalypse, and now it was time he forced the evil genie back into the fucking bottle.

Chapter Twenty One
SPLIT SCREEN

MIDNIGHT ETERNAL

1.

The figure stood over the bed, masked in the shadows of the gloomy bedroom. He stared at the couple lying under the covers. The young woman was beautiful as she slept, snoring lightly. She'd pushed off the blanket, and the sheets hinted at her exquisite curves. The man had an eye for talent.

He was lying flat on his back, eyes covered in a black sleeping mask, shallow chest rising and falling. Sleeping like a baby. Amazing the tricks a mind could play to allow one's consciousness to accept absolution and rest, no matter the crime. A quick poke of a talon to the forehead would do it.

The man suddenly sat upright, and wide-eyed, babbling incoherently about a weird dream and "someone there."

"I need you to get dressed and contact Spyder. We need to have a little talk." The familiar voice made The Geek snatch the sleeping mask off his face. Even in the shadows, there was no mistaking the hulking figure. The smell of sulfur assaulted The Geek's nostrils. He glanced at the still-slumbering beauty sharing his bed.

"Forget her," Andre told him. "She'll be there when you get back. Unless she wakes up and comes to her senses."

The Geek finally exhaled and rolled out of bed. "Good. I'm coming back."

2.

The figure stood over the bed, masked in the shadows of the gloomy bedroom. He stared at the couple lying under the covers. The young woman was beautiful as she slept, snoring lightly. She'd pushed off the blanket, and the sheets hinted at her exquisite curves. The demon wearing flesh had an eye for talent.

He was lying flat on his back, eyes covered in a black sleeping mask, shallow chest rising and falling. Sleeping like a baby. Amazing the tricks a mind could play to allow one's consciousness to accept absolution and rest, no matter the crime.

The business end of the .45 automatic pushed gently into the man's covered right eye. "Get up. Slowly."

"I'm not asleep."

A black-gloved hand snatched the mask off his face just as someone else flipped on the light. The sudden glare was startling. It took a moment for Straitjacket's eyes to adjust. The broad-shouldered man in the black overcoat holding the weapon to his face was the aptly named Gunn. Crossing the room toward the bed was Priest. The serial killer's eyes twitched toward the shiny butcher knife and cleaver lying on the bedside table.

"Oh, please do," Gunn prompted with a grin. Straitjacket glanced at the still-slumbering Courtney.

Priest started humming "When the Saints Come Marching In."

Chapter Twenty Two

THE SPYDER AND THE GEEK

The Won Ton Café was located on the northeastern edge of downtown San Angeles, bordering the Skid Row area. Looking like a stereotypical greasy spoon to those not in the know, the Won Ton actually served the best Chinese food outside of Chinatown. Party catering and deliveries to all the downtown corporate offices made the restaurant one of the most profitable in the city.

The crowded dining room was furnished with mixed-and-matched tables and chairs purchased at garage sales. The tile floor wasn't the same from end to end. Customers spanned the spectrum from twenty-something junior execs to rough-edged panhandlers sitting at the counter enjoying a large, one-dollar bowl of white rice and a tall glass of bottled water with a lemon slice. Despite the citywide smoking ban, cigarette smoke hung along the ceiling by the two chess tables in the corner, which were always occupied by some of the city's best underground players.

At the entrance, a silver bell rang when The Geek walked in. The owner, a tiny woman named May, offered him a welcoming smile as she took a lengthy phone order.

The Geek wove his way through the dining room and straight through the swinging doors that led into the kitchen. The kitchen help continued to hustle about, not giving the man a second look. He walked straight to the rear of the prep area toward two large refrigerators. He pulled at the handle of the one on the left, and stepped into the empty metal box. As the door shut behind him, the rear wall of the container slid open, revealing a pair of well-armed female guards from Old Scratch's army.

Both women looked him over, but did not stop him as he passed between them and headed straight to what appeared to be a bank-vault door. Another woman guard turned and quickly pressed a code into a number pad. There was an echoing release of large sounding metal locks, and the door swung open. The demon waited inside.

Andre stepped aside for the genius to move into the room, which allowed Andre to stay between the closing vault door and the two criminals at this particular meeting.

The Geek cautiously took a seat at the small table with a single comfortable chair. He had to swing his head around until he found Spyder. She crouched in the farthest corner of the ceiling, looking more as if she were ready to scurry away than leap to an attack.

The Geek waved at the spider woman, but she didn't respond. Her eyes continued to dart around the room, looking for an escape route that didn't exist.

The vault door closed and sealed with an echoing, definitive metal-to-metal sound.

The Geek's large Adam's apple bobbed nervously. "So, what's up, boss?" he finally managed.

Andre remained quiet, but smiled as he leaned back against the vault door.

"Time is short, so I'm going to get right to it. I'm going to tell you some things that are going to sound insane, and you can choose to believe me or not. But after I'm done talking, your answers will determine if and when you leave this room alive."

The Geek glanced over at Spyder, sighing deeply. "I've always been on your side, Scratch. You know that. And I didn't go to the meeting Scarlett called either." He gave the spider woman a sideglance. "Unlike some."

"Shut up," Spyder hissed defensively.

"This isn't about the meeting, at least not directly. It's about the future. Yours and the city's." Andre paused, trying to determine if there was a better way to say what he wanted to say. There wasn't. "You're not talking to Old Scratch," he blurted. "You're speaking with the guy who used to be Midnight."

The near-silent vault room got even quieter. A dropped pin would have sounded like a gunshot. Moments stretched out before The Geek clapped his hands and started laughing. "Oh boss, you're so full of shit, man."

Spyder continued to stare.

Andre returned Spyder's hard look. She knew.

"It's the truth, you fucking bookworm," Andre said.

The Geek stopped laughing so suddenly it was as if someone had flipped a switch. He shifted anxiously in his chair. "Fucking Midnight called me bookworm all the time. The piece of shit."

"Shut up and listen, Geek," Spyder warned.

"It happened the night of the storm. The lightning torched my body, but my consciousness jumped from my body into the demon's."

"And Old Scratch?"

"Gone, as far as I know."

The room fell silent again. Andre shrugged the demon's massive shoulders. "I don't expect you to believe me. Catfight didn't. Starlight figured it out, but she's dead."

Spyder pushed herself out of the corner and crept down the wall. Her eyes never left the demon.

"That's not even possible," the Geek said, shaking his head as his massive intellect tried to formulate possibilities.

"What, like the possibilities of a real hell full of demons?" Andre retorted. "Or the possibility of a human/spider hybrid?"

Spyder stopped crawling down the wall.

"Whatever. Like I said, I knew you wouldn't believe me, so forget that shit. Let's talk about the important stuff. I know you've heard I've ordered a crime stoppage until further notice. Scarlett's been suspicious of me since the accident, and now she's planted the seed within the rank and file. You know— my weird, erratic behavior since the storm."

The Geek's mouth dropped open slightly, but he didn't speak. The dots were starting to connect.

"And that's my plan— to use the demon's power to end crime in San Angeles."

"But why would you do that?" The Geek was still fighting the obvious conclusion.

"Because he isn't the demon," Spyder whispered.

"Have you lost your mind?" The Geek pointed at the demon. "Of course this is our favorite hell demon. He's fine, he's just testing us, you know, using the situation to see who's loyal and who's looking for an opportunity to exploit him."

"I'm in love with Catfight," Andre said.

"With that ass, who ain't?"

"I enjoyed killing The Coroner," Andre continued.

"Uh huh. Sure you did. The word on the street is that the media cooked up that execution story to pad Midnight's vigilante rep after The Bat came on the scene. You know, a little one-ups-manship."

Andre stared at the man, and a thought made him grin. The change in the demon's expression from frustrated to amused caused The Geek to shift nervously in his chair again.

Spyder continued her patient descent.

"Remember what happened in lock-up after your arrest on the pyramid scam?"

The Geek pushed his glasses back up his nose. He stared back at the demon, but didn't speak.

"Jon-Jon delivered a message from me to you, didn't he?"

The Geek climbed out of his chair, whispering under his breath. It sounded like "Shut up."

"How long were you in that supply room? Almost an hour, right? Just you and Jon-Jon having a deep, intimate discussion."

"Shut up." The words were barely audible.

"What'd you say?" Andre asked, cocking his head.

"Shut up," the Geek said softly, stepping toward the demon. Andre smiled and continued to taunt the genius.

"You didn't like the message, but you never stole money from senior citizens again, did you?"

The Geek's eyes blazed with malice. "No."

Andre glanced at Spyder, and then back at the mad genius. "Believe me now?"

Chest heaving with emotion, The Geek stood for several seconds before sitting back down. He turned his laser stare onto the table. His head slowly began to wag from side to side.

"It's not possible. Can't be," The Geek whispered under his breath.

Spyder looked back and forth between the two men, and then slowly began to back up. "You believe him?" she asked The Geek.

The genius shrugged. "Maybe. I don't know. Fuck!"

The female mutant continued to stare, but her demeanor changed from a mix of fear and respect to shock and awe. "Fuck me," she gasped, her mind working to wrap itself around the unbelievable premise.

The vault room fell silent a third time.

"So, while you'll mulling over my impossible reality, here's my deal for the both of you. Use your talents and help me clean up Dodge, and," Andre pointed at the Geek, "I'll turn over a significant amount of the demon's accounts to your control. I just need you to be my eyes and ears."

Andre addressed Spyder. "I will allow you free rein to feed and expand your army, as long as your nourishment comes from members of the crumbling empire."

The woman with the spider's face contemplated the offer.

Andre shook his demon head. "No more innocent babies or young children. Only criminals."

"What about mobsters' children?" The response came back so fast it caught Andre off-guard. He didn't have to think about it. "Mafia families are fair game."

"I'll do it under two conditions," she negotiated, moving closer as if to further convince herself of the demon's true identity. "The first is that I want a new place for myself and my army."

Andre nodded. "No problem. And the second condition?"

"I want to kill Scarlett." Spyder smiled and exposed all those moist and shiny and poisonous black fangs.

"I'll consider it," Andre replied. "But I might need her if my plan falls through."

"Fair enough. She won't be valuable forever," the mutant hissed, satisfied.

"And what if I say no?" The Geek questioned. "You gonna kill me?"

"Nope," Andre answered, crossing his arms across his chest. "I'm going to let Spyder have you."

The answer blindsided him. The Geek's expression turned comically horrified. When he looked over at Spyder, she smiled back at him, digestive goo dripping from the corners of her mouth.

"Oh hell no," he announced, waving his hands. "Fuck that. I'd rather use a nail gun on my own balls. I want some assurances and a new crib. And a fucking shitload of money. So much money I could pay Paris Hilton to lick my ass!"

Andre frowned. The Geek was nothing if not consistent.

"What happened in lockup wasn't right, man."

Andre chuckled. "A change of teams might just do you some good."

"And stop looking at me that way!" he cried out in protest to the spider woman. The sound of what passed for her laughter was nothing less than bone-chilling.

Chapter Twenty Three
EXORCISING EVIL

Andre perched on the partially destroyed roof of the now-vacant Blackledge Tower, scanning the downtown area. Inspectors and investigators had spent the day going over the ruined remains. Some of the roof was still intact, but several floors had been affected, many curtained off in plastic to ward off exposure to the elements. It certainly looked like a bomb-blast area.

A paranoid ex-military zealot named Airstrike had become the target of a massive manhunt for his involvement in Starlight's murder, though the media had still found a way to implicate the demon. In fact, more than one cable news program looped footage of his outraged wail moments after Starlight's death into a bloody victory cry. Andre almost couldn't remember how well the media had treated him all those years as Midnight. Being on the other side, with negative news coverage, was like being dropped into a dark hole and having the whole world lined up to piss on you. It never took long for speculation to become truth in the court of public opinion.

He didn't care about the possibility of Tatiana or any of the other heroes return to the scene of the tragedy. This was where he wanted to be, amongst the scattered dead and ruined tributes at his back. The skyscraper was the only place where he could feel the city's support. Demon body or no, he was going to finish what he'd started years ago. He was going to make San Angeles safer for everyone. And he was going to use the twist of fate to enforce his promise.

He had worked a transformation like no other. In less than twenty-four hours the tidal wave of crime he'd established had diminished to a leaky faucet. Law enforcement and National Guard vehicles had been cruising up and down the streets, but in the last several hours, there'd been no explosions or mob action or arson.

In Skid Row, the homeless had gone underground, literally seeking shelter under the streets. Compared to a normal evening, only a sprinkling of streetwalkers plied their trade, and the few that dared to work had been smart enough to stay in well-lit areas like the bus station or the corners illuminated by the major mission buildings. No dimly lit streets or alley mouths. Not tonight.

Street beggars had taken the night off.

The city was as quiet as a city could be, compared to the previous hell nights. The basic symphony of crime— sirens, screams, and gunfire— had ceased for the time being. But Andre waited, patient in his belief that there were going to be crimes, and even more certain there'd be crimes he'd be able to put his own personal brand of intolerance on. So, much like an ornamental gargoyle, he perched, watching, waiting, and listening.

He heard the scattering of birds on the far side of the partially collapsed roof. He wasn't alone. Catfight, maybe? Scarlett? Starlight's ghost? Instead of stirring up even more drama, he chose to sit and continue to scan for trouble. If they wanted his back, they could have it.

The light footsteps continued to cross the rooftop, neither hesitant nor rushed.

When Catfight spoke, her voice was much closer than he'd expected. "What are you doing here?!" she challenged with a shout. His lack of a timely response infuriated her. "Why are you here?!" It felt like she screamed the question right into his head.

When he turned, she skipped back a few steps, already in a fighting stance. An instant later, she split into three, each feline fighter holding a slightly different posture. Andre knew Catfight's gleaming claws couldn't do real harm to him, but they were all she had, and she appeared ready to go down fighting.

"Tatiana, please..."

Catfight flashed forward, raking her claws across his upper back and shoulders. "Speak my name again and I'll claw your fucking eyes out!"

Andre sighed. "I didn't kill N'eve. Airstrike had been after her since—"

Andre flinched at Catfight's scream. It was so emotionally charged, it was really a screech. "Now you're fucking innocent?!" The trio of Catfights launched into a frenzied attack on the demon, clawing and kicking and pummeling him with a fury Andre had never witnessed before. He warded her off without any offensive aggression.

One of her incarnations leapt onto his shoulders and shrieked in a battle-fueled rage. Both her sets of claws ripped and slashed at his large eyes, and without thinking he struck out, sending the feline fighter across the roof in a line drive. The Bat would have approved of the hit.

The other two Catfights paused to watch the fate of their sister. Catfight twisted herself around in the air like her namesake animal, landing in a balanced three-point pose. He could hear her angered hiss across the roof. The other two Catfights turned on him again. Before they could relaunch their attack, he jumped to his feet and pushed the duplicates down, his wings popping open for effect. They both scrambled backward as he stepped forward.

"N'eve came to me! She knew what I tried to tell you was true! I'm not Old Scratch! I'm Andre!"

The trio gathered themselves, all growling low in their throats. "I knew Andre hated you, but I never realized why his hatred was so deep." The original stepped closer, while the other two hung back. "Titan is hesitant to leave New York unprotected. Maybe beings will come from Starlight's world to avenge her death and I will point them straight at you. But one way or another, I will see you dead."

In a flash she had morphed back into a singular Catfight.

Andre stood, arms hanging at his side. His wings slowly flattened to his back. He dropped his gaze to his monstrous feet. "Not very long ago, you looked into my eyes and told me you wanted us to have a little girl first."

Catfight's whole body wavered as if she were standing against a gale-force wind. Her eyes blinked and blinked and blinked, stunned.

"You wanted to name her Nadia."

Her savage scream was demon-like, and she launched herself at him with murderous intent, claws and teeth bared.

But just as it had been in his persona of Midnight, the demon's size was not indicative of his quickness. Andre sidestepped the vicious but clumsy attack and watched as Catfight hurled herself over the roof's edge. In true cat fashion, she howled her way toward the pavement hundreds of feet below. Andre leaned out and watched her fall, and couldn't resist giving her a little wave goodbye. He knew she would land on her feet.

Gunshots rang out from a nearby street.

Andre lifted into the air, and swooping over the edge of the building toward the gunfire without a thought. Outside of one of San Angeles' last single-screen theaters, it looked like two rival gangs were manning up after a screening of *The Warriors*.

Great movie, but didn't theater owners ever read the newspaper or catch any news online? Violence seemed to break out every single time that film showed in a metropolitan area.

He sorted it out quickly. One group fired their weapons from the windows of a vintage boat car— a caddie or Buick— at a group that looked to have just left the theater. Other patrons lay on the ground. Police sirens approached. Apparently, no one in law enforcement followed the film's reputation, either.

Andre recognized the similarly-dressed patrons exiting the theater as part of the Badges vigilante group. The handful of Badges members had all dropped into classic police firing postures.

Their outfits, work overalls made to look like classic SAPD patrol uniforms, were form-fitting but not skintight. The silver badges pinned over their hearts glittered in the night. Each of the men and women Badge members wore simple black Robin-style eye masks to disguise their identities.

Andre chose the easy solution, swooping down from the night sky with a wicked smile.

In the midst of the gunfire, Andre dropped to the ground in front of the boat car. He lifted the front end as easily as someone lifts a spread to look under a bed. He grabbed the front axle and pushed the car straight back, up into the air.

"It's Old Scratch!" Someone yelled from inside the car. The gunfire from the car turned on him. The small-arms fire felt like mosquito bites.

"Now, now, boys," he chided. "I'm sure word got to you about my order to chill out." He flapped his wings and rose in the air, carrying the now-vertical car, and them, about a dozen stories high.

A head popped out of the front passenger window. "They called us out before the movie even started," a young man tried to explain.

"And that made you forget my order?"

The young man had no reply.

Andre flashed his demon smile. "Seat belts on?"

Andre let go of the car. "Ooops."

The Cadillac crashed onto its roof about thirty seconds before several police cars pulled up. Any survivors would be a miracle.

Due to the relative lack of crime that evening, the emergency response was overwhelming. The other gang members were dropping their weapons as the SAPD cars skidded to surround the theater front.

Andre hovered over the car ruins. He couldn't resist. "Click it or punch the big ticket."

The demon took to the night sky in the direction of the Blackledge Tower, wondering how the media was going to twist this incident. Screw them. It felt good to be back in the crime-fighting game again. And he had zero remorse for dropping the car.

Saved the taxpayers some coin.

#

Courtney cowered in the corner of the guest suite. She was terrified, and had been for hours. The priest was performing a real-life exorcism on Dr. Reese. The things she'd seen. The things she'd heard.

Being a student at San Angeles' most notorious prep school sounded like the greatest thing in the world right now. Fuck this badass bitch shit. Fuck it entirely. She hadn't cried this much since her Uncle Frank had fucked her the night before her fourteenth birthday. In fact, he'd used her every which way that night, stuffing her underwear into her mouth to muffle her cries in the pool house.

That episode had seemed to last forever, and the smallest details had been seared into her brain. She remembered staring up at the ceiling, tears in her eyes as he took her virginity. She remember her dog Bluto barking outside, probably looking for her. She remembered all the horrible things he'd whispered to her, and she was so fucking sorry for having teased him for so long.

She'd developed curves early, and her mother had warned her about men, young and old, who would do anything—ANYTHING— to try and have an excuse to touch her. She remembered laughing in her mother's face and calling her stupid. Courtney had thought she knew everything. Like *Cosmo* magazine was the Bible.

She remembered Uncle Frank growling at her, and then flipping her to her stomach. She'd tried to crawl away, but he'd pinned her down, grabbing her neck with his hand and squeezing. He was too strong, and she was getting every bit of the punishment she suddenly thought she deserved. All the times she'd been disrespectful to her parents. Lied to them. Called them horrible names. Did bad things to her little sister. Bad things to her so-called rich-bitch friends.

She'd thought the pain between her legs was terrible. The moment he'd pierced her ass, her scream sounded almost like someone else had stepped in the room and witnessed the atrocity happening to her, the little teasing slut that liked to jump onto the laps of her father's cop friends and rub her ass into their crotches. She loved getting men hard and laughed at their reddening, embarrassed faces. Then she'd hop off, and sometimes reach back and give them an accidental squeeze for when they jerked off thinking of her later.

And the ways she'd tormented Uncle Frank.

She'd once pretended to have hit her head on the edge of the pool. She'd crawled between his legs and put her face in his lap so he could look at the back of her head. He'd hardened instantly, and she'd raked her nails over his hardness. Then she'd stood and smiled. His expression mixed both anger and embarrassment, and he'd quickly dived into the pool to hide himself.

Courtney remembered his wife appearing just then, and the look on her face. Aunt Lydia was suspicious and irritated, but clearly wasn't sure what had happened between the two. Uncle Frank's lame excuse for not immediately getting out of the pool wasn't helpful for his cause.

And even as Uncle Frank had fucked her ass, he'd growled and grunted Aunt Lydia's name. After he'd done the same to her mouth, he'd stood there watching her crawl and drag herself into the restroom, half-lying on the toilet as she threw up. For every whispered rumor or compliment about her having a sweet ass, she had first-hand evidence to the contrary. Her ass was not sweet at all.

So here she was now, pressed into the corner of a room that could have been the size of a football stadium, and there still wouldn't have been enough space between her and what was happening.

Her eyes darted around the room.

Gunn was still there. He hadn't moved much in the last few hours. He'd hung his long coat behind his chair, exposing the multiple holsters he wore. Occasionally, he'd look across the room at her, but that was just to check her position. Courtney had experienced enough men checking her out across rooms to know when they were looking at her, and when they were looking AT her. He looked at her, then checked his holsters, then checked his pocket watch, and then looked casually over at the priest and Straitjacket and the ceremony. All with the same expression. Everything seemed the same to the gunslinger. Detached, almost bored observation.

Courtney had been wrapped in nothing but a thin white sheet from the moment she'd been awakened, early, by the doctor's voice. None of the men seemed to notice or care.

She wasn't a morning person, but had clearly heard the priest mention an exorcism. *The Exorcist* was her all-time favorite movie, along with this old black-and-white movie called *Kitten with a Whip*. A real-life exorcism had to be the coolest thing ever to watch, or so she'd thought, but she'd been dead wrong. At one point she had been sure something was trying to crawl inside her. There had been a sharp pinch at the bottom of her right foot, then a weird, creepy sensation, almost like a worm struggling to burrow into her foot. The priest had been especially loud and forceful during this part of the ceremony, and at one point had stood over her and dowsed her with cold water. She'd guessed it was holy water, but whatever it was, the worm stopped bothering her foot.

Courtney had starting reciting the Lord's Prayer. There'd been a high-pitched squeal, and she'd squeezed her eyes shut because she didn't want to see what was making the sound. It didn't sound like any person or animal or insect she knew of. The sound caused chills to run up the middle of her back, and a frozen balloon expanded in her stomach.

After that, she'd mostly kept her eyes closed.

A couple of hours ago, hot piss had splashed on her. She'd actually dozed off at some point, and then steaming urine had sprayed on her face. She wasn't going to leave her corner, so she just put up her hands to deflect the stream. Through half-closed eyes she saw that the piss was streaming in an arch from the bed. The doctor was pissing on her. And the first thought that sparked in her mind was that he'd already done much worse to her than that. So she dropped her hands and ducked her head into the top of her pulled-up knees until it stopped.

It smelled so fucking awful. Like rotten eggs and sulfur.

Not long ago, she'd heard movement on the bed, and then the doctor's other voice was crying out in a lot of different languages. Some she even recognized, like Latin and Spanish and German. But there were plenty of others she didn't recognize at all, that just sounded really old. Ancient. The doctor sounded like he was in a lot of pain, but he wasn't giving up. The priest, who'd taken off his jacket early on, had a big Bible in one hand and was drizzling holy water on the doctor with the other. The doctor's body was arching off the bed. At some point, he'd been tied down by his wrists and ankles.

Courtney looked long enough to see something had happened to the doctor. His body would arch off the bed, straining at the metal shackles, but his body looked all wrong.

Impossibly wrong.

His elbows were pointing in the wrong direction, as were his knees. And she was positive that his straining, screaming face had turned all the way around to point down toward the pillow instead of up where his chest was.

Lucius was the name of the demon inside of the doctor. It was the disembodied evil spirit who directed the doctor to become a serial killer and do all those awful things to women. And children. And her little sister.

Ohmygodohmygodohmygodohmygodohmygodohmygod.

She'd just stood around while he did things to her. She'd even helped tie her at one point, telling her sister over and over it was going to fun, it was going to be fun, it was going to be fun...

Courtney had laughed while he'd skinned her alive. Her little sister had screamed until she'd passed out.

Courtney loved her little sister. She'd been the only one who'd never judged her. Always smiled and hugged her and liked to be around her.

They'd left her on the cold tile of the entryway. Straitjacket wouldn't allow her to cover her up.

Courtney had lived up to every ugly thing anyone had ever written online or tweeted about her.

Now she sat frightened and shivering, listening to the quiet room. The priest had stopped talking. There were no movements from the bed. She couldn't make anything out, so she allowed herself to open her eyes.

The priest was crossing from the bed toward Gunn. The holy man was holding a clear globe about the size of a bowling ball. Inside of it was a swirling red...thing. There were flecks of other colors like silver and white and black, but mainly it was bloody red. It looked like a mist or gassy thing, but it also had an eel-like quality. How it seemed to be both made her stomach feel queasy.

Gunn held open a leather bag, almost like an old doctor's bag, and the priest carefully placed the container inside.

The doctor's body was still on the bed. It looked smaller than it had earlier. It appeared broken, like a toy given to an uncaring child.

Courtney hadn't been a good sister or daughter or friend. The doctor had said she'd been the best pet he'd ever had. A day ago, she'd been so proud to wear that badge of honor. Now she was a pathetic orphan who'd made a gift of her sister to a psychopath.

Gunn sat the bag down and reached for his coat. Courtney pushed herself from the floor and started across the room, leaving the sheet on the floor. She'd been on the floor so long her legs had all but fallen asleep. Her joints were stiff and creaky. With no makeup on and emotionally worn out, she passed a mirror and didn't recognize herself. A strange young woman wearing a dog collar stared back at her. A dog collar?

Her movement caught Gunn's eye, and he turned to face her.

Courtney tried to smile as she approached him, but she sobbed instead. Gunn looked to Priest, then back to the young woman.

She was naked, but Gunn looked her straight in the eye. She was naked, but she didn't feel sexy. She was naked, but she wasn't trying to tease him or the priest with her nudity or sexuality.

She was naked, but she ignored the small twisted body of the doctor. She was naked, but she wasn't wanting to climb back into bed with the serial killer. All that craziness was over.

She was naked when she stopped in front of the handsome, bearded Gunn. They shared a look, and she was able to offer him half a smile.

"Thank you," her voice was a quiet croak. Too much crying; too much emotion.

Courtney Robertson, daughter of the deceased director of the Allenby Asylum for the Criminally Insane, was naked except for the dog collar when she reached out, undid the strap securing the .45 automatic on Gunn's left hip, and withdrew the weapon.

"God in heaven," Priest whispered as Courtney placed the gun inside her pouty mouth and, an instant later, pulled the trigger.

MIDNIGHT ETERNAL

In the quiet room, the sound of the single shot made Gunn flinch.

Both the pistol and her body fell to the ground and were still.

The modern gunslinger reached for his weapon, but then left it on the floor, untouched. He could barely make eye contact with his friend. "The weapon is now cursed. God's will be done," the world's greatest marksman whispered, crossing himself and leaving the room, holding the satchel.

The armed SAPD officers stationed outside peeked into the suite. Smoke was still drifting from the entry wound.

"The demon's lair is clear," one of the riot-helmeted officers reported to Gunn and Priest. "Very few casualties, no officers among them. Over one-hundred-fifty women taken into custody. Scarlett was not among them."

"Call an ambulance," Priest directed, pulling on his jacket. He couldn't take his eyes off the young woman's body. It had almost become the next vessel for Lucius. She'd been ripe for possession, but he'd been able to complete a protective chant to block the demon's attempt. Such a waste of a blossoming young life.

So sad.

Courtney was naked, and for the first time in her life, a man looked at her nudity and felt only sorrow. Priest left the room he'd entered nearly a day before and promised himself there would be no more fighting evil until he got some rest and regained his strength. When that would truly be, he had no idea.

Chapter Twenty Four

AN ITSY BITSY SPYDER

It was another postcard-perfect day in sunny Southern California. Routine for those living there. Incredible for those visiting from harsher and less beautiful locales.

In downtown San Angeles' Little Tokyo, Councilman Charles Itou arrived via black stretch limo to the Itou Mall, a three-story shopping and entertainment center. It had taken him nearly a decade and a lot of backroom deals to make his dream a reality. With the demon's empire crumbling, this was the perfect time for his own enterprise to come to fruition. And the demon had zero involvement. Itou could retire a rich man with legit cash flow, and still head up the San Angeles Yakuza. Things were coming together perfectly.

He looked across at his personal assistant, an ex-wannabe porn star who happily satisfied his variety of sexual desires. Amii was a slim, five-foot tall African-American and Japanese biracial beauty with a honey complexion. Hair braided and wearing what he'd ordered— a white sheer blouse, short black leather skirt, and black pumps— she'd accompanied him to the mall's grand-opening ceremony.

They'd arrived an hour prior to the ceremony so Itou could rehearse his speech and relax. The word "relax" was code for his driver/bodyguard to park the limo in a shaded, secure spot and give them privacy for approximately forty-five minutes. No interruptions. Occasionally, Old Scratch himself had seen fit to intrude, but he was known to rest during daylight hours, so the Yakuza boss was looking forward to an undisturbed "rehearsal."

The driver, an ex-sumo wrestler, parked the limo in the shady side of a San Angeles avenue parking lot run by his brother. The driver left the customary crack in the one-way bullet-proof glass partition between the driver and the rear section. He also cracked open the rear-compartment side windows and the tinted sunroof. The councilman didn't like to get too hot or sweaty prior to a speaking engagement. The limo's air conditioning was also left on at a comfortable seventy degrees. Combined with the low-seventies outdoor temperature, it was a spectacular day for the mall's grand opening. The limo was then coned off by the parking attendant so there were three empty spaces to each side of the vehicle. It wasn't an unusual sight in the neighborhood. Itou averaged two morning "relaxation" sessions per week.

The driver and the attendant met at the small attendant booth, where they each took an envelope full of cash duct-taped under the valet key box. They both walked briskly away from the parking lot.

Inside the limo, Itou's assistant was putting on his favorite shade of red lipstick while he adjusted himself accordingly.

Outside the limo, everything seemed normal on a Monday morning heading toward Christmas.

As soon as the woman's face dipped into Itou's lap and his eyes closed, the manhole cover the driver had parked over lifted silently from its resting place and was eased carefully to the side.

Inside the limo, Itou mumbled a jumble of Japanese and English as his assistant went to work with superior skill.

Under the black stretch, there was movement. From the busy street nothing could be seen, but if someone had been standing close to the vehicle, it would have looked as if something was… spreading. But not spreading as a liquid would. This dark wave almost made a sound, and moved erratically. This darkness moved on eight legs.

The flood of spiders raced out in all directions, reaching the car's tires and flowing up them as if the darkness from the manhole was trying to swallow the limousine.

Inside the passenger compartment, Itou's assistant was teasing him, changing up the pace and talking to him just the way he liked. Itou's fingers dug into the door arm and the leather seat as the sensations continued to mount.

The spiders continued to envelop the car, reaching the cracked passenger windows and flowing in from both sides. More spiders moved toward the slightly open sunroof.

Under the limo, Spyder herself squeezed out of the manhole, flattened enough to scurry out from under the car, and watched her ravenous army of assassins cover the limo. She hopped from the ground into the air…

Itou's eyes popped open. Something had landed on the roof.

And then he saw the crawling horde covering the ceiling of the car's interior compartment. His panicked scream only made Amii chuckle around his manhood. Wide-eyed, the Yakuza boss realized the whole compartment was blanketed in spiders. Tiny ones, tarantulas, black widows, wolf spiders…He turned his head and stared into the multiple eyes of a yellow-and-black garden spider half the size of his hand.

His next scream was a mixture of fear and massive chest pain. The woman glanced up at the man's enthusiastic reaction to her work, and kept at it.

There was the sound of metal rending above her. When Amii looked up, Spyder had popped her head into the opening where the sunroof used to be. The female mutant smiled at the servicing assistant. "I like to suck, too."

Amii glanced at Itou, who by now was in full cardiac arrest. A split-second later she understood the eight-legged hell surrounding her. The assistant's scream filled the compartment as Spyder squeezed through the roof opening and her arachnid army swallowed up the councilman and his assistant as they had the limo.

Spyder looked at the man's still-exposed member. "That's as good a place to start as any," she hissed with a hungry, malignant smile. But when Spyder's face dipped into the Yakuza boss's lap, he didn't come.

He went.

Chapter Twenty Five
MEETING ONE'S MATCH

Match smiled ear to ear as he appraised his reflection in the floor-length mirror in his guest suite. He'd been eager to get out of the warden's sloth-like body once they'd successfully escaped the asylum and gone underground. He'd felt really drawn to the young woman warrior in the demon's female guard, but hadn't been stupid enough to go against the direct wishes of Old Scratch.

The raid on the demon's underground lair had been a desperate situation that turned out to be a wonderful stroke of Providence.

When the intruder alarms went off, law enforcement had already penetrated the hideout's outer defenses. The Damned seemed in disarray, and it wasn't until later that Match found out that neither Old Scratch nor Scarlett had been at the base to direct their forces. Law enforcement had a relatively easy time capturing and controlling the base.

Match had thought about attempting an emergency transformation, and then realized he was actually in a good position in the guise of the asylum director. He rumpled up the suit he'd arrived in and shoved it under the bed. He'd sat on the floor at the end of the bed in his dress socks, underwear, and woman-beater. Match put a worried, dejected expression on his face, and waited for the SAPD team to reach his room.

The four-man team arrived a few minutes later, kicking in the door, their red laser sights sweeping the suite. They covered the bedroom and bathroom quickly, calling out "Clear!" in less than thirty seconds.

One of the officers immediately identified him, and after checking to be sure he was unharmed, sent the other three forward to check out the rest of the rooms, including the suite where Straitjacket and the girl were at.

The officer who stayed with him took off her helmet, revealing herself to be a pleasant-looking female. She had closely cropped, punkish black hair. When she smiled to reassure him of his safety, a pretty set of dimples appeared. She had good size for a woman, about five-foot-nine, maybe ten. Even in the SAPD jumpsuit, she looked athletic. She had coat-hanger shoulders, and her carved facial features looked like they belonged to a gym rat.

She'd asked if he had any clothes to put on, and he shook his head no and started to sob about the inmates killing his wife and kidnapping his daughter. The officer turned and pushed the door to the hallway closed. When she turned back around, Match was on her. His right pinkie fingernail was actually a stinger, which remained usable throughout any transformation. He jabbed her on the back of her neck, and the quick-acting poison rendered her unconscious and paralyzed in seconds. He dragged the unconscious woman to the bathroom, stripping her uniform off, then his undergarments. He positioned himself over the top of her, propping himself like he was going to do a push-up. He lowered himself until his skin was barely touching hers. He closed his eyes and let his ability run its course. He did his best to push the transformation as quickly as he could.

Once he'd duplicated her body, he quickly put on the officer's uniform and gathered up her equipment. He locked the bathroom door, then stationed himself outside in the hallway. When one of the team came back down the hall, he informed the officer that the asylum director was upset and waiting for some clothing to be brought to him by emergency services. With the media circus already building up outside at street level, she thought it best not to have the director portrayed in an embarrassing position. The other officer agreed, informed her that Priest and Gunn had subdued Straitjacket and a young female, and had asked SAPD personnel to guard the room until they came out.

When Match heard the word "Priest," he couldn't help but glance up the corridor. He wanted to try and help Straitjacket, but what could he do? He didn't hesitate, following the other officer through the maze-like structure of the long abandoned underground power plant and subway maintenance station before reaching the wide stairway that took them back up to the surface. The morning sun was shining brightly, and reporters called out to them from the other side of a barricade.

"We're rock stars," the other officer dryly joked as they headed back to the police unit's van.

Match's lack of police procedure knowledge didn't get in the way of him being able to follow his team back to the station and clean up after the mission. In the shower, Match happily confirmed what he'd already observed— the female officer's body was indeed fit and athletic. She was muscular but not bulky, and her torso was flat and strong. Her breasts were small, but perky. She also wasn't wearing any jewelry, which would make his relatively brief life in her skin a much easier transition. He'd learned it was her partner's turn to do the paperwork, which allowed him to walk out of the station into a beautiful San Angeles day with her I.D., money, and car keys.

The police woman drove a sporty pickup with license plates

that read "deadsht." He used the vehicle's GPS to locate the address on her driver's license. She lived in a small apartment complex in North Hollywood. There didn't appear to be an alarm for her place, but he was cautious as he turned the front-door key.

Before he could shut the door, a large German shepherd strolled out from a room down the hall. Match quickly stepped back out and locked the door. Match could duplicate humans, but not their scents. The dog would know she wasn't its master in seconds. Shit. And he was kind of afraid of dogs anyway. Especially bigger ones. Well, so much for the perfect scenario, but all was not lost. Match hadn't planned on playing the role of female cop, anyway. He'd just use her body and do what he knew best.

Hustle.

The hustle brought him to Hollywood Boulevard and its wide selection of costume and hooker clothing shops. It would take him up the West Coast to San Francisco, or maybe across the desert to Las Vegas. With a great body like this to wear, why not show it off?

So Match smiled ear to ear as he appraised himself in the floor-length mirror. The cop had a nice slim figure, and her ass looked great in everything he tried on. Her long, toned legs were going to look fantastic in all kinds of freaky stockings and knee-high socks and boots. Match squeezed his new breasts. Small ones with great nipples meant no bras and sheer blouses.

He couldn't wait to get strolling tonight. He'd figure out which hotels had the largest foreign tourist groups and work the exchange rate to his favor.

Match turned gracefully on the glossy, over-the-knee, high-heeled pirate boots. Big fun was coming. And some extra pocket change. He closed his eyes and smiled, spinning in place as if he were a child playing on a sunny day, soaking in the sun.

The front door customer alarm went off, which caught Match's brief attention. He stopped spinning on the heels long enough to glance toward the front of the boutique. He couldn't see the front door, but he did hear the metal deadbolt lock into place over the background pop music. He would have ignored that, except for the sudden descending of the outside metal shutter that protected the store's large display window.

The store's lights were on, but the closed shutter choked off a lot of the additional light. Match's euphoria flipped to caution. The edges of the store were now a bit threatening in their gloom.

"Hello?" he called out, cautious but not fearful. If this was a robbery, he could turn it to his advantage. An unexpected cash bonus.

When neither of the sales ladies answered, Match stepped back so he could see the unmanned checkout counter. He peeked down the small changing area. All the curtains were pulled open, and it was quiet. He hadn't noticed when the super-thin street pro had left.

"Hello, Match," a woman's voice said into his ear.

He turned so fast he teetered on the four-inch heels. A pair of strong hands

Grabbed the front of the sheer black blouse he'd tried on.

Match looked straight into the eyes of a tall brunette. Her dark eyes were humorless. Her attractive features were a blend of beauty and hardened strength.

"Be careful, Babydoll," called another woman from the rear of the store. "You ruin it, you buy it."

"Get your hands off me," Match demanded, eyes twitching from the Amazonian warrior in front of him to the as-yet unseen owner of the second voice. "And by the way, I don't smoke."

"Nice try, Match, but the authorities have already found Officer Grant. She's at the hospital waiting for us to find you."

"I don't know what you're talking a—"

The uppercut to Match's gut forced the air out of him, dropping the mutant to his knees. Babydoll jerked his head up by the hair. "You stupid bitch," she threatened.

"Match is a man, sister," Truth said, stepping into view from the rear alley exit.

"Whatever." Babydoll rattled the mutant copycat.

Match didn't resist. "What do you want?" he gasped between shallow breaths. "Just take me in. Whatever."

Truth moved down the aisle like she was enjoying a Sunday stroll in Beverly Hills. "Oh, the first stop will be the hospital, so you can return Officer Grant to full health."

Match smiled like a shark. "Fuck you! I'm not giving up this body."

"Sure you will. You just need the proper motivation." Truth stepped right up to the still-kneeling mutant. Without the black leather outfit and half-mask, she looked almost normal in her jeans and white tee shirt.

Babydoll was still sporting camouflage khakis, but she'd replaced her lingerie top with a simple black tank top. It showed off her impressive upper-body physique. Her mask was gone too, but her sheer presence kept most people from looking her square in the face.

Truth spoke slowly. "So here's the deal. We take you to the hospital for the SAPD officer, and then to lockup isolation. Or, if you want to play hard ass, we just take you straight to lock up and say 'Screw you' for a day or two."

"I really like 'Screw you'," Babydoll growled, almost bouncing Match's new face against the tile floor.

"How'd you find me?"

"Oh, let's just say it was a nice blend of multi-agency work and technology," Truth replied. "Plus the fact you're a freak when it comes to playing hooker. This store opened the earliest. So predictable."

Match slapped the floor in frustration. "Well, might as well take me straight to lockup. I'm not giving up this great set of tits."

Babydoll chuckled at the comment, than glanced at Truth. "This is gonna be so much fun." She grabbed up Match, and after quickly cuffing the faux woman's hands behind his back, the ex-Israeli commando half-walked, half-dragged the imposter out the rear of the store. Truth followed.

The two female crime fighters secured Match in the rear of a SAPD-paneled van, and started driving. Match didn't speak a word the whole trip downtown. When the van finally pulled to a halt and the engine stopped, Match could hear dogs barking.

The rear van doors jerked open. Babydoll climbed in and unlocked the wall cuffs.

"Where are we?" Match asked, his anxiety growing as he listened to the chorus of barking dogs.

"At the lockup," Truth replied, pushing the van doors shut.

Match started to walk, then froze as he read the sign over the front entrance.

San Angeles County Animal Shelter

Babydoll barked, and then laughed as Match nearly jumped out of his skin.

"I'm not going in there!" he shouted, resisting Babydoll as she forced him forward.

"Oh, the dog thing is in your file too, Match."

Match refused to walk, so Babydoll dragged him, resisting all the way, toward the entrance.

"You can just take me to lockup, 'cause I ain't giving up these great titties!" Babydoll taunted him with a pouty face.

"You can't take me in there!" he cried. "I'm not an animal!"

"The jails are overcrowded, dude. Don't worry, though— you'll still get your three squares and daily yard time," Truth pledged.

"Just watch your step in the yard," Babydoll said, laughing at her own joke.

"I'm not going in there!" Match screamed like a two-year-old in a supermarket. As they got to the entrance, Match jumped up and planted a boot on each side of the door frame. Babydoll dropped him to the asphalt parking lot as Truth took out her lock-pick set and worked on the front door.

It only took seconds for her to pick the lock, and Babydoll spun Match on his ass and then started dragging him inside, where the barking audio levels jumped several decibels.

"Okay, okay, okayokayoakyokayokay," Match gave in. "I'll give back the body!"

"What?! After we spent all this time driving downtown, and NOW you want to go with the program?" Babydoll yelled. "Oh hell no!"

"You're here for at least the day and night," Truth stated. "You had your chance, but you decided to get hard."

Match struggled with a fury only absolute fear for one's life can bring. "Don't put me in there! Please!"

"Convince us," Truth said.

Match looked at the pair of heroines, trying to think, pleading. "I don't know…"

Truth nodded to Babydoll, who reached down and grabbed Match by the cuffs.

"Okay, okay!" he shouted, "Something is happening with Old Scratch. He's called a stop to all crime under his control. Scarlett thinks he hasn't been right since the lightning strike. She called a secret meeting, but he found out and he banished her, which is why she wasn't caught in the raid earlier. Money says she's going to try to kill the demon before he offs her."

Truth and Babydoll looked at each other, then down at Match.

"If the demon wanted her dead, why didn't he just kill her at the meeting?"

"I don't know, I wasn't there. Straitjacket told me."

"Straitjacket's dead, and so is the director's daughter," Truth confided. Match's body slumped with the news.

"Straitjacket was the scariest thing alive," Match whispered.

"Scariest thing?" Babydoll asked, puzzled.

"The doctor shared his body with a demon named Lucius. Gave him great evil ideas."

Babydoll looked to Truth, who nodded. "I always wanted to meet up with that sick fuck," Babydoll said.

"He'd have sliced your tits off, shaved your head, and made you his bitch," Match spat.

"Before or after I bit off his tiny little dick?"

"Tough talk now that they're gone."

Babydoll didn't disagree. "So, are we taking him in, or back to the hospital?"

Truth sighed. "Better get him to the hospital. She was really hurting."

Babydoll jerked Match back to his feet, then shoved him toward the van.

"Thanks for keeping your word," Match said as he climbed into the van. Babydoll handcuffed him in, then secured the rear doors. As they drove to the hospital, both women knew that as soon as the police officer had been restored to full health, the duo were bringing Match back to the animal shelter until his Monday morning arraignment. He might be really insane by the time he reached court. But there was plenty of available space at Allenby Asylum for the Criminally Insane, including Match's old cell.

"By the way," Truth asked, "what do you look like when you're not doing the body-snatching thing?"

"Let me think...I kind of look like fuck you," Match said.

"I heard he looks like a giant maggot. All pale and wrinkly and oozy," Truth commented, faking a shiver.

"Figures. That would explain his breath," Babydoll said.

Chapter Twenty Six

OH WHAT A TANGLED WEB WE WEAVE

Priest lay in the grass under the shade of a pretty flowering tree. He'd tried to go home and rest on his own bed, but his mind kept replaying the young woman's suicide. He'd seen so many horrible things, long before God had summoned him from His spiritual army into His warrior army. So much hatred and loss and despair amongst the people he worshiped with and protected.

He just hadn't been able to sleep. Sometimes his mind skipped to the grueling exorcism with Lucius, and sometimes it took him back to the roof and the very strange conversation between Old Scratch and Catfight. The demon's expression had been filled with a desperate loneliness. And its serpent eyes…something about the demon wasn't right. Or maybe it was more about something not being horribly wrong about what was supposedly evil incarnate.

Very strange indeed.

So, after tossing around in bed for a couple of hours, he finally got up, got dressed, and started walking toward the San Fernando Mission Memory Garden in Mission Hills. It was a lovely place where outdoor weddings and parties took place. The flowers were beautiful year 'round. Every color of the rainbow was represented.

So he'd picked a lovely tree to rest under. He stared up into the red and white blossoms, enjoying the sunshine finding its way through the branches. Those scattered rays warmed his face, relaxing him. Soon he closed his eyes, and not long after, his breathing slowed. The sounds of the world dropped lower and lower. The passing traffic. The movement and laughter of playing children. The whispering of young lovers from a nearby bench. His mind unlocked the doorway to sleep.

A second later, five minutes later, an hour later, the man of God wasn't sure how much time had gone by when the woman's soft voice reached out.

"Excuse me."

Priest awoke, his mind skating on the edge of deep sleep. He opened his eyes and stared up at the woman. She was tall, and she wore a San Angeles Dodgers ball cap. Her oversized sunglasses covered the top half of her face like a hero's mask. It was obvious she was hiding her true identity.

"I apologize for bothering you, but we have a mutual problem."

Priest propped himself on his elbows. The woman's dark jeans were too tight to be comfortable. Her black tee shirt barely reached her waist, straining to cover her full chest.

As his mind cleared, he repeated her words. "Mutual problem?"

"Old Scratch."

And as soon as she said the demon's name, her voice sent off terrible alarms. Without her provocative crimson costume, he hadn't recognized her.

He casually climbed to his feet, his mother's Bible clutched in his right hand for strength. "If you're looking for a battle, I'd ask you'd be mindful of the small children nearby," he said softly. There was no misunderstanding the underlying warning.

She nodded. "I'm not here to fight. I could have attacked you as you slept. I'm here to ask for your help."

Priest stared at Scarlett for half a minute. "Take off your glasses."

She hesitated for a moment, then pulled them from her face and hung them down the front of her tee. Her eyes were clear, sharp.

"Let's walk," the holy warrior said, showing the way. The two fell into step.

"The last couple of weeks have been crazy," she began. "And it started with the thunderstorm and Midnight's death." She took a few more steps before continuing. "I'm not sorry about Midnight. I hated him. But something happened to Old Scratch that night, and now the demon is going to kill me the next time he sees me."

Priest stopped walking, and couldn't help but stare. "And this is a bad thing?"

"Aren't you a priest? Aren't you supposed to care for and protect everyone?"

"I care for and protect the innocent. You made the mistake of forsaking your God and associating with a hell demon. You are the lowest of human life. You have the nerve to come to me stinking of sulfur and brimstone in an attempt to save your own skin when your mad dog finally turns on you."

"I can help you kill him," she offered.

Priest exhaled. "I don't kill."

"Semantics, Priest. I don't steal; I just take things that don't belong to me. You had no problem dealing with Straitjacket."

A stab of pain pierced Priest's temple. Guilt? "Exorcism isn't murder," he defended himself.

"Tell that to the doctor."

"Open your soul to the devil and reap the consequences."

The two stood looking at one another. Scarlett blinked first. "So do you want Old Scratch gone, yes or no?"

"And besides your life, what else do you want?"

She smiled, and her beauty was undeniable, even to him. "Right now I'll take my life."

Priest stood, waiting for the rest.

"And later, I want the money in the demon's vault. And I will disappear for the rest of both our lives."

"Must be millions," he whispered.

"You have no idea, Priest. You have a ceremony to send an evil spirit back to hell. Can you do the same to an actual being from hell?"

Priest was quiet, thinking through how he wanted to word his response. "How do I know you're still not working for the demon? He knows that with Midnight gone, I am the biggest threat to him outside of Titan."

Scarlett chuckled. "No offense, but Old Scratch doesn't even think about you or your Bible. The only threat that crosses his mind is Titan, but I think we both know Titan isn't coming to San Angeles."

"Titan," Priest sighed, "is a coward." The words slipped from his brain to his mouth faster than he could edit them. But the truth was the truth.

"Exactly. I believe Titan is afraid if he somehow were to be defeated by Old Scratch, the Christian community around the world would crumble. That's a lot to risk when you're the world's greatest hero."

Priest nodded. "I have been working on something to contain Old Scratch. Give me twenty-four hours, and find me again." Priest started to walk away, then stopped. "If your treachery reveals itself, semantics will not factor into how you're dealt with."

Scarlett hitched her shoulders. "I'd give you my word, but we both know that doesn't mean shit, so expect a fucking double-cross and be surprised when there isn't one." He watched her jog across the boulevard and onto the back of a waiting motorcycle. The driver wore a helmet with a tinted face shield, so he couldn't see who it was, but he guessed it was another woman. The cycle burst away toward the freeway.

Gunn, dressed as a custodian, walked up. Priest looked at his friend and couldn't help but chuckle.

Gunn grinned. "My service doesn't always require bullets."

"But sometimes a shower, amigo."

"What did the witch want?"

"She wants me to kill Old Scratch."

"Cool," Gunn said with an approving nod.

Priest looked sternly at his associate. Gunn raised his hands in surrender. "I know, I know, you don't kill."

Priest turned and walked away, already thinking about the massive challenge to come.

"But don't tell that to Straitjacket," Gunn whispered under his breath before following his fast-walking friend.

Chapter Twenty Seven
THE ENDGAME

It was the third night of Old Scratch's crime embargo. The city's downtown had gone graveyard-quiet. The incident two nights ago at the theater, along with a handful of other crimes interrupted by the demon himself, had the city buzzing, and the criminal underground paralyzed.

Catfight wasn't sleeping. The past week had been too chaotic. Too much travel over too many time zones, too many deaths, and all this craziness with the demon. She really hadn't slept well since Andre had died, but she hadn't slept at all since her return to San Angeles. She felt so tired, and her eyelids scratched like sandpaper. Her lithe limbs were cement-heavy, but she couldn't keep herself from returning to Blackledge skyscraper night after night. She sat on the roof's ledge, not so much looking out for criminal activity, but trying to clear her head.

Word had reached her about Old Scratch's crime ban. What was the demon up to? What was his endgame? What he was doing made no sense. Why set the city on fire and then douse the flames? Why protect her and try to convince her he was actually Andre?

The demon was a natural trickster.

N'eve had thought there was something wrong about Old Scratch, and had tried to convince her before she'd been killed.

Tatiana's head bobbed on her neck. So tired. She swung her body around and stretched out on the skyscraper's ledge. The possibility of rolling off never passed through her mind. She might as well be stretched out in a hammock in her den.

A crime stoppage could be chalked up to an egotistical demonstration of power, but that didn't begin to explain what the motive was behind the demon's personal crusade to enforce his order.

But the latest and strangest piece of this insane puzzle had come earlier in the evening, when an informant left her a message stating that, upon closer inspection, the demon's much televised, so-called "victory scream" moments after Starlight's death actually appeared to be a cry of anguish. The informant didn't know what to do with the revelation. Tatiana hadn't returned the voicemail. She was too tired to think straight, and there weren't enough clear facts to provide her with solid possibilities. Whatever the demon was up to, it was his craziest scheme ever.

She sighed and let her eyes close. How did all the pieces add up? What had Starlight stumbled onto? The alien had gone looking for the demon, and found him right here at the scene of the original crime. The demon kept coming back there, just like her. Why was he drawn there? Was he stalking her?

Then her mind screeched to a halt. She'd been so tired, so angry, so aggravated, she'd only listened to half the bullshit the demon had spewed. At the same moment, two thoughts collided.

The first was the aura-read Starlight had done. Not only had the demon's aura been different from Old Scratch's, but it had been familiar to the alien.

The second was the startling realization that Old Scratch had mentioned a personal detail only she and Andre had shared. Her mind replayed the memory.

It had happened after one of their rare tender lovemaking sessions. There'd been no sexual acrobatics, no biting, and not a word of profanity. She hadn't raked his back with her claws, and he hadn't been his normally aggressive self. They'd both been slow, tender, and loving. There were hushed whispers, and breathy prodding. When they had both reached satisfaction, Andre had flopped to his back, his chest heaving and glistening with sweat. She'd pounced on him playfully, her chin jabbing into his bellybutton. She'd baby-kissed her way up the middle of his chest, taking a teasing nip at a nipple.

"I want us to have a little girl," she'd whispered with a hungry smile. "I want to name her Nadia."

Andre had just smiled, and then kissed her fully and deeply. The subject hadn't come up again.

How could the demon have known about that?

Shit.

Catfight's eyes flashed open. Scarlett was standing above her. She was in a fighting stance. Her hips twisted and dropped, and her fist rammed into Catfight's face. Even with her superlative quickness, there wasn't time for Catfight to avoid the smashing blow.

#

Darkness replaced night.

Andre stayed high in the sky, scanning the San Angeles streets. Three nights into his crime stoppage, and the difference was startling. From downtown San Angeles into Mid-Wilshire, down through Watts, up through Hollywood, and just over the hills in the shallow of the Valley, not only was crime all but nonexistent, but traffic was extremely light. A pimp and a small harem of prostitutes were hanging south of Sunset Boulevard on Western Avenue. When the demon's shadow passed over them, the pimp screamed like a surprised prom-queen winner. He herded the girls into his tricked-out, pearl-colored Escalade and quickly found the freeway.

There wasn't a nook or corner or crevice dark enough for all the cockroaches to hide. As Midnight, Andre had only sipped at this kind of menacing presence. There was always a dumb-ass gang member with an UZI dreaming of being the one to kill him, but as a hell demon, his inherent ability to strike fear into the hearts of everyone— good, bad, innocent, guilty, young, and old— was almost intoxicating. No one was immune to the terrifying, real-life Boogeyman that Old Scratch was.

He wasn't a costumed representation of a twisted mind. Old Scratch was THE villain. He was evil incarnate. He was a living nightmare capable of anything because the rules and morals of human civilization meant less than roach piss to him. Scratch wasn't the devil himself, but he might as well be.

It was actually kind of cool. And Andre was going to use the demon's dark power to cloak his city into a darkness where even the hungriest of vermin were too afraid to tread into the light. Imprisonment was like a Club Med vacation compared to the license Andre could take, the punishment he could deliver, wearing the hellspawn's skin.

Things he'd daydreamed doing to the most heinous of criminals, but hadn't ever seriously entertained. Tossing a notorious rapist/murderer through a window into traffic wouldn't even sniff at the top one-hundred acts of retribution he'd contemplated over the years.

And now, he could enact such punishments to those that dared to ignore the demon's direct order.

He blinked.

Not Old Scratch's. His own orders and warnings.

Shit. Things were so twisted up.

He swooped down Santa Monica Boulevard, heading west toward West Hollywood. An alternative club featuring a Goth night was closing its doors late. Many of the exiting patrons spotted him, and actually cheered and whistled. To those whose image of hell was that of an imaginative domain of the darkest pleasures, he was a symbol of a real hell somewhere out there.

The positive attention was too weird for Andre, and he veered back east, rising into the starry late night, satisfied his threats were still holding. Downtown looked relatively dark from this distance, but he could see Blackledge Tower, and his wings carried him toward it like a moth to a flame.

On the way back to San Angeles' center, he caught a sight that made him hesitate. A homeless woman with a string of several shopping carts was heading up Vermont. A pair of hoodie-wearing teens flashed out of nowhere and snatched up a few of her trash bags. Lord knew what was in them, but before Andre could decide whether to get involved, more out of boredom than the need to impose his will, the woman cried out a vile curse worthy of any veteran longshoreman, and then released a monstrous white pit bull on the thieves.

The dog only had to bark once to make both teens gasp in shocked disbelief. One kid immediately tossed the bags back toward the shopping caravan, then put his head down and ran like an Olympic qualifying sprinter.

The other, a tall gangly youth, tried to dart out into the moving traffic, but got clipped by a taxi's front bumper before he could clear the second lane. The teen was spun and tossed to the asphalt, and the dog was on him before his body had even rolled to a stop.

The very light late-night traffic stopped, drivers watching as the dog grabbed a bony shin and went to work. The young man's screams actually contained a lyrical quality when they reached the demon's ears. Andre couldn't stop his smile. Some folks didn't need protecting, and other folks were too stupid to distinguish the ones that did from the ones that didn't.

Andre wore the same smile as he flew uninterrupted to his favorite perch on Blackledge Tower.

But he never got a chance to do his best gargoyle imitation. As he approached the damaged rooftop, he saw that all the flowers and gifts had been removed. The part of the roof that was still intact was just bare concrete.

At first glance Andre thought some gangbangers had drawn graffiti on the roof, but as he dropped closer he realized it was a crimson painted message left for him. He hovered over the single sentence.

You know where to find us.

His first impulse was that it was a threat from the crew he'd hurt when he'd intervened outside the theater. None of the five gang members in the Caddie had survived the ten-story drop and resulting explosion.

Then his eyes stopped reading and he dropped all the way to the roof, his large feet straddling the "I" in the word "find". The dot over the "I" wasn't painted. It was actually a wadded-up ball of material.

As he bent to pick it up, he realized what it was.

It was Catfight's mask.

Andre scanned the painted message.

It was blood. It was drying, but still a bit tacky. There was no way of telling if the blood was Tatiana's, but there was no doubt about who had left him the message. Scarlett had made her move.

He knew the "us," and he certainly knew the "where." Or at least he thought he did. There was only one way to find out.

The demon's right hand was already a dead woman walking, and she knew it. It was just a matter of whether he could save Tatiana, if she weren't dead already. There was nothing worse than going willingly into what would clearly be a deadly trap, but he had no options. If he got too cute or too cautious, Scarlett would simply kill Tatiana. No doubt about that.

With a growl, Andre burst into the sky. He was so close to making his plan for San Angeles into a reality. What if he had to trade his life for hers? He still loved her, but was her life alone worth all the lives he could save over the expanse of time he could survive as the demon? Tatiana was no innocent victim. She was a superhero, and allowed for the flirtations of death that came with the job. The best ending would require saving her, and surviving whatever Scarlett had in mind. Her deadly power had no sway over him directly, but that didn't make her any less dangerous.

But too much thought was a waste of time. So often, as Midnight, he used to say, "Time to show up, kick ass, and save the girl." This was the perfect example of a situation that fit his patented answer. He flew toward Hollywood, touching his earpiece.

"Geek, I need for you to listen to me carefully." Andre could hear the genius's fingers blurring over his multitudes of keyboards.

"Talk to me."

And then the hero wearing the demon's skin did just that.

Andre completed his conversation with The Geek long before he dropped down into one of Hollywood's darkest alleys, created by the black paint covering all the surrounding garages, sheds, and structures, including the street itself. With a complete lack of any street or garage lighting, a single manhole cover sat off to the side of the alley. Andre moved the cover and dropped down onto the manhole, quickly squeezing down under it into the darkness beneath the street. He pulled the heavy cover back into place without a sound.

In the darkness, even the surrounding silence felt like as if it were stalking him.

"Central control is shut down," The Geek whispered in his ear. "There are no eyes on you."

Andre didn't acknowledge the info. It was still quite a ways to the compound and his master chamber. The cool air felt frigid to the demon's sensibilities. One of the things Andre had liked best about being a creature of the night was that, with San Angeles being a desert city, the nights were nearly always a pleasant temperature. And it was easy to forget Old Scratch was not a true creature of the night like a vampire. He was a hell demon, and as far as Andre knew, neither heaven nor hell had seasons, day, or night. Hell was simply hell all the time. Odds were, if the hell Old Scratch used to call home was even vaguely like the hell of most human civilizations, weathermen were probably not in high demand. And the cooler city nights might actually seem frigid to a creature used to living in such an extreme-heat environment.

Decembers in Southern California were typically warm. The annual Rose Bowl game on New Year's Day was usually played on days that would pass for summer weather in the Midwest. December nights made for wonderful evening strolls at the beach. Andre and Tatiana had taken their share of motorcycle rides along Pacific Coast Highway, taking time off the bike to walk along the surf in Malibu.

The underground air around him had a cool seaside dampness, but without the wonderfully fresh ocean fragrance. There was nothing like an ocean breeze. Air-freshener companies could try all they wanted, but there was no reproducing the real thing.

Andre didn't think much about where he was going. He let instinct guide him back to the fringe of Old Scratch's vast underground compound. Once he reached one of the main entrances, finding his way to his master chambers would be easy enough.

His night vision made the dark voyage easy. Being as at ease in the demon's body as he'd ever be, he also felt a complete lack of fear about the coming battle. There was no way to anticipate what Scarlett would have set up. She was desperate, but smart and ruthless. Having been separated from the demon's side, the sense of danger she could bring had been severely kneecapped.

But Andre would be a complete fool to underestimate her. Even if she'd gathered every street soldier in the city and had set up the granddaddy of all ambushes, they had no hopes of gunning him down. A bazooka would only slow him. Napalm and flame-throwers, to him, were the equivalent of stepping into a sauna. Oh, what could she have cooked up? He stopped walking.

A nuclear weapon.

Could she have gotten her hands on one, and was luring him to the detonation point? Even the demon couldn't survive that kind of fire power at ground zero.

What if the weapon was counting down right now? It wouldn't really matter if Tatiana were still alive or not. There would be no way to protect her from the blast. Hell, she wouldn't allow him to, anyway.

Scarlett could be headed out of the city right now. Getting herself clear of the blast radius. San Angeles would be wiped from the map, Old Scratch would be dead, and she could return and own the ruins of one of the world's great former cities.

The nuclear weapon theory was a distinct possibility. Andre started to jog, and found the notion of fear creeping back into his consciousness. Fear not for himself, and not really for Tatiana, but for all the innocent people of his city. He'd gladly give his life a second time for San Angeles.

But outside a nuclear device, what else could Scarlett have conceived and be ready to execute in such a short amount of time?

Had she found a way to get Titan involved? That pious prick would never stoop so low as to team with the Mistress of Blood in order to destroy him. There wasn't a deal she could offer that Titan would accept.

None of the other local heroes had the power or connections to capture or destroy him. The U.S. Army might have some secret weapon they might be willing to test out on him. Who really knew what those secret government think tanks were working on? Problem was, how could they develop a weapon to kill a creature they had little information on? Unless they had a genuine demon stashed away somewhere. That seemed unlikely. Hellboy was just a fictional comic book character.

But the demon could be captured, contained, and then perhaps exiled into deep space. That thought gave Andre some pause. He certainly didn't think there was a prison or containment unit on earth capable of holding Scratch for any amount of time. But space was a different matter. He and Starlight should have explored that option more thoroughly. If Scratch were transported to the moon, would he be able to escape? Andre certainly didn't know. He wasn't even sure the demon needed air to exist. Then again, the extreme cold and pressure of space would probably extinguish the life out of most every living creature.

Andre felt like smacking himself in the head. How could he have been so stupid? Fuck. All those nights he'd spent trying to figure how to take out the demon, and space never crossed his mind. Shit, he'd spent more time fantasizing about the devil himself coming to earth, taking his rogue son by the ear, and dragging him back home to hell like a spoiled child.

Andre heard the demon chuckling, and realized it was him. No one had ever accused Midnight of being a master tactician. He was a master ass-kicker, plain and simple. It was what he did best. Hell, it was what he did better than anyone in the whole friggin' world. And it was time, even in the demon's body, to get back to basics.

When Andre reached an unguarded steel-plated access door

into the old subway maintenance facility, he barely paused in front of it.

"Fuck you," he growled, grabbing the chained door handle and ripping the heavy security door from its hinges. He tossed the door aside like a used tissue, ignoring the fact it made for a noisier-than-necessary entrance.

"I'm coming for you, Scarlett!" he yelled, his demon's voice echoing out into the darkness in front of him. He started running. The demon's body wasn't made to run, much less to run fast, but Midnight forced the body into a lumbering pace that would have made any NFL offensive tackle proud.

He might be trapped in Old Scratch's body for the rest of eternity, but the time of game playing was over. It didn't make any difference if the world didn't believe who he really was. He knew.

It was time for Midnight to go to work.

The compound was empty, which explained why Andre didn't have The Geek kibitzing in his ear. He hadn't passed a soul since he'd dropped underground. He paused briefly to look into the communication center, but the room was dark and unmanned. The demon's army barracks looked dark and deserted. The authorities had swept through the facility like locusts. There were minimum signs of struggle or hostile takeover, but without the demon or Scarlett to coordinate the warriors, the superior invading force had had it easy. It had been a ballsy move on the city's part to put that kind of offensive into action with the chaos of the prior nights. Good for them.

Andre walked the remaining stretch from the com center to his private quarters. When he reached the final length of corridor, he was surprised to see lit torches spaced along the walls. Instinct screamed at him to slow down and ready himself, but instead he roared at the top of the demon's lungs and strode through the gloom like the prince of hell he was.

There were no guards outside his private chambers. The heavy double doors were ajar. An odd, dancing light pierced the narrow opening.

Andre was feeling way too much like himself to not just walk into the cavernous chamber. And that's exactly what he did. If his entering the room was going to spring a trap, let it be sprung.

But there were no tripwires or false stone pressure plates.

Thankfully, there also wasn't a nuclear device.

It was not at all what Andre was expecting. He actually had to squint against the bright lights inside the room coming from both the flames in the large fireplace and another, unexpected source.

The heat in the chamber was stifling, but the demon's body

relaxed in it like a mud bath.

Scarlett, wearing her classic red outfit, stood across the room, waiting by the large slab of stone that had once been the demon's bed. The stone had been lifted and now leaned against the rear cavern wall, revealing a rough-edged pit that the slab had concealed. Fiery steam and illumination poured from the opening, which was covered by a metal grate. Staked across the metal grating was an unmasked Catfight. She struggled in vain against metal restraints on her wrists and ankles.

Scarlett's expression was hard to read as she watched for the demon's reaction, her right hand gripping a long, metal lever.

On the left side of the room, by the huge fire pit, was Gunn. His long coat was swept open, his hands hovering over the holstered weapons on each hip. His wide-brimmed hat hid his eyes, but Andre sensed the gunslinger was nervous. He was certainly sweating.

Priest waited at the chamber's far right side. He held a small tablet. His Bible was nowhere in sight. His white shirt was drenched in sweat.

Priest started reciting something in a whisper. Gunn shifted in his stance, ever so slightly.

"Hello, Scratch," Scarlett greeted him. "Nice to have you home one last time."

Andre took a step forward, but stopped when Scarlett waved a warning finger.

"Take another step and I release the catch holding Catfight, and down she goes."

Andre frowned. "Down she goes?"

Scarlett laughed, and it sounded sincere.

Priest continued to speak in hushed tones. That couldn't be good for a demon's health.

"Since the lightning strike, you've developed quite the sense of humor," she responded. "It was nothing short of a miracle when the lightning didn't kill you, but you've been full of surprises since you came out of the coma."

It was hard to ignore Priest's focused incantations. Andre focused on Scarlett. "So, the deal?"

"I want to live, of course. But I'm not comfortable with my life expectancy while you're around, so I'm going to make you a deal." She glanced down at the hissing Catfight. "Whatever she is to you now, I'm not sure, but I will spare her life if you return freely whence you came."

"Whence I came?" he repeated, momentarily puzzled at the request. Then the answer sparked. "You want me to go to hell?"

"If that's what it's really called. In truth, the world would be a safer place without you."

"Let me loose!" Catfight screamed at Priest, but he was totally absorbed by whatever ceremony he was performing.

"He really didn't want it this way," Gunn said, seeming to speak to Catfight as much as to the demon. "But he couldn't pass up the chance to extinguish the greatest evil in the world."

"I'm flattered," Andre said.

"I'm sorry." Gunn spoke evenly to Catfight. "Sacrifices must be made in order for good to triumph over evil." Catfight spat and hissed, a furious feline.

The volume of Priest's incantation started to rise, and he slowly lifted his arms.

Andre glanced at the clergyman. "Can I ask what he's doing?"

"He's the world's most accomplished exorcist," Scarlett answered. "And he's taken the challenge of vanquishing your evil spirit back to hell." Andre looked back over at the clergyman. "Okay. That makes sense," he said. "But can we talk about the barbeque grill you've got Catfight tied to?"

Scarlett smiled.

"Are you saying that pit leads to hell?"

"Of course it does. You know that better than anyone."

"And if I go willingly, you'll let Catfight go, and then everyone goes about their merry way?"

"Simple plans are the best," she replied.

"And if I don't go, you drop her and send me to hell anyway?"

Scarlett nodded, though she looked a little less assured.

Andre looked Priest over again. "Exorcism rite." And then Andre started to laugh. His voice rose and rose, until his laughter echoed off the walls of the earthen chamber.

Gunn shifted his stance, looking around to make sure the ceiling wasn't going to come down. "Come on Priest," he encouraged nervously.

Suddenly Priest knelt and placed the tablet on the floor. He removed a gold crucifix from it and walked slowly toward Scratch, his right arm extended. He began reciting the Lord's Prayer. "Our Father, which art in heaven, hallowed be thy name. Thy kingdom come, Thy will be done in earth, as it is in heaven..."

The absurdity of the situation continued to fuel Andre's laughter. He couldn't stop laughing, and he realized his crazy behavior was probably as much like the demon's as he had pretended all along.

Priest continued the Lord's Prayer until he was almost close enough to touch the demon with the cross. His faith was unshaken as he pressed the blessed artifact against the middle of the demon's chest. Andre's laughter eased a bit, but he made no move to avoid the contact. Priest's eyes were squeezed shut and he grimaced with focus and determination as he completing the prayer. "And lead us not into temptation, but deliver us from evil: For thine is the kingdom, and the power, and the glory, forever. Amen."

The chamber went silent for a split second, except for the crackling fire in the massive fireplace. Priest stood, his teeth gnashing, his body trembling as he continued to hold the crucifix against the demon's chest, well within the lethal reach of perhaps the world's deadliest creature.

As the seconds stretched out and nothing happened, Andre stopped laughing. Priest slowly opened his eyes and looked up into the truest face of evil he'd ever known.

The demon's face split wide in a treacherous smile.

Across the room, Gunn whispered in startled shock. "Oh shit."

Andre whispered as he gently covered Priest's hand and the cross with his own massive one.

"Exorcisms are for banishing evil spirits. You were trying to banish a flesh-and-blood demon. Problem is, the evil spirit that possessed this body is already gone."

Priest slowly crossed himself, softly speaking in Spanish. He didn't move an inch back, but instead looked strongly into Old Scratch's eyes.

"Then who are you?" Priest asked, his lean body taut as piano wire.

"I'm Midnight," Andre answered, loudly enough for everyone in the room to hear.

Gunn flinched. Scarlett didn't move a muscle. Priest's expression shifted through a number of emotions before he shook his head. "That is not possible," he mumbled, fear driving more Dominican accent into his tone.

"Then why haven't I ripped your damn head off?"

Across the room, Scarlett jerked the long lever. The shackles released as the iron grating over the pit dropped away in two halves. Catfight dropped from sight.

Scarlett shrugged.

For a second, everything and everyone froze. Even the flames in the fireplace stopped moving. Andre could only stare at the result of the magic trick. Scarlett had made Catfight disappear.

But before he could move, Priest, Gunn, and Scarlett did.

Scarlett sprinted for the doorway. Priest and Gunn raced toward the pit. For a second Andre was torn between love and hate. He took a step to cut off Scarlett, but turned away and took to the air toward the pit.

"The mouse is loose," Andre said to no one in particular,

watching as Priest ran and dove headlong into the hole. Gunn skidded to a stop at the pit's edge, his eyes following the flight of his friend. The gunman's cry was of startled anguish. Andre hovered above the opening, and had to quickly twist himself out of the way as Catfight swung herself back out of the pit, somersaulting into a three-point landing.

Andre glanced at her, then back down into the glowing, smoking abyss.

The putrid smoke and fumes forced Gunn back from the edge, but Old Scratch's body had been born into a world of reeking excrement and the airborne remnants of charred remains. Andre stared with unaffected, unflinching eyes down in the pit, watching the man called Priest descend, now screaming as his clothing and flesh burst into flames, his eyes bursting from their sockets.

Andre suddenly realized the man wasn't screaming in agony, but was actually yelling the Lord's Prayer. When Priest's body exploded into a million shards of charred flesh and bone, his battle-cry prayer continued to echo.

"Jesus Christ," Andre said, and all

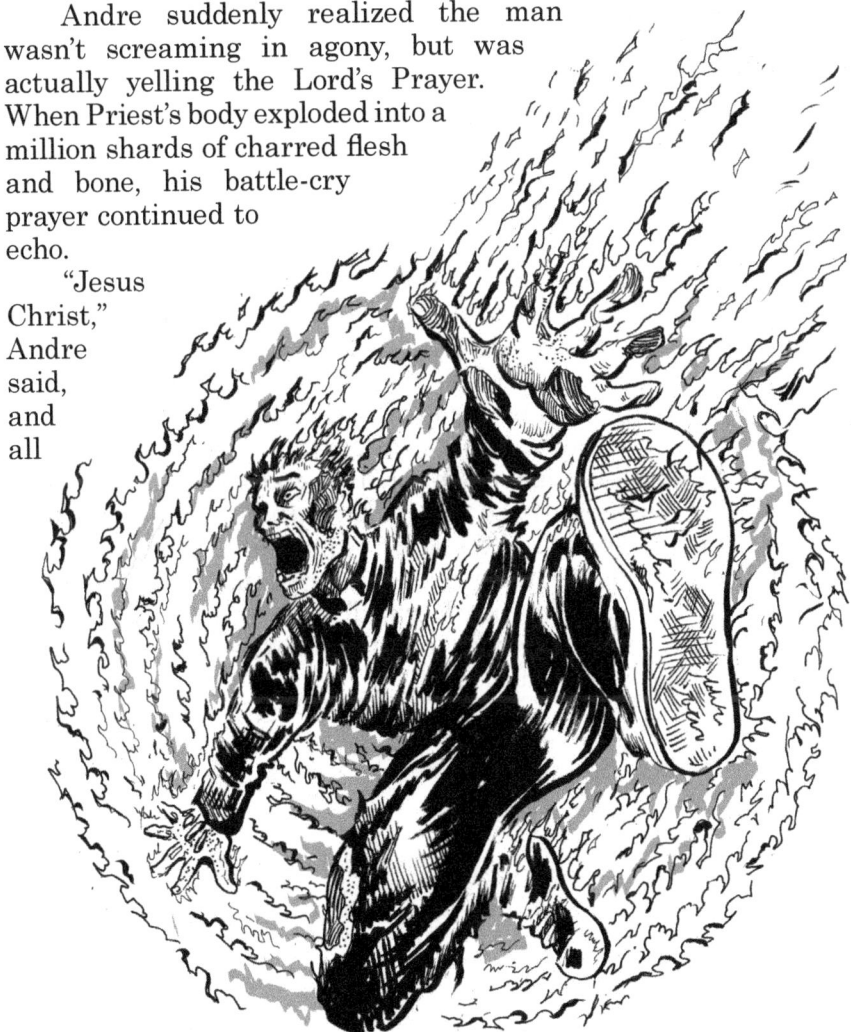

he could do in his startled state was grab the massive stone slab and slam it down over the pit to cover it. But instead of the thunderous crunch he'd expected to hear, the stone seemed to pause just over the opening for an instant, then settle without a sound, sealing it off. He stared at it, afraid of what might try to move it aside from underneath. When seconds passed and nothing came for him, he released the breath he'd been holding.

"Did you really just say that?" Gunn's voice was serious. Andre turned, seeing that the gunslinger had drawn both weapons from his hip holsters. "Did you just say Jesus Christ?" Gunn's voice had ascended to a disbelieving shout. Both his weapons were pointed squarely at Scratch's face.

Andre slowly raised his hands. Gunn's hands were trembling just the tiniest bit. Sweat dropped into one of his eyes a split second before Catfight pounced on him, driving a hard knee into his face. Catching him by surprise, she followed the blow with a series of sharp punches. A nasty head-butt finished the gunman temporarily. But even as she delivered the blow, she felt the air above her move, and only caught a glimpse of Old Scratch flying from the room.

Panting heavily, she dropped the unconscious Gunn's head to the dirt floor. Her attention swiveled between the huge slab covering the pit and the doorway. Almost casually, she pulled her legs up and sat Indian-style on Gunn's chest while deciding what to do.

"We have a fix on her movement," The Geek said into Andre's ear as he lumbered through the dark facility. Andre stopped moving for a second. He listened. Nothing. No one was following.

He ran again, moving through the maze of the compound until he reached the ladder leading to the alley's manhole. He leapt upward and blasted though the manhole into a different, but much more familiar darkness. He dropped the manhole cover back onto the opening as if he were pitching a penny. Then he flew into the night sky as high as his wings would carry him. He wasn't close to the beach, but after getting a whiff of hell, the stale funk of Hollywood might well have been a breeze straight off the water.

And the relative chill felt good.

Chapter Twenty Eight

GOODNIGHT, SAN ANGELES

Scarlett made it back to the Silver Screen Motel, entering her room from the back-alley bathroom window. She'd removed the screen and left the frosted glass slider unlatched. It wasn't easy getting in, but it wasn't supposed to be.

She dropped into the tub and moved into the main room. She sat for a few moments on the edge of a bed well past its prime. The mattress squeaked in protest as her upper body slumped back against it.

She didn't have much time. Even without his network, it wouldn't take the demon long to find her. A day. Maybe two.

Her eyes slid in their sockets to look at the trash bag, filled with meager possessions, leaning against the cheap dresser. It was all she had.

She closed her eyes, and a tear escaped. She was exhausted. Her plan had been a crap shoot, and it turned out to be shit. She'd killed Catfight, and Priest had died trying to save her, but her problems— well, one big problem— was still out there, and would be coming for her very, very soon.

She'd get some sleep, and then grab a ride from a college kid to Salt Lake or Phoenix or San Fran or the Mexican border, and then she'd dive deep from there. Waitress, hooker, hotel maid. So many juicy choices for her immediate future.

Her heartbeat was finally beginning to slow. She hadn't felt this way since she was twelve, when that creepy carnival barker had taken her into the tent between performances, and...and...her mind hitched, then skipped through an ugly myriad thoughts and sensory snippets she hadn't visited in years.

Even as she shed the nightmare before it fully enveloped her, the rest of her mind and body finally gave in to the rest it desperately needed.

Something crawled across her face. Scarlett's eyes flittered awake. She swiped across her cheeks, and then wiped at her eyes. How long had she been asleep? Her vision was still foggy. She blinked to clear it, staring up toward the hazy white ceiling.

Hazy.

Almost like lingering cigarette smoke, but not exactly. And then at the edge of her sight, she caught movement.

Scarlett sat up, and her instincts screamed. Spiders scrambled across her hands, and she shook them off as she bounced off the web-strewn bed. She turned and gawked, not believing her eyes. Her cheap motel room was blanketed in spider webs. She could barely make out where the front door was. While the web covered walls were empty of spiders, the floor was a deep carpet of movement. Spiders of every size, shape, and color writhed on top of each other. They quickly covered her boot tops and surged upward. She kicked out in frustration, then froze.

Where was Spyder?

As the question formed in her mind, her chin lifted and her eyes rolled upward toward the ceiling.

The woman/spider hybrid was dropping from the ceiling directly above. Before Scarlett could react, her adversary was on her. The mutant's fangs sank deep into her bare shoulder, and Scarlett could feel the icy poison forced into her flesh. Scarlett grabbed and twisted, but Spyder leapt away, jumping off the bed and onto the far wall.

Clutching at her seeping puncture wounds, Scarlett almost forgot about the waves of spiders scrambling up her legs, nearly to her waist. She stumbled, losing feeling in her extremities. She pitched to the side, flopping into the moving, eight-legged carpet. She thought she'd experienced every ugly thing in the world before the

demon had found her, but when a small spider scurried across her eye and her scream came out only as a breathy whine, she acquired a terrible new scar. The paralyzing ice spread throughout her body, and now unable to close her mouth, spiders quickly discovered the warm, moist opening. She gagged, and then the feeling of all those little legs entering her was lost, too. All she could do was stare blankly into the squirming tangle.

Spyder's voice hissed quietly into her ear. She had probably crawled on top of her, but Scarlett couldn't feel the mutant spider woman's weight.

"I know what your secret power is," she teased, her mouthparts scraping over Scarlett's pearl white flesh. "You have the power to feed the masses."

Scarlett could no longer could speak, mouthful of spiders or no, but her visual perspective changed as she was rolled onto her back.

Another tear leaked from the corner of her eye as Spyder took her time stripping away her outfit and baring her flesh. Soon, so many spiders covered her face she was all but blind. As they slowly consumed her eyes, she soon was.

As her life drained away into a thousand mouths, she tried to remember a prayer her mother used to say with her when she was a child. But her mind was getting black around the edges, darkness seeping in like a permanent stain. She could see her mother's pale, pink-lipped mouth moving, but she couldn't recall—

#

Andre hovered over the Silver Screen Motel, high enough that the casual stargazer couldn't see him. He stayed in the sky, wings tiring. Part of him wished he could witness the end of Scarlett, and part of him was so glad he couldn't.

If there was really a hell, that meant there might be a heaven, and if there was really a God, he'd have the good graces to let the two women kill each other and solve two problems at once.

If Spyder lived, Andre knew he'd have to deal with her eventually, but not tonight.

No more tonight.

He turned and headed toward the Hollywood Hills and home.

Andre had flown for less than half a minute when he spied a large balding man dart into the shadows toward the rear of a closed parking lot. Andre adjusted his flight for a quick look.

The overall-clad man squatted in the corner of the fenced-off lot and dumped the contents of a large purse. An amazing number of items piled on the ground, but he was only interested in the pocketbook. The man stuffed a change purse into his pocket, and then took a moment and opened up the owner's eyeglasses case. He slipped on the small rectangular framed pair, squinting to see if they could be of any use. They certainly weren't, because he didn't see the large, gargoyle-looking monstrosity swooping out of the starry sky.

Andre's foot claws bit deeply into the man's shoulder, and then he and the man rose in the air. The man's cries of both pain and fear of heights wailed like a siren, awakening many of the slumbering folks in the neighborhood.

When Andre reached the North Hollywood police station, he spiraled downward tightly, making the man lose his dinner to the ground below. Landing, the man crumpled to the ground and quickly curled into a frightened ball.

A patrol car pulled up, framing the man and his deliverer in its headlights. Andre lifted the whimpering man's head and, using his talons, slowly carved the letters T-H-I-E-F across the man's forehead.

"Freeze!" one of the cops shouted, but Andre only smiled and let the thief collapse back on the sidewalk before taking to the skies again. The cop didn't fire at him, and Andre wasn't surprised. A bullet from a .38 was going to do little more than tickle.

The encounter with the purse-snatcher had actually worked in his favor, taking him into the Valley. Andre wasn't far from home now.

Chapter Twenty Nine

MIDNIGHT ETERNAL

Sunrise was still a couple of hours away. Andre suddenly realized he didn't know how many days were left until Christmas. For a second, a rush of panic coursed through him when he realized he hadn't done any shopping. Money wasn't an issue. He'd just been so fucking busy dealing with Old Scratch.

He was a fucking idiot.

If he'd just kept it simple and stayed a crimefighter. But the fucking demon had changed everything. No, The Coroner had changed it all.

No, what had changed was he'd chosen to take the easy way out. It was easier to be cruel than have the strength needed for understanding, compassion, and the imperfect criminal justice system.

Now he was living the hell he'd created for himself. But he was going to live it the right way, wrong body and all.

He dropped down through the trees, slipping from one darkness into another. He landed near the boulder entrance to his home, leaving himself less than a minute's walk.

The demon's body was feeling heavy, which meant it was time to get some rest. Andre missed his strong but much more agile frame. He missed walking. Missed his motorcycle. Missed his life.

He could see the boulder straight ahead, and the demon's long strides ate up the ground quickly. Andre started to bend and do the rock sequence when a twig snapped close by.

He spun and dodged, which must have been a funny sight for whoever was approaching. A soft laugh came from his back.

Tatiana stepped forward. She didn't have her mask, but wore a cautious smile. She looked genuinely entertained by the demon's startled movement. "Awful jumpy for a hell demon."

Andre stood back up, but didn't speak. Other than the smile, she looked like hell. Smelled like it, too.

"So..." she began, looking at the ground, then all around him, measuring her words. "You know the secret entrance to Andre's place. Interesting." She stepped forward, and he caught her attention flickering toward his exposed groin.

He chuckled. It was amazing how easy it was to forget that he was always naked, much less packing enough hanging man meat to make all the other demons jealous.

"You know, you really ought to wear something, demon or not."

His body flexed unconsciously, and she sensed it. "Don't fly away." Tatiana stepped within an arm's length of him. Andre's stomach started to twist. "Is it really you in there?"

He dropped to one knee, and his arms slowly encircled her. She stepped closer, touching the top of his rough head.

"Oh, my God." she whispered as he started to sob. It wasn't long before he felt her tears drop onto his back. They felt like kisses. "Oh, baby," she sobbed.

They didn't move for a long time.

A MONTH LATER

Andre sat perched on the edge of the parking garage across from the hospital's emergency room. The sun was all but down. It was late in the day for a patient discharge, but he was going on the information Tatiana had managed to obtain.

And sure enough, a pair of uniformed San Angeles police officers stepped out of the emergency entrance/exit, both casually looking around. One officer signaled back inside.

In a few moments, a broad-shouldered, athletic-looking man rolled himself out in a wheelchair. He was clean-shaven. He had a small duffel bag on his lap. He offered his hand, and one of the officers shook it reluctantly. The other cop totally ignored the individual and re-entered the hospital.

A taxi van pulled up, and the man eased his sizable length out of the chair, which the remaining officer wheeled back inside. The driver stepped around the vehicle and opened the sliding door for the patient. Andre thought he caught a glimpse of the man's expression brightening as he climbed inside. As the cab started away from the hospital, Andre took wing.

The van wove its way toward downtown, eventually stopping in front of an older, nondescript brick building. It looked like it might once have been a commercial building, but had been converted to lofts.

An attractive young woman got out of the street side of the van and settled the fare. She went inside the building as the man eased himself out of the sidewalk side and stood, one hand on the van for support.

Andre landed on the front edge of the building's roof. He sat, thinking about what he was going to say and do. "Fuck it," he said, dropping from the edge. The four floors passed and the demon landed with a heavy thud on the sidewalk near the cab.

The man turned, and his smile evaporated. A couple of seconds later the young woman emerged from the building, propping open the entrance door. A wheelchair sat at the ready just inside. Her beaming smile wavered when she first saw the man's face, then disappeared completely when she saw the demon.

She froze.

"Stay there, Ivy," the man, once known as The Bat, called to her.

Andre had to do a double-take at the woman. It was Ivy, all right, but she'd completely changed her look, her hair color and style, and her happy smile totally transformed her appearance.

Andre stepped closer to The Bat, who took a teetering step toward the demon. "You here to kill me, her, or both?" The Bat's glare was hard and certain. "She doesn't work for you anymore. Never again." When Andre didn't respond, The Bat took a side step and put a hand back on the van for support. "Been watching the news. Don't know what you're up to, but whatever it is, leave her out of it."

"Doesn't appear you could do much to stop me," Andre spoke flatly. "Even when you were one hundred percent." The demon glanced at Ivy. He couldn't get over the change. It was wonderful.

The Bat smirked. "So? Do what you came to do."

Andre frowned, caught by The Bat's unexpected bravado. He started to say something, then stopped. This wasn't going the way he thought it might.

"I'm getting stronger, but I'm out of the game. I want a real life." The Bat looked over at Ivy. "I don't want to end up like Midnight. Someone else can have it."

The comment stung, but Andre understood.

"And I've heard rumors," he continued. "Everyone is talking about how crime is practically down to nothing with you prowling."

"That almost sounds like a compliment," Andre answered. His wings lifted him off the sidewalk.

The Bat frowned, looking confused. "That's it?"

"Enjoy your retirement, Bat," Andre told him, taking to the sky. He watched as Ivy moved to her man's side, and he smiled as The Bat leaned on her for support as they moved slowly toward the door of their home.

#

Andre settled on the edge of Blackledge Tower, looking west toward the ocean. He didn't perch as he was apt to do. He actually sat down and let his wings flatten to his back. He looked at one of his right-hand talons. It was his writing claw. The blood was still drying.

On the way to the tower he'd caught a man dragging a middle-aged business woman behind a cement mixer parked near the building. His intent appeared obvious as he began tearing the clothes off her at gleaming knifepoint.

The assailant now hung unconscious and shirtless from a streetlight half a block away, his belt hitched under his armpits. The letters R-A-P-I-S-T were carved into his forehead and down his torso for the world to see.

Andre was kind of hoping the guy would fall and break both his fucking legs before the police and fire department cut him down. Would serve the shit bag right.

Andre loved the middle of the night, though he missed the charge he used to get as the evening progressed. He'd always feel like he belonged under the stars.

Starlight.

He missed her.

Andre was still admiring the gleaming sky when Catfight dropped down next to him. She smiled as her gaze dropped to his groin. "How are the tights working out?"

Andre looked down at his black, skin-tight shorts. In order to accommodate the demon's monstrous organ, the length went down

VINCE CHURCHILL

to his knees. But he was covered, and felt more human for the modest adjustment.

"Thank you for them. Snug, but all right."

"I miss Starlight too, Dre."

The two sat in silence. Catfight let her head lean against his upper arm.

"Watch the horn," he warned of the sharp bone spur on his shoulder.

Catfight giggled, then purred, nuzzling.

Andre sighed.

He wished midnight *was* eternal.